COOKING WIT

Also by Katharina Marcus

Eleanor McGraw, a pony named Mouse and a boy called Fire

The Boy with the Amber Eyes

Boys Don't Ride

Katharina Marcus

COOKING WITH CAROLINE

For my Molly who begged me to write a book without horses in it then promptly fell in love with the Hawthorne Cottage crowd while she was waiting

Also for my Mum without whom I wouldn't know what good food should taste like

And for Steve, my chef

PART I : BENCH

They keep asking me what I'm doing here, and I don't really know what to say.

The first thing that pops into my head is They don't know about us. But I think they would look at me even funnier if I suddenly belted out a line from a song. It's by the singer my mum named me after. Kirsty MacColl. She got hit by a speedboat when she was forty-one. Shoved her kid out of its path, took the brunt, died instantly. That's my namesake. Did I ever tell you that? Probably not. Let's face it, it's a bit random and we don't know each other that well, really.

So, instead of giving them some random song lyrics from a random song by a dead singer I just look at them as they approach, put on my best gormless face, and they frown or shake their heads and leave me alone again.

No, backtrack, that's too simplistic. Nice word, simplistic. So much more complicated than mere simple.

Here in order of appearance the actual reactions to my being here:

Your mum — doesn't see me.

Sophia — doesn't see me. I'm not surprised though. She was

1

hanging over your mum's shoulder as they rushed past and she kind of looked at me, but I don't think she has the visual range yet.

Your dad – checks me over with a dismissive frown.

Twin 1 (George) – "Oi, Fat Face, what are you doing here?"

Twin 2 (James) – sniggers.

The pea brains of Tweedle Dumb and Tweedle Dumber obviously haven't caught up with reality yet. I wish I'd asked you when I had the chance if it was actually physically painful living with such morons.

So, in the stark light of day, the 'they' who 'keep asking me what I'm doing here' is only George, really. I'm not sure that makes me feel more comfortable, though. It means that the rest of 'them' are in my head. The voices that tell me I'm making a fool of myself, sitting here like someone who may be somehow important to you.

But I tried leaving and I couldn't.

I'm not joking.

As soon as I stepped through the gates and tried to head home my blood started racing around my body in total terror. I thought I was going to have a heart attack. Seriously. I've tried it three times now. Different exits, same effect. It's like I am doomed to stay here, my fat bum parked on this recycled-plastic slat bench, until you... I don't know... release me?

Sounds crazy?

I don't care how it sounds.

I know I can't leave. I know I need you to come back or I'll sit here till the end of days. And since it looks like it'll be a long time either way, I've decided I'm going to write 'us' down. I've discovered that my brick of a music player, generic middle-aisle-crap that it is, has a word processing function and roughly nine hours of juice left. That's the beauty of cheap with no frills: the battery lasts forever.

2

Nevertheless, either the end of days, or you, could hurry up a bit.

I haven't got all life.

Tap. Tap.

In the meantime, I'm not quite sure where to start. Also, if you don't mind, I'm going to switch narrative format in a minute. I don't really like reading stuff in first person perspective. My old-fashionedness doesn't stop at The Kinks, Dusty Springfield and The Animals. I prefer my books that way, too. Even when I'm daydreaming, I dream of myself in the third person. Like, say, when I'm fantasising about someone kissing me, I'm always observing myself in their arms. I see what's happening, rather than imagine what it feels like.

The other thing about changing perspective is, I could make us both a bit, well, more palatable. You know, dress the plate a bit, use better ingredients. I wouldn't need to be me and you wouldn't need to be you.

I could be smaller than I am, hell, I could be actually skinny, positively dainty, if I so decreed. I could be honey blonde and straight haired with cornflower blue eyes rather than have this mane of dull-as-dishwater brownish curls hanging down my back in a thick bread-like plait and common-as-muck brown eyes. And I could think before I open my mouth rather than open my mouth without thinking. I could be a deep-thinking, cornflower-eyed, blonde beauty with a solid future in unspoken philosophy.

And you? You could be dark, dashing and noble with a future (any kind will do at this juncture) rather than surprisingly okay to be around, snub-nosed (sorry), slightly pig-faced (sorry), with muddy boring-blonde (sorry) hair, fat girlish lips (sorry) and that silly line of freckles along the nose that just looks like splash-back from stirring the tomato sauce too hard.

I wouldn't change your eyes for the world though.

At which point it all falls down.

Greenish-blue like the ocean in postcards from the edge of the globe doesn't really go with dark and dashing (I realise that a globe has no edge but neither has it got corners and people always go on about 'every corner of the globe'). It would make dark and dashing look effeminate and not in a good way. In an ailing sort of way. You know, withering away while coughing prettily into a silk handkerchief. Can you imagine? You, of all people, coughing prettily into a handkerchief?

Yes, I clearly see the flaw in my plan now.

I guess you're just going to have to be who you are.

I might still photoshop me a bit though.

Ah, hang on, that doesn't work either.

Because if I was that cornflower-eyed beauty queen, we would never have met. Or rather, we might have met but the context would have been completely different. Your brothers wouldn't have been such total expletives to me for starters. They would have fallen all over themselves to get some with the skinny blonde babe.

Oh man, I shudder at the thought of one of them trying to stick his tongue in my face. You know what? On second thoughts, I'll stay exactly who I am, thanks.

Kirsty Matthews. Sixteen years old. Too chubby from being fed too much beige food over the years, but not grossly overweight yet, and cooking hard to keep it that way. Not totally unfit either as her karate instructor will verify. Pancake-faced, which always makes her look bigger than she actually is. Light-brown, curly, long hair that falls to the small of her back and is so thick she only washes it once a week since the process takes two hours. Brown eyes, lips even bigger than yours, and a nose.

There we go, done.

I guess I'd better start the story now.

4

This bench is bloody uncomfortable.

∞

Kirsty was shocked.

Up close, or rather from Kirsty's vantage point half way up the auditorium where the special year eleven and sixth form assembly was being held, Caroline Connelly seemed seriously gaunt, almost translucent.

Under her trademark, short-cropped, auburn hair, Connelly's face appeared skull-like and her hands, which were nervously kneading each other in front of her navel, bore little by way of meat between bones and skin. Standing next to the solid frame of Anthony Simm, head of Gull Cove Secondary School and Sixth Form, the woman appeared more like a brittle leaf than Kirsty's favourite TV chef.

While Simm carried on relentlessly waxing lyrical about the unique opportunity presented to the young people in front of him without actually saying what it was, Kirsty's brain tuned out and tried desperately to catch up with reality. As her cogs turned she could sense Phoebe, who was nestled into the chair next to hers, try just as hard to assimilate the sudden appearance of *their* Caroline at their school. Kirsty wondered if Phoebe, too, felt the strong desire to drag the woman off the stage, feed her some sandwiches and then put her back in the box where she belonged.

Their box.

Caroline Connelly may well have been considered a staple in late afternoon British broadcasting, with a career that spanned decades, but as far as Kirsty was concerned the presenter was private property. Phoebe's and hers, to be precise.

The two friends had watched *Cooking with Caroline*, Connelly's most recent show, which saw her knock on random people's houses and cook their dinner with them, religiously since the first season. But while they had been waiting patiently for season four to start it had been announced that Caroline would not be returning to the screen. Nobody seemed to know why. The official *Cooking with Caroline* site merely stated that Connelly was taking a sabbatical to dedicate more time to her personal life.

And now she was here.

In their school.

And clearly not pregnant, as Kirsty and Phoebe had speculated for a while. No, having seen her in the emaciated flesh now, Kirsty realised that the chef was far from expecting.

Kirsty was still trying to tally the frail woman by the podium with the presenter she adored when her focus was called back to the action on stage, where Connelly was finally being invited to take the microphone. Simm, three-piece-suited leader of them all, stood to the side and ushered her to take his place with an encouraging smile. The woman took a deep breath and stepped up, her eyes remaining on the head.

"Thank you, A—", Connelly corrected herself swiftly before the man's given name could slip over her lips, "Mr Simm. And may I just say that I am truly honoured by this o—."

The chef's haughty, melodic voice, that could make cheese on toast sound like a three-star meal, came to another abrupt halt when she turned away from Simm to face the students.

Kirsty thought the woman looked terrified.

While Connelly shut her eyes for a moment to gather herself it occurred to Kirsty just how off kilter it was for somebody who was used to performing in front of the camera and whose job it was to pressgang total strangers into cooking with her to be so nervous addressing a bunch of inconsequential teenagers.

When the chef looked out at them again her stance had changed and she appeared to have found at least some of her professional patter.

"For years, it has been my dream to return to Gull Cove and give something back to what I still, to a large extent, consider my community," the chef recommenced her speech. "I live mostly in London now, but as you all just heard, I was born here and went to school right here in this very building. My parents still live down the road, and I spend a great deal of time visiting. So when I look at the national obesity figures—" As Connelly paused, for effect this time, Kirsty felt an absurd twinge of guilt deep in her gut. "And year after year our little town keeps ranking in the top ten, it feels personal. I can never shake the notion that I should be doing something about it."

Kirsty glanced away briefly, only to catch Mrs Elliot, performing arts teacher extraordinaire, and by default always present in the wings whenever something was happening on *her* stage, do her finest interpretation of a nodding dog.

"So that's what this is about," Connelly continued. "I am inviting twelve people from your year groups to take part in an exciting challenge. The idea is simple. I'm going to teach you to cook." Kirsty sat up straighter. "I am aware that you should all have garnered some basic knowledge in food technology at some point. But what I am planning is a little different. We're decidedly *not* going to look at the science of food, nutritional values or any of those things. Personally, I don't believe any of these things are remotely useful. No, we are simply going to cook. Good, old-fashioned, healthy meals, from scratch. So that when you go out into the world soon you won't ever," Connelly emphasized the word with a sweeping gesture, "need to rely on ready meals and processed fodder." The chef took a side glance at Simm and he gave her a nod. Connelly smiled at him then carried on. "We're talking about a ten-week course, spanning the whole of this term," she began spelling out the details. "You need to be free on Thursday evenings between 6pm and 8pm, you don't need to have any culinary skills already, and it doesn't cost anything to take part. The ingredients will be provided for you. But I expect you to be one-hundred percent committed once you're in." Connelly seemed to be rapidly running out of what little steam she had mustered to begin with now, making her voice change tone from the learned presenter's pitch to a darker, more honest note. "And for the cynical among you, I assure you this is not some secret camera set up or some publicity stunt. I'm here privately, purely for the experience. We haven't even told the local paper. So I don't want any of you who might consider taking part to be put off by the idea of cameras. Absolutely none of this is going to be filmed. It's not what this is about. In short, I don't want anyone not taking part because they think they'll be on TV, or," she ran her eyes over the crowd, "anyone putting themselves forward because they desperately *do* want to be on TV, for that matter. Understood?"

A murmur went through the audience.

"Any questions?"

A couple of hands in the lower rows shot up.

"You!" Connelly nodded encouragingly at a blonde boy just in front of her.

Oh no, no, no, no! Bad mistake! Kirsty screamed inside as soon as she realised who it was.

"What's the prize?" George Deacon asked loudly.

Caroline Connelly was visibly thrown.

"Pardon?"

A couple of rows behind George, his twin brother James started sniggering.

"The prize, Miss," George said, feigning innocence. "If it's a challenge there must be a reward, right?"

"Oh, well," the chef said, flustered. "I might have phrased that wrong. Let's call it a project rather than a challenge, shall we?"

"So, there is no prize?" George confirmed, hamming up disappointment now, while his twin had begun breaking down in a heap of laughter. "You're saying we don't get *anything* at the end of it?"

Kirsty could see the woman crumble inside. Simm came forward and leant in to whisper something into Connelly's ear. He was clearly about to step in when a different voice rang through the auditorium, all the way from the back row. It sounded just like George's but louder, rougher and more jaded, spiced with a sincerity that made Kirsty's neck hair stand up.

"Your prize, you imbecile, is that you'll know how to feed yourself at the end of it without opening a cardboard box first. So shut up, and let the lady tell us how to get in."

Kirsty saw Connelly smile up gratefully at the speaker while the twins turned around to glower at him. She didn't need to look to know who had spoken. Neither did anyone

9

else.

The only Deacon who could shut up a Deacon was a bigger Deacon.

"Yes, thank you, Jake," Simm took over resolutely. "But please watch the name calling, even if they are your brothers and I think you might have a point." The subdued laughter that statement reaped from the crowd made a smirk play on the man's lips. "What we agreed on is to invite anyone who is interested in joining Miss Connelly's cookery class to write her a short letter by this coming Friday, explaining why they want to be chosen, and then it is down to Miss Connelly to make her selection. I would highly recommend participation even for those of you with GCSE and A-level exams coming up. Gull Cove's revision schedule is one of the most robust in the country. If you regularly attend your classes leading up to and especially *during* exam season you should not need any more study time outside school." Audible groans went through the rows behind Kirsty where most of the A-level students were seated. "But I fully endorse that you carry on with your extra-curricular activities during that time. I've said it before and I'll say it again, you need to relax your brain in between study periods. One of the best ways to do so is by acquiring a new skill. And cooking is a life skill. However, please remember only to apply if you haven't got any other commitments on a Thursday night, which means anyone involved in this term's play is automatically out. Rehearsals for *The Little Shop of Horrors* start next week and those will coincide with Miss Connelly's class. The same goes for anyone on the football team. As ever, there will be matches on Thursday nights. For the rest of you, this is a golden opportunity. I strongly suggest you get writing. Dismissed."

"Well, there aren't going to be many of us left then, are there? They didn't think that one through, did they?" Phoebe muttered, while she and Kirsty slowly lifted their butts out of the flip back chairs. Kirsty's best friend parked her miniscule behind down again on the small edge of the seat to retrieve her bag from the floor, ignoring the throng of people to her right, who were trying to pass through. Kirsty could tell that Phoebe was seriously cheesed off and putting gallant effort into refraining from kicking the back of the chair in front of her.

Of course, both girls would have jumped at the chance to cook with Caroline, but Phoebe had sold her soul to Mrs Elliot in year eight, and was not going to be released from any cast until such time that she left Gull Cove. Phoebe Faulkner was the best in song and dance the school had to offer, and in an educational establishment which came fitted with its very own, purpose-built theatre, that amounted to absolutely no get out clause, ever. While Kirsty wondered how she could possibly join Connelly's club without losing her friend's affections, a cacophony of subdued shuffling, moaning and nagging ensued from said friend's right. It was quenched by a sharp side look from Phoebe.

"Get a life, sheeple. If you can't wait, go the other way," Phoebe snarled. "Morons," she added acidly, looking back at Kirsty before they began shifting towards the exit. They reached the stairs, and Kirsty waited for a gap in the flow of people who were making their way down from the back rows. She watched Jake Deacon filter through among them, floating in an invisible exclusion zone, forged by years of being, well, Jake Deacon really, and clearly demarked by the stupid lime green and white motorcycle jacket he insisted on wearing, regardless of the fact he didn't own any vehicle that would warrant such attire. He seemed withdrawn, Kirsty noticed, not his usual cocky self, despite having just delivered a masterpiece in public humiliation of his kid brother. Kirsty hadn't seen much of Jake since after the Christmas holidays or, come to think of it, for most of this year so far, and it crossed her mind how strange that was. Jake Deacon's job description at Gull Cove was to be in everybody's face at all times.

When he was there, at least.

Not so much when he wasn't there, smoking spliffs on the playing field, nicking fork lifts from the local supermarket for joy rides, setting the village green on fire or banging Mia Mayo in the derelict guesthouse at the A-road junction — or vice versa. Nobody really knew for sure who had been doing whom there. But at all other times, being the school's prize peacock was his foremost occupation.

"Oh, don't be so damn polite, Kirst, just go!"

Phoebe gave Kirsty a non-too gentle shove into the traffic of human bodies. Kirsty stumbled forwards, stalled and turned.

"Drop it, Phoe! It's not my fault you've got rehearsals Thursday nights. But I tell you what, I won't try and get into Connelly's club either. Solidarity and all that. Satisfied? Now stop copping a strop."

While the people behind Phoebe squished themselves through the narrow gap that had opened up between the end of the seat row and her back, the girl's eyes suddenly lit up.

"Awh." She slung her arms around Kirsty's neck to give her a brief hug. "You're the bestest." She drew back. "And a complete idiot. *Of course* you are going to try and get in.

One of us *has* to. Look!" Nearly poking a squeezer-by's eye out, Phoebe turned dramatically to point at the chef, who was still standing with Simm and Elliott by the stage. "It's *Caroline Connelly.* In *our* school. How fab is that? I mean, I know we knew she was from around here somewhere. But who knew, right? Come." She grabbed Kirsty by the elbow and dragged her towards the steps. "Let's go and say hello."

∞

And that's exactly why I'm friends with Phoe.

Oh, dear, I hate stories with ever changing narrative perspectives even more than continuous first person drivel. But I need to explain this, you see. I need to explain this. Because I know that people look at her and me and don't get it. I think they mostly think I am the duff. The thing is, I'm really not.

Well, yeah, underneath all that Goth make up, Phoe is infinitely prettier than me, that's for sure. I could look into those big blue eyes forever, and I would kill for straight black hair that can be cut into any shape and then bloody well stays that shape. And that bone structure! Cheekbones. I'd so love some of that cheekbone action. But see, it's not always been that way. I've known Phoe since reception. And, boy, was she an ugly four-year-old! I can't even begin to describe just how much of a freakazoid she was. So I'm not going to.

Suffice to say, back then I was the popular kid out of the two of us, because I had the longest hair in the playground. And I had the best nail varnish collection because my Nan still had the salon then, and I always got to pilfer the nearly empties. That's the stuff that counts at four. Not to mention having free access to the salon's office and knowing exactly where the Blu Tack was kept.

That's currency at infant school. Hard cash. And I was loaded.

Phoe? She smelled of wee and only really kind of blossomed in Year 6, just in time for secondary. The little traitor.

I say that with all my love, because the thing is, when the tables turned, she never turned her back. I know she isn't exactly Little Miss Popularity Contest Winner at Gull Cove, abrasive as she can be. But people respect her, they know who she is, while I, well, I'm just wallpaper, aren't I? Part of the general ambience. One of the people you need for others to stand out.

She could have done. Turned her back on me, I mean. Easily. Without bad blood. Because the thing is, other than watching food porn together, we haven't really had much in common for years. Pretty much nothing at all. But she didn't, and whenever we have a class together she'll still automatically sit with me. Because for some absurd reason, to do with me plonking myself down next to her at our first ever carpet time, she loves me. Loyally. So loyally she wasn't even angry when I did get into Connelly's club for real. She was totally over the moon.

That's Phoe.

And that's why we're friends.

∞

"So, what are you going to wear?"

Phoebe swivelled in half crescents back and forth on Kirsty's desk chair, facing the room.

"Clothes?" Kirsty answered from the bed where she sat, cross-legged, her back resting against the cold blue wall and her pillow in her lap, scrunched into submission by anxious hands.

Kirsty still couldn't believe she'd actually got into Connelly's club, and each time she thought about the first class, which was starting in ninety-three minutes, her stomach lurched with nerves. She had no idea who else had got in, and she hated new-group dynamics at the best of times. The last thing she needed was for Phoebe to give her a headache about cooking fashion.

Phoebe stopped mid-motion to stare at her with raised eyebrows.

"You need a new scriptwriter — your jokes are getting tired."

"Thanks."

"Seriously though, what *are* you going to wear?"

"Don't you have drama to go to?"

Phoebe glanced at the old train station clock above Kirsty's head, so big and dominating, it had a habit of becoming invisible as a time piece, and jumped off the chair.

"*Merde.* I'm gonna be late."

"*Hasta la vista*, Audrey."

Phoebe grabbed her jacket from the floor and grinned over her shoulder as she left the room.

"Not if I see you first."

Kirsty listened as Phoebe ran down the stairs, shouted a 'Bye!' at Kirsty's mother, and opened and shut the front door noisily. She sighed heavily into the suddenly empty space around her, then got up and stepped over to the pine wardrobe opposite her bed to pick out a pair of nondescript jeans and a dark-coloured tartan shirt that would hide any food stains better than the white uniform one she'd been wearing all day.

∞

15

An hour and twenty minutes later, Kirsty was walking slowly down the road towards the school and staring at her music player, torn between The Animals' *Don't Let Me Be Misunderstood*, a solid staple in moments of anticipated dread, The Rolling Stones' *Paint it Black*, always a good reminder that no matter what she was facing there were worse things in life (like death), and Petula Clark's *Downtown*, the ultimate happy tune antidote. Just as Eric Burdon won the debate and his molten baritone began submerging her eardrums, she caught a flash of lime green and white in the corner of her eye.

It rounded her and started disappearing briskly into the distance.

Irritation surged through Kirsty.

That bloody jacket.

It was so *stupid*.

It had always riled her. Always. Not that she was a member of the fashion police or anything, but it was such a ridiculous item as everyday clothing, with its inbuilt spine protector that made the wearer look like a humpbacked insect. He'd worn it continuously since year nine, back then over his *uniform* for goodness' sake, and way too big for him. By now he'd grown into it, filled it out alright, and when paired with faded jeans and work boots, like it was presently, the less knowledgeable might even have believed that he had his bike parked up just around the corner.

The words pretentious and prat mixed themselves into Burdon's plea for understanding of a soul whose intentions were good, just in time with Deacon stopping in his tracks for no visible reason.

Kirsty slowed down, not entirely sure what to do.

Stop and wait until he carried on walking? Carry on

walking in the hope he'd start moving again in a second? Carry on walking and overtake him? Turn around and walk in the other direction?

She could circle the school and approach the entrance from the other side. But that seemed a tad extreme. This particular Deacon had never been mean to her, after all. And this one wasn't known to be a bully either. He was a general pain in the arse but not really a plain arse like his brothers, as far as Kirsty could tell. Plus, she doubted he even knew her name. It was just, he was Jake Deacon and the road was deserted other than the two of them. It felt awkward.

Where on earth were the other cooking class people? Surely they couldn't all be early or late?

All the while she was considering her options, she kept snailing forwards and within a minute, she found herself only a couple of paces behind him. She squared her shoulders and sped up in preparation to walk past him, when he suddenly turned around to face her. She saw his mouth move as he addressed her. Kirsty stopped dead in front of him, almost too close for comfort. She clawed the headphone buds, and with them Burdon's voice, out of her ear canals, hiding them in a clasped hand so he wouldn't be able to hear what she was listening to, and looked up into his eyes.

"Sorry. What did you say?"

"Kristy, right?"

"Kirsty."

"Sorry. Close enough though, yeah?"

It should have come across as belittling but, actually, he seemed genuinely apologetic. Kirsty shrugged.

"I guess. If you're dyslexic."

She could see him do an inner double take before his eyes twinkled with amusement. She got that a lot. People usually thought she should be as plain and thick on the inside as she appeared on the outside. Often *they* turned out as plain and thick on the inside as she appeared on the outside. And didn't get it. To her surprise, he'd got it. She found herself do an inner double take right back at him, while she waited for him to speak again. It was obvious he wanted something. She was tempted to pre-empt him with an 'I don't smoke,' but kept herself in check. Benefit of the doubt and all that.

"Erm," he began, looking over her head for a second as if trying to find words in the air above the frizz halo that always snuck out of her pleat. Finally, he made eye contact again. "Are you doing the cooking thing?"

"Yup."

Kirsty nodded, instinctively bracing herself for some comment about food and moon faces and butts like sofa cushions. But the expected missile didn't come. Instead, he gazed down at her feet almost shyly before he gave her a well-practised, charmball smile, somewhat at odds with the eyes that seemed to be pleading with her for real.

"Would you ... would you mind if we went in together?" He watched her intently as Kirsty's face contorted itself into a one part frown and two parts eyebrow raise cocktail before he explained himself further. "It's just, I'm a bit nervous. I *hate* walking into these afterschool lynch mobs."

∞

Hi. Me again. First-person-voice. Annoying, I know. But I thought I'd better butt in here before you get the hump with what

I've written about that stupid jacket. Hump – see what I did there? Just to say, I did absolutely despise it. Then. Now, of course, I love it half to death. It's the best jacket ever made. I hope.

∞

They walked in silence through the school and towards the cafeteria where they were to meet the rest of Connelly's guinea pigs. Kirsty was loath to admit it, but walking into this thing next to Jake Deacon felt kind of good. The anxiety she had battled all day dissipated as soon as they fell into step with each other, and there was the very real reassurance that nobody would mess with her or make snarky comments while under *his* protectorate. A snicker escaped her when she thought about who had asked whom for safety in numbers here. Jake shot her a side glance but didn't break his stride.

"You okay?" he mumbled, as they stopped to survey the tables from the top of the short staircase that led down to the expanse of the cafeteria floor.

"Uh-huh," Kirsty replied, although it was a lie.

Her heart had started pumping faster as soon as she had spotted the group of eight students, sitting at a table at the head end of the cafeteria and being handed drinks by Caroline Connelly. While she watched them from afar as they wrote their names on sticky labels, Kirsty did a quick evaluation.

So far there was nobody else from her year, only year twelves or thirteens. Great. Unless the missing two turned out to be other year elevens, she was going to be the baby of the bunch. There were five girls and three boys. The latter surprised her. She hadn't reckoned on that much interest

19

from the y-chromosomes. If she was honest, until she had accumulated the strange travelling companion next to her who was currently gripping tightly onto the banister with poled arms, she had assumed it would be an all girls club with maybe one, maximum two, token males thrown in.

"Great," Jake hissed with an undertone of humour. "I've only slept with one of them."

"Which one?"

Kirsty nearly tripped over her tongue as she asked but it had slipped past her censorship chip regardless. He'd done that somehow. With his disarming honesty about hating to walk into scenarios like the one laid out in front of them, he'd instantaneously become — she struggled for the right word until *a conspirator* popped up in her mind's eye, in friendly Comic Sans lettering. And there was no shame, no airs and graces between conspirators. No censorship. A bit like friends, but for a temporary arrangement. She could live with that. As long as he didn't drop her like a hot potato as soon as they'd settled in. But just in case that was the plan, she reminded herself to stay in the emergency landing position for the eventuality, and almost missed his reply in the process.

"The cute one in the short black leather jacket."

Kirsty scanned the people again but the only one fitting the description was a boy called Ronan, whose special niche at Gull Cove was to be year thirteen's poster gay boy. She glanced at Jake sideways just in time for a huge grin to light up his features, his arms to bend at the elbows and his shoulder to give hers a nudge.

"Sucker," he scolded her amicably, in between subdued laughter. "I'm not as much of a manwhore as people around here make me out to be, you know. Although, it's kind of true. I shared a tent with that guy during our year ten residential. Back then he was still quite sweet. Kind of shy. Wonder what happened to him. Come on, let's go cook some shit."

∞

"I thought we'd make our lives easy on our first evening and give ourselves some time to get to know each other."

Connelly was sitting on the table opposite the one her little group was gathered at, swinging her legs and smiling down warmly at the round of faces. Kirsty thought the chef looked a little less gaunt than the last time she'd seen her, but there was still something off about her. There seemed to be constant shivers running through the woman that reminded Kirsty of those silly trembling handbag dogs. Connelly's eyes took a sweep of her charges again, then travelled back to Kirsty and squinted at her name tag.

"Yes, Kirsty?"

Kirsty flinched out of her contemplation. She hadn't been aware that she had made any movements showing a wish to say something, but luckily she could think of an obvious question that didn't mention either handbags or dogs.

"I thought there were twelve places, Miss. Aren't we still waiting for people? It's not even six o'clock yet. I think we should give them more time to turn up."

She heard the Ronan boy snort and saw his obligatory female shadow, a girl clad in black called Aimee, who Kirsty vaguely knew through Phoebe, send her a sharp look. Kirsty raised her eyebrows at her and shrugged defiantly. It was true, it wasn't six o'clock yet, not even in wannabe-Uber-Goth land.

"Call me Caroline or Chef, but not Miss, please, and, yes, you are right, there were twelve places but this is it. We couldn't fill them. Everyone who wanted a place got a place. The reason every one of you is here is because you were the only ones who applied."

Connelly paused to give Kirsty another opening, but the girl was too shocked to say anything else. Kirsty looked down at the beige Formica table top instead. She couldn't believe it. She had spent *hours* writing and rewriting that letter.

"Which has messed up my plans a little where cooking in teams of four is concerned," Connelly carried on. "But we'll cross that bridge when we come to it. I guess we could do two threes and a four. We'll see. For now, it doesn't matter. Most weeks you are supposed to be cooking in pairs. Not today though. Today, we cook as a whole group. If you want to call it cooking at all. As I said, we'll make our lives really easy tonight. After that you can find yourselves a cooking partner and rest assured, I'm not planning on shaking it up every week. When I was still at school I used to hate having to work with anyone other than Anti—that's Mr Simm to you and if he ever finds out I've told you his nickname, you'll be cooking *me* for dinner next. So, if there are people here who already come with a partner that's fine by me, I won't tear you apart. I want you to be happy about doing this, and there'll be homework sometimes, so people might need to meet up outside school. What I'm saying is, if you want to call dibs on a specific person to work with, now is your chance. If you haven't got someone I'll pair you up during tonight's dinner."

Kirsty felt shuffles ripple along the bodies around her but kept her gaze down, busy examining a tiny biro-drawn flower on the table which she had currently framed in a triangle formed by her two thumbs and index fingers. When she finally looked up she was once again amazed by how quickly allegiances could be formed in the face of otherwise random selection.

Ronan and Aimee weren't much of a revelation. Neither were a guy called Zach, who'd come in a Batman comic strip shirt, showing the caped crusader as he fried eggs for Robin and Batgirl, and his sidekick Noel, who was sporting a long-sleeve with the image of a knife and fork crossed and *Food Fight* lettered around it. The two year twelve, graphic novel geeks were a respected fixture at Gull Cove, and never really did anything apart. Once she'd got over the unexpected number of y-chromosomes present, Kirsty hadn't actually been terribly surprised to see them here. There was something both foodie and Youtubie about them. She could envision them running their own whacky food show channel one day, complete with animated clips to slide from one section to the next and onomatopoeia like 'SIZZLE!' appearing around the cooking action.

The impromptu pairing of a redhead in a jumpsuit called Poppy, who Kirsty had never noticed before, and Maisy Miller-Makambe, head of the student council and future first alliterated black female right wing prime minister was a little more noteworthy.

Possibly the most interesting marriage of necessity, though, was that of Gemma Smith, year thirteen's most ambitious Barbie doll, and arguably the thickest person in Gull Cove, and Catalina Amado, a Spanish exchange student with eyebrows like caterpillars, the wrists of a man and a bottom wider than Kirsty's. Much as Kirsty adored Caroline Connelly, why a Spanish girl would want to learn to cook from a British TV personality was beyond her. Kirsty had been to Spain on holidays every year since she was six, and as far as she could tell, Spanish babies were born clutching a tiny frying pan in their little fists. A three-year-old Spanish child could out-omelette any British three star chef in its sleep. Why Catalina would want to pair up with such a complete airhead was even more intriguing but there it was, the evidence right in front of Kirsty's nose. She was taken aback when she realised that both of them were staring at her with equally annoyed expressions on their faces, but the penny didn't drop until Kirsty suddenly became aware of the last person in the mix, on the edge of her space. The last person, who during the general shuffle when Kirsty had been preoccupied with staring at the flower, had apparently turned a quarter on his seat next to her in order to face her sideways. The last person, who was now sitting with legs spread wide apart and despite having left a generous exclusion zone between himself and her had managed to encompass her entire right side below the waist in that manner, while shielding her top half with an arm sprawled out on the table and curved lightly around her territory.

Gemma might have fancied herself a stint with the wild boy of Gull Cove, and Catalina might have hoped to team up with the other fat girl in the group, but the evidence was clear.

Jake Deacon had staked his claim.

∞

And here we go again.

I give up. I clearly need to have these little intervals, this 'me'

24

time. So be it.

The problem is, I'm kind of stuck here. I've been staring holes into space for the last half an hour because I don't know where to go next with this. It's such a strong sentence, 'Jake Deacon had staked his claim'. I'm not really sure that's how it felt to you at the time. Or to me. But in retrospect, it's kind of what happened, isn't it?

Anyway, it's such a strong sentence, I don't know how I get from there to all of us standing in the school kitchen looking at those chickens that Caroline had brought in as if they were, I don't know, raw food or something. And though I'll never ever forget Ronan's face when Caroline told him to peel his own bloody carrot and cut up his own bloody potato and not let Aimee do it, I have no idea how to describe it. Really, I'm not writer enough to do any of it justice. Yes, English is my favourite subject and, yes, Mrs Dodson keeps going on and on about how I should really do something with my creative writing and, yes, I probably have twice the vocabulary of most of the people in my year, but right now, words fail me.

I still think it was really clever, the way Caroline made us make a roast that first night. Because she is right, it is the easiest meal in the world. Cut potato in four, peel carrot, drape around chicken in lightly oiled dish, add sprig of rosemary, put cooking cupboard on, open cooking cupboard, put food in cooking cupboard, shut cooking cupboard, do something else for an hour, take food out of cooking cupboard, make a sauce, eat food.

It was genius because the only things she really taught us that day were how not to be afraid, and to make gravy from scratch, and the thing is, once you know how stupidly simple that is there is no way you'd buy granules, right?

Strike one against prefab fodder accomplished and we didn't even realise.

But it was also clever because it gave us time to get used to each other, and to look around the kitchen in peace, and for Caroline to explain utensils to us. But mostly because of how she made us share with each other why we were there, without really making a big deal of it, just asking people as we went along to remind her why they wanted to cook. As if she hadn't memorised each letter.

I felt bad when Aimee said both her parents had started working nights, and if she didn't learn to cook she'd have to live on frozen pizza for the rest of her life. It's kind of like I felt, only my folks didn't work nights. They just didn't cook. Funny girl, Aimee. When she is not busy being a cliché, she's actually quite sound.

I also remember feeling really smug when Zach and Noel admitted that they were thinking of doing their own cooking show one day. I'm good at this stuff. Casting people, seeing into their dreams. I hope they make it. I think they deserve it. They really are cool, those two. And, yes, blah blah, I know what you think of Noel. But I still think he's kind of cute and maybe I should have, you know. I mean someone's gotta do me one day, right? But I'm jumping way too far ahead now.

I did think it was hilarious when Catalina said she wanted to learn about English cooking, so she would know how to cater for English tourists in her parents' guesthouse back home. I don't think she really knew what she was saying there.

I'm wracking my brain here, but I can't for the life of me remember what Gemma proclaimed her reason for being there was, but I don't really think it matters what she said. Everybody knew she hadn't got the memo that there really wasn't going to be a TV crew, not even a teensy-weensy little camera man.

Neither can I remember why Ronan, Poppy and Maisy said they'd wanted to do it. To be honest, I think I've edited a lot of *their contribution from my memory. Ronan because all he ever seems to do is gossip, or moan, or both. Poppy because she is soooooooo quiet she kind of edits herself. And where Maisy is concerned, it's pure survival mechanism. I simply developed the capacity to block out her constant know-it-all commentary about half an hour into the first evening in order not to throttle her and ruin my life. Man, that girl is a pain in the backside. I know her big brother Robbie quite well because their mum used to work for my nan's salon doing the hair extensions, and he used to come in to help out on Saturdays. Total sweetheart, says about three words a day and smiles the rest. Bright, too, just like Maisy. He went to a public school on a scholarship. Big little girl crush of mine. But his sister? Drives me up the wall. Go figure.*

I know, I'm digressing talking about people who have no bearing on our story whatsoever now. If I'm honest, I'm stalling because I still don't know where to pick up again, what to leave in, what to leave out, what's important. I mean, at this point every little detail I can remember about you seems like it needs to be pickled and preserved for eternity.

∞

When Kirsty left her first ever cooking with Caroline class, happily swinging her homework in the shape of a chicken carcass, a leek, a carrot and an onion in a plastic bag, she felt invigorated rather than stuffed silly, despite the sizable portion of food she'd just eaten. She also felt a little lonely.

Jake had been kept back by Caroline after the chef had ushered out the rest of them, and while the others had filtered out in pairs, Kirsty had been left to find the exit on her own.

When she hit the playground, it was getting to the end of

27

twilight outside, and a lot chillier than it had been earlier in the evening. She stopped just past the school gate to button up her jacket, then pored over her music player to select a homewards tune. Lost in choices, she didn't hear Zach, Noel, Aimee and Ronan approach, and only realised once they started their interrogation that they must have waited by the fence for her.

"You got any idea what Deacon is doing here?" Aimee asked curiously.

Kirsty scanned the crescent of nosy faces around her.

"Cooking?" she dead-panned but it didn't seem to cut the mustard. They kept staring at her, so she shrugged. "Nope. Why should I?"

"Erm, because you came with him?" Ronan said, raising his kink-plucked eyebrows.

Of course, that would have got their tongues wagging, and normally that would have amused Kirsty no end, but something else more intriguing occurred to her that same instant. It was only now, prompted by their question, that Kirsty realised something. While everyone else had been lured by Caroline into talking about why they had applied for cookery club, the chef had distinctly left Jake out of her efforts.

"I didn't come *with* him. I came *in* with him. Big difference. Anyway, what does it matter?"

"It doesn't, we were just wondering," Noel answered, already half turned away. He ran a hand through his plum-coloured, spiky hair and gave Zach a 'Let's go' nod at the same time. The two walked off, raising their hands above their heads in simultaneous goodbye gestures. Aimee and Ronan, however, weren't as easily satisfied.

"You know what Connelly wants with him?" Aimee

carried on her line of questioning.

"I haven't got the faintest," Kirsty replied. She could feel herself bristle. She hated this kind of crud. People sticking their noses in other people's business. "And even if I did, I wouldn't tell you. Why don't you ask him yourself?"

"Whoa, easy there." Aimee held up her hands. "Just asking."

"Someone's got the hots," Ronan taunted with a giggle. "Shame Jake's probably playing lucky dips with the dishy TV lady in the store room right now. Didn't you know he's got a thing for older dames, that Deacon? I'm sorry, honey."

He gave Kirsty a mock pitying look then dragged Aimee away by the sleeve, still laughing affectedly. Kirsty stood frozen to the spot, not sure if she was more furious about the inference that she fancied Jake, or about Ronan's blatant attempt to perpetuate an ancient Gull Cove myth that two years previously had caused one of her favourite ever student teachers to move placement to another school. Or maybe she was just angry with herself for the tiny, niggling fragment of doubt that Ronan had managed to plant with one foul sentence. She was still fuming, still torn between going with Nancy Sinatra's boots to walk all over them or with the more peaceful *Everbody's Talkin'*, when Jake materialised by her side.

"Hey. You're still here. Someone picking you up?"

She didn't turn to face him. She wordlessly shook her head, which was suddenly full of the kind of imagery that Ronan's suggestive comment had left behind.

"Are you walking or on the bus?"

"Walking," she answered thinly, trying her hardest to push the X-rated film in her mind aside.

He stepped around to face and block her at the same

time, bending his head to try and get her to make eye contact. Considering what she'd just seen in her imagination, she really, really didn't want to meet his gaze.

"Okay. Then I'll walk you home."

"What? Why?"

Her face shot up to look at him aghast. The shock of the offer had vacuumed all the unwanted pictures out of her mind, which was a significant blessing.

He shrugged.

"'Cause you're on my team now, and I don't want you walking home alone at night."

"I'd hardly call this night. There's still light in the sky. It's not even nine o'clock yet. You go home, I'll be fine."

Even while she was listening to her own voice, Kirsty couldn't quite believe she was in the process of fending off chivalry from Jake Deacon, of all people, a thought which seemed almost more absurd than the fact she had spent the evening in the company of Caroline Connelly.

"Man, you are hard work. Are you always this argumentative? I tell you something, that's probably why my brothers pick on you, you know. If those two idiots know they can get a reaction out of somebody they're all over it like a bad rash. Take my word for it, if you didn't rise to it, they'd leave you well alone. They haven't got the guts to go after someone who ignores them. Here's some intel for you: in my house they're nicknamed chicken and shit." Jake took a deep breath and frowned heavily. Then he slowly leant in and scrutinised her more closely, searching her eyes. "Or is it that you don't want to be seen with me?"

"What? No!!!" She took a step back but forced herself not to evade his gaze. "Don't be stupid. But I'm a big girl. I

30

don't need a babysitter. And I've been walking by myself for a good few years now. Thanks for the offer though." She smiled gratefully for the last part. "Go home, Jake."

He straightened up again, cocked his head and let his eyes roam freely over her shape, so blatantly body scoring her that it didn't even feel intrusive. Insulting, maybe, but not intrusive. Somewhere in the back of her mind a voice screamed that she should be livid, but just as an appropriate tirade of ranting feminism wanted to roll off her tongue he cut her short.

"I've seen bigger," he stated dryly. Then he moved back around to flank her and hooked his arm through hers. "Come on, don't be stubborn." He tugged gently, indicating the plastic bag on her other side with a jerk of the head. "I'd never forgive myself if something happened to our future stock in there."

∞

You know what I remember most about that walk home? How easy you were to talk to. I would never have expected that, you being a Deacon and all. I can't actually remember a thing we said, just that we were chatting back and forth the entire way. No, that's not right, I do remember you laughing till your eyes welled up when you asked how come I knew so much about people at school and I said 'I don't watch soaps, I watch Gull Cove'. As if that was actually funny. And I recall how amazed I was at how much you knew about the twins targeting me. There was this absurd sense of gratitude towards them, because clearly without them making me the butt of 90% of their jokes, you wouldn't have had heard of me. There was also this slightly warped sentiment that actually by knowing about it you had kind of looked out for me for a while. At some point I suddenly knew for certain that if the twins had ever really gone to town on me, or anyone else, you would have taken their heads off and that because they knew that, they'd never turned on me or anyone else properly. I hate to say this because they are your brothers, but those boys have it in them to be nasty. Really, really nasty. And, no, I have no evidence for that statement. They never really did anything truly horrific to me, other than when they posted that picture of my backside on Instagram. Actually, that was mortifying, even if Simm made them take it down almost immediately. But what was way worse than that was the constant commentary. Every day. Since year seven. Like Chinese water torture. Drip. Drip. Drip. 'Oi, fat face, you sure you want to eat that?' Drip. 'Fat girls don't cry. They don't cryhyhy.' Drip. 'Here comes Kirsty. Ahahahand here comes Kirsty's butt'. Drip.

And I don't get why me. I mean, I heard what you said but, still, why even start on me in the first place? I'm not really that large. I mean, yes, I'm a bit podgy, sure. I'm soft to the touch. But it's not like I wobble or can't see my feet or have difficulties running for the bus or anything. I'm big and taut with tits and arse and a bit of a belly in between. That's me. I've seen girls from school in bikini tops who were miles bigger than me hanging around with your brothers in the park. And not a word said. Well, maybe they weren't bigger as such but easily on par. Only less firm to be honest. I mean, you know, they had extra wings under their wings. At least I don't have those.

So how does that work? Why me and not them?

Did, I should say. How did that work?

Because, of course, as if by miracle, as of the day after our first cookery class, they practically stopped. The occasional 'Fat face' notwithstanding. I can live with that though. When it lacks the rest of the onslaught it's practically a term of endearment from those two.

∞

"**Y**ou're kidding, right? Jake Deacon is actually picking you up?"

"Yup, that's what he said to me in the cafeteria this morning, and if you sound any more surprised, I'll take that as an insult."

Phoebe and Kirsty were sitting opposite one another on the floor of Kirsty's room. Having horsed around with applying, removing and reapplying nail art all afternoon they both felt a little light-headed, and a bit sick from varnish and acetone fumes. Phoebe carefully finished painting a last bat onto Kirsty's big toe nail, then looked up sharply.

"Come on, Kirst, you know that's a bit strange, to say the least." She leant forward, concern written all over her face. "Are you sure it's not a set up?"

For a split second, Kirsty's blood pumped faster with fear as her body contemplated the possibility once more, but her brain proved more self-assured. When Jake had sauntered over earlier in the day and casually asked if they could go to cooking club together tonight, there had been a moment when she'd entertained exactly the same thought. But then she'd remembered the walk home the week before and suddenly noticed the pleading in his eyes. Like he actually *wanted* her company.

"You have to stop watching those godawful movies, Phoe," Kirsty said, almost too casually. "Really. Stick with the horror flicks, goes better with the image anyway. This is not *Hollywood High*, this is Gull Cove. And he's actually a

33

really nice guy. Go figure."

"What? Jake Deacon? *The* Jake Deacon? Same guy who got Mr Livingston suspended for decking him one because he wound him up *that* much? Same guy who made Miss Richardson leave because they were having an affair? Same guy who—"

Kirsty wouldn't let her finish the sentence.

"Allegedly having an affair," she pointed out, soberly. "And if you think about it, it was Livingston who did wrong there and not Jake. Also, have you not noticed that he's changed somehow? I don't know, he's way less obnoxious than he used to be, don't you think? Like he's trying really hard not to be, you know, Jake Deacon anymore." She hesitated before she voiced the thing that she hadn't even noticed had been bothering her ever since Caroline Connelly's first appearance at Gull Cove. "Do you recall seeing him around at all last term?"

Phoebe shrugged, pretending to have lost interest already by picking a bottle of dark purple nail varnish out of Kirsty's make up box.

"Nah. Not really. It's not like he's really on my radar unless he's trying his hardest to be on *everybody's* radar. Nice colour."

"Have it. But that's exactly what I'm saying."

Phoebe pocketed the little bottle, and took a deep, exasperated breath.

"All I'm getting at, Kirst, is: be careful. You like him. Don't deny it. I can see the attraction, too. You're weirdly similar people. You're both as pompous as each other. In your own way. You're both sickeningly sure of who you are. You both walk around as if you're untouchable. You both sound as if you swallowed a Thesaurus for breakfast.

You both—"

"Says the woman who just used the word pompous," Kirsty interrupted.

"A word I adopted from Deacon, I believe," Phoebe continued dryly, "after I heard him use it in the context of 'Mr Livingston, sir, you appear to be mistaking pomposity for intelligence'. I was *there* that day, Kirsty. Now stop interrupting, I'm having an epiphany and I'm having it for *you*. Where was I? Ah, yes. You both have somehow managed to turn having no fashion sense into a distinct style. You're both arrogant as hell. You both—"

"I think you covered arrogant with pompous already."

"Shush. I'm not finished. What I'm saying is, you both march to the beat of a different drum. Actually, make that an entire drum kit. But, and this is important, Kirst, that's where it ends. That boy is just bad news. And I'm worried about you. Talking of bad," she added, suddenly jumping up to leave, "I have a date with a carnivorous plant. *Tot ziens.*"

Phoebe slipped through the door before Kirsty could properly process even a fraction of her monologue. One day she would have to thoroughly question how her best friend saw her, but for now she just felt a bit stunned.

And strangely flattered.

"What language is that?" Kirsty just about managed to shout after her.

"Dutch, I believe," came the muffled reply from the landing.

A minute later Phoebe had left the Matthews' abode, but the echoes of her voice had not. Kirsty got ready to the tune of her friend's words in her ears, oscillating between irritation, disbelief, wonder and indignation as she turned each comparison over in her head again and again. By the time she heard the knock downstairs, her brain felt like a scouring pad and her nerves stood on end.

They settled the moment she opened the front door and saw Jake smile at her in a wordless greeting. She stepped outside to join him while he turned towards the road and crooked his elbow for her to hook in. Without hesitation, Kirsty loosely slung her arm through his and then they were off.

∞

Following the instructions Caroline had given them at the end of the first night, they didn't wait in the cafeteria but walked straight to the kitchen. This time, Kirsty and Jake had arrived long before the others and though there was a heap of shopping in bags on the counter, Caroline was nowhere to be seen.

They hesitated at the threshold.

It still felt more than a little rude, this taking over of the dinner ladies' domain. Gull Cove's kitchen manager, Gina, was a fierce woman with a seriously territorial side, and normally even leaning in too far over the serving area would get a student's head bitten off. It had been glaringly obvious during their induction evening that even Caroline seemed to live in fear of the resident chef's wrath. They had left the kitchen spick and span, but Caroline had still seemed nervous about having left any utensils in the wrong place, the wrong switch on, or equipment unplugged that should have been plugged in and vice versa.

After a minute of just standing and staring into the empty space in front of them, Kirsty put a foot out onto the blue anti-slip lino on the other side, as if testing the water, and then nodded reassuringly to Jake. There was something satisfying about hearing him chuckle as they crossed the border into the forbidden realm. It was nice to be able to make someone other than Phoebe laugh, to have someone other than Phoebe who got her sense of humour, who got *her*.

Kirsty went to the counter, put down the bag containing the frozen stock she had brought with her, and vaulted herself up to sit next to the shopping. The move made her suddenly feel both quite naughty and kind of cool. She couldn't remember ever feeling cool before. Somewhere between Phoebe's monologue and the company she was currently keeping she'd stopped feeling quite so much like wallpaper.

Jake raised his eyebrows.

"You got guts, Kirsty Matthews, I give you that." Kirsty didn't really get long to revel in the knowledge that he must have memorised her surname at some point, as the content of his next sentence hit home. "Imagine if Gina walked in right now. We'd have a special 'special' tomorrow, and nobody would ever know … " He let his voice trail off ominously while Kirsty made to jump off. He held his hand up in front of her chest to stop her. "Stay." He grinned. "Just winding you up. I'd hazard a guess that Gina is back in her lair by now, nursing her young. What's in the bags?"

"I'm pretty sure Gina is past childbearing age. I've heard once you're past one hundred and eighty your eggs shrivel up," Kirsty replied, while poking a finger into one of the shopping bags and pulling the plastic to the side so she could take a peek.

"You don't know much about dragons, do you? They can

give birth until well into their thousandth year. Go on, spill."

"I see tomatoes and carrots and onions and some green fresh herbie type thing," Kirsty answered, then leant closer over the bag and inhaled deeply. "Coriander," she decided before moving on to inspect the next lot of shopping. "And a packet of something and a couple of those things that look like huge yellow pears but are actually a kind of pumpkin."

"The word you are looking for is squash," Caroline said from the door where she'd just appeared, in the process of tying her apron. It was long and black, hugging the chef's skinny frame in a way that almost turned it into a garment of elegance. As the woman walked over to join them, Kirsty wondered how that worked. When Kirsty wore an apron, no matter what colour, she always ended up the spitting image of a stout, pre-revolution, Russian peasant crone, as depicted in her year nine history book. She nearly forgot to jump off the counter as she mused, mumbling an apology for peeking into the bags when she finally did.

Caroline chuckled.

"It's okay. I'm thrilled you're taking an active interest. We're already one down. Gemma's dropped out. Maisy said she was going to be late tonight, but as you can see," the woman paused to turn and spread her arms, indicating the empty space around them, "none of the others take it seriously enough to be on time either."

If Kirsty detected a smatter of dejection in the chef's voice, she didn't get around to feeling sorry for her because just then the others did show up in bulk.

It was soup time.

∞

Out of the five different soups the teams cooked that evening, the potato and leek won hands down in the taste test. Kirsty didn't think it was entirely fair, since due to the absence of Gemma, Caroline herself had joined forces with Catalina to produce something that didn't even taste of its main ingredients anymore. It tasted divine. And marginally Spanish, although that could have been Kirsty's envious imagination.

Second, without a shadow of a doubt, came Aimee's and Ronan's carrot and coriander. Mostly, Kirsty thought, because, again, Caroline herself had had a hefty hand in that creation. They'd been given one of Caroline's own stock tubs to work with since they'd failed tragically on the homework. Kirsty couldn't for the life of her imagine how you could mess up boiling a chicken carcass and some vegetables until the water tasted of chicken and vegetables. But after some gentle probing it transpired that Aimee had forgotten about the pot on the hob while she had gone to dye her hair, and when she had come back she'd found all the fluid had evaporated and the bones baked to the bottom. The way Aimee told the story was so funny and animated that Kirsty found herself rapidly warming to the girl, especially when Aimee delivered the kicker.

"And look at this," Aimee exclaimed, having come to the end of her tale. She lifted her newly black hair into a ponytail to reveal a pair of thoroughly dyed dark purplish ears, setting off her multitude of silver piercings nicely. "To add insult to injury, I get this. First, I forget about the chicken and then I forget about the dye while frantically trying to clean up that bloody pot so my mum doesn't effing kill me. It's a LeCreuset. You know, one of those ugly orange jobs. A real one. Really expensive. I was sweating it, literally, and the dye must have run."

Once Kirsty had finished laughing, and Maisy had been done berating Aimee for saying 'effing' on school grounds, which had sparked a short but heated debate about whether that could technically be counted as actually swearing, an offence like no other in Simm's book, they had moved on to Maisy's and Poppy's tomato soup. It had turned out so mediocre that Kirsty had had to rein in the impulse to perform a dance of joy. Beastly though it was, it delighted her no end to see Maisy fail. Flipping goodie-two-shoes.

Zach's and Noel's lentil broth had been thick and hearty and good. They had basked in Caroline's appreciation of it, and for the rest of the evening it could happen at any point that one or the other of them would appear with a spoonful of their dish in front of any of the others' mouths tempting them with an enticing, "Lentil soup?"

To begin with it was kind of funny, but by round seven it had worn a bit thin. Although, looking into Noel's dark eyes as he once again pushed the tip of the spoon gently at Kirsty's lips, she thought for a moment that she could well live with a boy like him feeding her. The first couple of times he'd attempted it, she had flinched, the fat girl in her automatically assuming she was being teased. Then she'd reminded herself that she was not the butt of the joke, just part of a general running gag, opened her mouth and swallowed. It had felt kind of good. It had felt even better when she'd realised that it was *only* Noel who was doing it to her while both he and Zach shared the rest of the group between them. She was just about to consider reading a deeper meaning into that, when she saw Jake's hand appear on Noel's shoulder from behind. A funny vibe sparked between the three of them as Jake looked at her while speaking evenly into Noel's ear.

"That's enough, Noel. It stopped being funny half an hour ago. Caroline says we need to clear up now."

∞

As they filtered out of the school gate, all of them bar Jake who'd once again been kept back by Caroline, Aimee nudged Kirsty amiably.

"You know, I really liked yours and Deacon's squash soup. I thought it went underrated because of those jerks." Aimee indicated Zach and Noel who'd just detached from the rest of the crowd to walk down the road.

"I agree," Ronan chipped in, managing to make it sound as if he was mortally offended by the matter, as if his personal friends Kirsty and Jake had been short changed.

Turncoat, Kirsty thought.

They watched Maisy get into her mum's car, and Poppy and Catalina cross the road together, heading for the bus stop. Kirsty thought it was nice to see the one person in the group who never said a single word chatting to the Spanish girl. They both seemed like nice people. She wished them friendship.

"So, what do you think Connelly is going to dream up for us next week?" Ronan asked casually.

Kirsty shrugged.

"Maybe something vegetarian?" she suggested. "I mean, she is a bit lucky that none of us *is* vegetarian. Everything's been chicken based so far, even the vegetable soups."

"True," Aimee nodded. "I used to be veggie. For about a year. But I couldn't hack it. I just love bacon too much."

"Yeah," Kirsty agreed dreamily. "A world without bacon

41

would be a sad place indeed. Nothing like a freshly made bacon baguette with little cherry tomatoes, lettuce and lashings of mayo and mustard. The perfect marriage of English and French cuisine. Got to be happy bacon though. Unhappy bacon just tastes... unhappy."

"Totally. *D'accord, mademoiselle.* Ze bacon has to be ze free bacon. Otherwise it is ze watery bacon." Aimee ran with it, with a straight face and the worst fake French accent Kirsty had ever heard.

She was starting to really like this girl.

They grinned at each other.

"Are you finished with the bacon thing yet?" Ronan asked, tersely.

"Never!" the girls shouted out, but the beginnings of a giggle fit were stemmed abruptly by Ronan jerking his chin at something behind Kirsty's and Aimee's backs.

"Shush," he hissed at Aimee. "Here he comes."

The sweetness of the unexpected camaraderie that Kirsty had felt suddenly turned sour. They hadn't hung around for a chat with her. They had been waiting to ambush Deacon.

"Hey," Jake addressed Kirsty softly as he arrived by her side. He acknowledged Aimee and Ronan with a curt nod then carried on talking to Kirsty as if they weren't there. "I'm glad you waited for me." He paused briefly, looking away from her profile to frown at the other two as if wondering why they were still cluttering the scenery. "Or are you going with them today?"

"Wasn't the plan, no."

"Cool. Well, let's go."

"Hang on a sec, Deacon." There was serious challenge in Ronan's voice and Kirsty wondered for a moment if the boy had a secret death wish. He was about a third the width of

Jake. Or, if one subtracted the body armour in that stupid bike jacket, at least half his size. "What's the deal with you and Connelly? Why does she keep making you hang back?"

"None of your business," Jake said with a cold smile. "Come on, Kirsty, let's move."

They walked most of the way in silence that night, and Kirsty cursed Ronan and Aimee for putting such a downer on the evening. She and Jake had been halfway through an interesting conversation when they had arrived at the school earlier, and without realising it she'd really been hoping they could finish it. Or at least carry it on, since she seriously doubted they'd solve the meaning of life in two short walks. Just before they turned into Kirsty's road, Jake suddenly shook himself, as if trying to shake the thoughts in his brain into a new pattern, and took a deep breath.

"Go on then," he said, exasperated.

"Go on, what?"

"Ask me the question."

"What question?"

"The question Ronan asked."

"Nope. None of *my* business, either. I figure if you want to tell me what that's all about, you will. But I don't stick my nose into other people's business. Not my style. I watch but I don't pry. Big difference. That's why my nan sold the salon. My family used to own a hair and beauty studio. She reckoned there was no point keeping it for the next generation 'cause I'd make such a lousy hairdresser."

She felt relief when she heard him laugh for the first time that evening.

"You're priceless, Kirsty Matthews. And so much more rock 'n roll than those twits."

They'd come to a stop in front of her house, and

suddenly she found herself in a hug that picked her up and lifted her feet off the ground. There was a quick "See you", but before she could even fully appreciate that this boy was strong enough to pick up her bulk without batting an eyelid, he had set her back down gently and was gone.

∞

Day two.

Yesterday's bench let me go in the end.

Not that it really had much choice.

My dad turned up around five in the afternoon and dragged me away.

I had to go to the police station and give a formal statement.

And ever since then I've been trying my hardest not to see the images that have been flashing through my mind on a continuous loop in the background somewhere. It's as if the shock delayed the retina memory until the police forced me to push the play button.

And now it won't stop.

I've battled with the visuals all night.

Whatever I see, I also see what happened yesterday at the same time.

Way home in the truck with dad, dinner with my parents looking worried, shower, getting into bed, mum coming to sit with me and trying to talk to me – and all the time: action replay.

Like ghosting on screen.

But I don't want to talk about it.

Ignoring it now.

If I let it through it makes me sick. And I mean physically sick. Bile and nausea.

So, anyway, I finally fell asleep at the crack of dawn, then woke up a couple of hours later and got on the first train over. It feels like I never left. Like the night never happened. Today, I'm on a different bench though. A bit further away from the entrance. I can still see people as they come and go, but it's more peaceful here. Astonishing amount of traffic considering it's only around eight o'clock in the morning. There is like a mini garden here, and then railings through which I can see the bus stops. It's quite a quaint front for such a huge building. I guess all the action is around the back.

My mum's already rung, telling me to come home again. I told her no. It might sound stupid but I really think that me being here, writing all of this down, is actually doing *something. Helping in some way. Maybe that's what praying is, really. Or 'sending vibes', if you are one of those people. For the first time in my life I actually get why people do it.*

Anyway, so I've been reading what I've written so far, and it occurred to me that the thing I said in the beginning about us not really knowing each other that well is a load of crap. Obviously. What I meant was, we never really said much about ourselves to one another. Like, I still don't know when your birthday is, or what your earliest memory is, or who your first kiss was, or anything like that. Or how much of the Jake Deacon legend is actually true. I do know that you have the most interesting theory about why time can't be linear, only our perception of it is, and that you were one of the only people to at least hear me out on my purpose of collective consciousness monologue. I know you love Star Wars *but hate everything else sci-fi, and will argue the toss that, strictly speaking, those films are not science fiction anyway. And I remember how astounded you were when I told you I had a big thing for Westerns, with* The Quick and the Dead *being my all-time favourite, and that you promised me that one day I'd own a dustcoat just like that. Nice sentiment, by the way, but I can guarantee you that a coat like that would work on me about as well as one of those aprons Caroline wears would. Not that it would make me look like a pre-revolution Russian crone, but what looked kickass sexy on Sharon Stone would probably turn me into the Golem. That's Golem, not Gollum, and you're the only other person in my age bracket in the whole of Gull Cove who I fully expect to know the difference. The actual difference. Not the retelling of the retelling of the retelling difference. Man, I wish I'd said that at the time. It would have made you laugh. I want to hear you laugh again.*

Please.

Please.

Please.

∞

"**S**o I lied," Caroline Connelly stated, smiling sweetly at her audience, the select group of eager young faces who were looking at her in anticipation from their stations on both sides of the centre isle hob.

While Connelly let the dramatic pause hang for a bit, Kirsty took stock of the chef's appearance this week. The woman looked heaps better. The constant shivering had stopped, and the hollows in her cheeks were slowly filling out. She didn't look downright ill anymore. The impression was underlined by the naughty sparkle that suddenly appeared in Caroline's eyes.

"I promised you quick and simple meals, but tonight's concoction is everything but. For tonight, ladies and gents, we'll be making lasagne, and that's one bitch of a dish."

A moment of hushed silence was disrupted only by Maisy uttering a shocked 'Miss!' under her breath. Caroline shrugged.

"Just calling a spade a spade. And lasagne is a spade, believe me. But it will teach you to make a bolognaise sauce, and roux, and from that roux a white sauce. Maisy, keep your hand down, I'll explain what roux is in a second." She took a breath. "Roux is any type of fat mixed with equal amounts of flour, heated in a pan. You can then stir in any kind of liquid to end up with a thick sauce. A little like when we thickened our gravy with flour a couple of weeks ago, but not quite. For the basic white sauce in lasagne, the fat you use is butter, and the liquid you use is milk. So, by the end of today, not only will you know how to make bolognaise, but also how to make a white sauce. And if you know how to make a basic white sauce you can make cheese sauce from that, simply by melting a generous helping of grated cheese into it. So then you'll also know how to make one of the two components that make up macaroni cheese. In other words, at the end of tonight you will be able to make three types of pasta dish. Spaghetti Bolognese, macaroni cheese and lasagne." Caroline took a breath. "Yes, Maisy?"

"But they are not very healthy choices, are they, Miss?"

Caroline rolled her eyes.

"Salad," she snapped.

Maisy looked at the chef like the proverbial rabbit caught in headlights.

"Pardon, Miss?"

"Anything cooked from scratch is healthy when consumed in moderation, and with a decent side of salad. And if you call me 'Miss' one more time, I'll throw you out of my kitchen. Let's get started, folks, we have a lot of cooking to do tonight. Maisy, Poppy, you'll need to work with Catalina today, I need to be able to switch between all of you to help out."

Half an hour later, the word 'bitch' kept running laps in Kirsty's mind in time with the circles her whisk was drawing in the butter-flour-milk paste she was desperately trying to homogenise into a sauce. It was hopeless. Each time she added a little more milk the stuff got lumpier rather than smoother as the milk evaporated more quickly than she could possibly stir. This was her third attempt already. On the first one she had let the butter-flour mix go brown, which apparently wasn't a bad thing if you wanted to make a red wine sauce for game meats or lamb, but not so great when the objective was to make a *white* sauce. On the second one, she had managed to keep the heat low enough for it to stay pale, but had put too much milk in at once. It had ended up with goo balls bobbing in a hot spa of liquid. Kirsty growled at the pot, sweat trickling down her forehead. She allowed herself a quick glance sideways at Jake, who was happily running a wooden spoon around the Bolognese sauce he had quietly produced next to her in the meantime. No hitches. She felt distinctly like she'd drawn the short straw. And like punching him for his smug contentedness. She squinted at the side of his nose, trying to determine which dots were freckles and which were splash back from the rather enthusiastic adding of tinned tomatoes to his fried beef mince earlier. He half turned to smile at her, then looked into her pot and tutted.

"Did you just tut?" she asked. It came out more acidly than she had intended but what normal person actually *tutted*?

"Maybe. Let me check." He did it again and smirked at her sideways. "Sounds like it. Yes, I think I can confirm that I did indeed tut. What of it?"

She couldn't help but grin back at him despite the uncomfortable feeling in the pit of her stomach that the sound had evoked.

"Real people don't do that." She turned her face away quickly, concentrating once more on what was rapidly threatening to become disastrous attempt number three. "The only real person I've ever known who actually tutted was Aunt Marjorie."

"Keep talking," he said, while turning his Bolognese down to a simmer and moving over to stand behind her. "Tell me about this Aunt Marjorie. She sounds like my kind of woman."

"Erm." Kirsty momentarily lost her train of thought as he covered her stirring hand with his palm and started helping her drag the whisk around her goo.

"You hold the pot," he instructed. She did as she was told, slightly dizzy from his sudden physical proximity. The moment of nausea passed, and then she just felt securely swaddled in his presence, her senses sharpened and the whole focus of her existence directed at the pot in front of them. He reached out with his free hand to pick up the milk jug next to her on the counter, and poured some more liquid onto the roux. He shook out her wrist before he guided her hand over the mix again.

"You're cramping. Relax the wrist. Pretend you are playing the drums."

Kirsty swallowed as she watched the mass in the pot finally transform into something akin to a sauce under his guidance.

"I've never played the drums in my life. I'm more of a triangle kind of girl."

"You crack me up," he chuckled next to her ear. "Now,

tell me about Aunt Marjorie."

"Nothing to tell. She was just this old woman who used to come into the salon every couple of weeks. She wasn't really my aunt. I'm not sure she was actually called Marjorie either. It's what she was referred to in the diary. She tutted. Like, all the time. At everything. But mostly at me."

"Why?" he enquired further, tipping a bit more milk in. "What did you do?"

Kirsty swallowed hard. She wished she hadn't mentioned it. She could feel heat and blood rushing to her cheeks. Standing behind her he stayed oblivious to her reddening face though and that was a small blessing in the immense embarrassment of the next few seconds.

"I ate," she confessed.

"Come again?" he asked distractedly because the sauce had suddenly demanded a higher gear of action. Kirsty could feel her whole body wobble slightly as he made them pick up the pace.

"I'd be there snacking on the complimentary biscuits, and she'd come in and she'd tut, and say stuff."

He took his palm off the back of her hand, stretched around her to switch off the heat under their suddenly miraculously perfect white sauce, stirred his Bolognese once with the other hand, and then turned her around gently by the shoulders, taking a step back to frown at her.

"Like what?" he demanded.

Kirsty could feel tears well up in her eyes, and didn't meet his gaze. For a moment, she almost hated him. The concern made her feel small and vulnerable, and she didn't like it.

"Like 'Is that child snacking again? Look at the fat rolls

over her wrists, she looks like Miss Piggy,'" she finally answered.

"What? That's awful. And your nan didn't say anything?"

Kirsty shrugged.

"She laughed it off. Told me not to mind the silly old bat."

There was a pause in proceedings, during which Jake just lightly shook his head.

"You know what? I've changed my mind," he said earnestly but with a glint of humour in his eyes. "That Aunt Marjorie woman? Not my kind *at all*. What a cow. I bet there was nothing wrong with you at all. And for the record, I always thought Miss Piggy's wrists were her one redeeming feature. Given a personality transplant, that pig could have been seriously hot in my books. In the light of this new information, I shall shun the use of the tutting sound forthwith and henceforth."

Making light of it could have been hurtful if it hadn't been for the squeeze he gave her shoulders at the same time. It made something inside Kirsty go suddenly soft and supple that hadn't been soft and supple in a long time. It said everything little Kirsty had so desperately needed to hear back then. That she was alright just how she was, that that woman had been mean and nasty, and a bitter old hag. And once again it left Kirsty marvelling at how different Jake was from his brothers, and at how the boy in front of her, who'd just managed with one kind gesture to eradicate some scar tissue that she had carried for most her life, just didn't tally with the sum of stories that were 'Jake Deacon'.

He took his hands off her shoulders and crossed his arms in front of his chest.

"You are trying to figure me out, aren't you, Kirsty Matthews?" He leant in, clenching and unclenching his jaw. "It's all true. I'm a liability and you probably want to steer well clear of me."

Before Kirsty could say anything, along the lines of how that was a bit like shouting 'careful' after the other person had already tripped over, his phone rang. He took it out of his back pocket, and seeing who came up on the display, sighed deeply. He suddenly seemed exhausted, sad and deflated.

"Excuse me, I have to take this, and then I'll probably have to go."

Kirsty watched him accept the call with a curt 'Hi,' and then glance across to Caroline, who was helping a lonesome Maisy with her fourth attempt at white sauce. Three cooks had proved just too much of a broth spoiling crowd, and Poppy and Catalina had paired off unceremoniously earlier on in the evening despite Caroline's instructions.

Jake exchanged a look with the chef that seemed to be loaded with mutual understanding, made the universal sign for walking, waited for her to dismiss him with a nod, went to grab his belongings and left the room.

A second later Caroline clapped her hands together sharply.

"Right, people, time to build your lasagnes. Maisy, go work with Kirsty. Try not to mess it up too much for her."

∞

The food had been good, but without Jake to share it with, Kirsty hadn't really enjoyed it.

While the other teams had happily chatted away during

52

the final prep, Maisy had quickly stopped trying to elicit a conversation out of Kirsty, and they had layered their dish in silence. During the three quarters of an hour in which everybody's lasagnes had baked in the oven, the two of them had made up a side salad and learned how to make vinaigrette before washing up the mountain of dirty pots and pans Jake had left behind, all without exchanging more than a few words. At the end of the evening, Maisy had been the first out of the door, refusing to take any of the leftovers home, not wanting to cheat her family into thinking she'd had any real impact on its creation.

Kirsty felt a little sorry for her, and a bit bad for not making more of an effort, but she decided quickly she could live with the guilt. She was too preoccupied with worrying about Jake. Whatever it was that had dragged him away in the middle of cooking, whatever it was that had made him not be overly present at Gull Cove last term, whatever it was that had made him toe the line of late, and by now Kirsty was convinced the three things were connected, it wasn't a good thing. She hung back, waiting for everyone to clear out until there was just Caroline left, doing the last nervous checks of the kitchen.

She watched the chef silently for a minute.

Something about Caroline's fretfulness around arranging everything to the kitchen manager's complete satisfaction reminded Kirsty of Phoebe and Ms Faulkner senior. Phoebe's mum, a lawyer, was so seriously obsessive-pedantic that ever since they had been tiny Phoebe had tried to spend as little time at home as possible, so as not to disturb her mother's order with her presence. That was until her mum had taken the next logical step and bought a house with a granny flat for her daughter, so the then fourteen-year-old girl could have her own space. A space Phoebe still didn't like unless she had friends to stay, and which she fussed over endlessly without ever feeling at home. Kirsty wondered if there was a kitchen somewhere that Caroline considered home. She hoped so.

"Chef?"

The word tumbled awkwardly off her tongue. Caroline didn't seem to notice though. She was kneeling on the floor, in the process of plugging a meat mincer back into its designated socket. She briefly looked over her shoulder at Kirsty.

"Yes, Kirsty?"

Caroline turned her face back towards the task at hand. Looking down at the crown of her head, Kirsty could see grey roots coming through in the chef's hair. She'd never realised that it was dyed before. It suddenly dawned on Kirsty that if the woman had been in the same year as Anthony Simm at school, she must be a lot older than Kirsty had always assumed. Around the same age as Kirsty's mum. It was a strange thought. In Kirsty's mind the chef had always been somewhere in her thirties. Not young anymore but far from past it. A hunch told Kirsty that the age question was somehow important. That it was at the heart of why Caroline Connelly was here in Gull Cove's school kitchen, on her hands and knees trying to find a plug socket behind an awkward shelving unit because she feared the consequences of not leaving the place behind *exactly* as they had found it.

"You know Jake had to leave early tonight?"

"Yes."

"Do you think you could let me have his address, so I can take him some of our lasagne? I mean, he practically made the whole thing. He should have some. It's really good. I'd take it home and give it to him tomorrow but I'm pretty sure he won't want to lug a Tupperware around with him all day."

It was a relatively feeble excuse for not saying 'I'd take it home and give it to him tomorrow but I really want to see him again tonight to make sure he's alright,' and Kirsty was pretty sure Caroline wasn't going to buy it for a second. Having accomplished her mission with the mincer plug, the woman turned and got up off the floor, frowning at Kirsty in obvious confusion.

"How come you don't know where he lives?"

"Erm, because I've spent my entire life so far trying to avoid being anywhere near the Deacons? So we're not exactly pally?"

Caroline's eyebrows shot up.

"Really? Could have fooled me. I was under the impression you two were really close. You work nicely together. Hm. I've got emergency details for all of you but I'm pretty sure I'm not supposed to hand them out."

Kirsty threw caution to the wind.

"Please?" she begged. "Considering we're a team?"

Caroline looked blankly at her for a second then smiled.

"I tell you what. The contact sheets are all in the front of the recipe folder in there." Caroline indicated a big black tote bag resting on the now otherwise clean counter. "I'm going to the loo. Why don't you do me a favour in the meantime and take out the recipe sheet for next week so I can go and photocopy it on the way out?"

She winked at Kirsty and started towards to the door.

"How do I know what next week's dish is?" Kirsty called after her.

55

"You don't." Caroline called back. "It'll be whatever you pick out."

Kirsty smiled to herself as she approached the bag with a wildly beating heart, despite the green light from its owner to go a-snooping.

Caroline Connelly in real life might have been older and frailer than the woman Kirsty knew from TV.

But she was also infinitely cooler.

∞

I need a breather before the next bit. I also need the toilet, but it means going in there and I really don't want to. It was bad enough yesterday. Twice I had to go and each time I thought I was going to have a heart attack from worrying about bumping into a Deacon en route. I mean, really, what would I say?

I could do with a drink, too. I'm parched. You would have thought that after yesterday I would have been clever enough to bring some provisions but I haven't. It's me and my stupid little jukebox again and that's it. Could have brought my laptop. Didn't. Thought it would be better to recharge this thing and carry on exactly as before.

Me? Ritualistic? Never!

Actually, I'm not sure I thought anything at all. I just kind of sleepwalked back to where I'm supposed to be.

On the subject of dodging Deacons, I actually did see your mum come out a few minutes ago. She was carrying Sophia, who was screaming her little lungs out. Didn't spot your folks go in, so I guess they either arrived before me or they have been here all night. Your mum looked awful. I mean really, really awful. Much worse than yesterday. I don't know what that means. I've been kind of assuming I'd know, you know. I mean, if my presence here suddenly became superfluous.

But it probably means nothing. She's probably just gone to take Sophia somewhere to get her fed or changed or something.

Right, breather over. And I can hold it. And staying hydrated is overrated anyway. Let's get on with it.

∞

The house was worth at least three times as much as Kirsty's parents' little terraced cottage. A detached mock-Tudor new build, set back from the road to allow for ample front parking on a red brick paved drive that carried on around the house to a double garage, it gleamed with all the cleanliness of a well-maintained trophy home, even in the misty darkness of an early spring evening. Kirsty glanced at its illuminated windows from across the road, where she had been standing under a lamp post for a good five minutes, pretending to be busy with her phone while trying to build up the nerve to actually go and ring the door bell.

About half a mile away it had finally dawned on her who the Deacons actually were. It was ridiculous, really, that she had never put two and two together. She, the person who knew so much about the population of Gull Cove Secondary School and Sixth Form, had remained oblivious to the fact that her tormentors and their big bad brother were the offspring of the company whose little plaques adorned practically every single fence in a fifty-mile radius, reading 'J.C. Deacon — Fencing & Decking LTD'. And she would probably still not have cottoned on, if it hadn't been for the fact that there were company trucks emblazoned with the same logo parked up and down the street.

57

She wondered how popular that made the Deacons with the neighbours. It really brought the tone down in an otherwise seriously polished neighbourhood. She wondered, too, if the J in J.C. stood for Jacob, making her Jake a 'junior'. Which would be both funny and tragic.

Her Jake.

The thought jarred a little and threw her right back into doubting the decision to come here.

What on earth had she been thinking?

They hardly knew each other.

She took a long hard look at the plastic bag dangling from her wrist, trying to decide what to do. If one of the twins answered the door she'd be toast. But then again, she'd coerced Caroline into breaking the rules for her and now she felt obliged to go through with it.

As if swallowing a spoonful of medicine and avoiding the taste, she finally took a deep breath, held it while crossing the road and didn't exhale until her finger had made an impact on the bell button. While she waited for someone to answer she debated what to do with the lasagne. Keep it in the bag, all casual? Take the plastic container out and present it by holding it up between her hands? Hang the bag from the door knob and leg it?

Just as the latter became more and more of an attractive option, the door opened, and a bald, chunky man with fat lips and a wild combination of laughter and worry lines crisscrossing his otherwise still boyish face opened the door. Kirsty guessed him to be somewhere around her own parents' age, but leathered prematurely from a life working in all weathers. Even if she hadn't already known what he did for a living, she would still have put him down as a builder type. He looked it.

"Yes?" the man she assumed was J.C. Deacon asked evenly, taking her in with furrowed brow.

"Sorry it's so late, but is Jake in?"

He didn't answer immediately, his frown deepening. She was about to hand him the bag and say, 'This is Jake's,' when he deigned to answer.

"No, he is not," Deacon said sharply. His disdain hit her like a punch in the gut. There was a short pause during which he began closing the door but then he abruptly seemed to change his mind, opening it a little wider again. "He is at Shannon's. They are getting back together. And the last thing that needs at this point is another girl sticking her oar in." He looked her up and down briefly as if to say, 'Not that you'd stand a chance,' before he carried on. "So do everyone a favour, girlie, whoever you are, trundle on and stay out of it."

A second later he shut the door in her face, this time without hesitation.

Too stunned to think or feel anything, Kirsty turned on her heels and began walking home. About ten minutes into the thirty-five minute walk, around about the same time the humidity that had hung in the air all day turned into constant fine drizzle, her brain slowly started to unfreeze. It began as a single thought, quite abstract at first, and ended in wondering how anyone could treat someone else with such utter contempt without any call for it whatsoever.

What a charmer.

At least now she knew where the twins got it from.

Then she started crying.

∞

59

Yup. I did. I cried buckets. All the way from Elm Street to Badminton Gardens. Not because you obviously had a girlfriend and I had this mad crush on you or anything. You can wipe that one straight off your ego chart, buddy. No, because it was so nasty. Your dad was just horrible. It felt like being told off for something I hadn't done when all I'd wanted to do was something nice. I mean, in hindsight I get it, I get why he was like that, but still. Really?!? What a ... you fill in the insult. You are better at that.

∞

The tears started to dry up when she crossed the little cemetery at the edge of her hunting ground and reached Badminton Gardens.

Kirsty loved this street. Somehow just entering here made her feel instantly better. The houses were semi-detached and slightly bigger than her own, well maintained with big bay windows but not ostentatious. Off the straight road that was Badminton Gardens ran Badminton Crescent, which curved around a little half moon shaped green in the middle, complete with beautiful wild cherry trees under which stood benches. In fine weather, the Badminton kids played here during the day until shift change, when the over-fourteens appeared after dinner and started fooling around. But with the eyes of the entire street watching them, it rarely got rowdy or loud. There was true community spirit in these houses. It was a place where the neighbours organised street parties, where Easter egg hunts were held and where people competed fiercely with each other about the best Halloween decorations. Kirsty adored all that stuff, and despite Phoebe, who technically counted as Badminton crowd by miscellaneous past boyfriends' association, teasing her endlessly about it over the years, she could well remember a certain Goth girl crawling around this very patch of land on her hands and knees in search of a chocolate bunny as recently as three weeks ago. The thought made Kirsty smile. She took a deep lungful of air and breathed out slowly, then dug around her coat for her music player which she had left off the entire way. For a brief while after turning away from the Deacon's house she had flirted with *Mr Pleasant* but in the end had decided that even Ray Davies' sarcasm couldn't save her. Somehow she hadn't really felt like putting a soundtrack to what she had been feeling and she never ever listened to music when crossing the cemetery. There was no point in being a black belt if you couldn't hear the attacker approach.

As she scrolled down her choices, still trying to decide if she was more sad or angry, an orange grocery delivery truck approached from behind, and slowly started crawling the kerb next to her. The small smile that had been brought to her face by the thought of Phoebe ripping holes in her best fishnet tights while sniffing out cocoa molecules on the green widened into a big grin.

How did he do this? How did he always appear at these exact moments in her life?

When she felt wounded.

The truck stopped. She turned to open the passenger door and climbed in.

"Hi Dad."

Her father's big, round face smiled at her before he pulled away from the kerb again, and she could feel the turmoil inside her settle down completely, everything falling back into its rightful place. She took a look at her father's bulk, at his hairy arms turning the steering wheel, at the glasses that always seemed to sit just a little too close to his eyes and felt safe.

"Are you still out on delivery?"

He shook his head.

"No, just finished the last drop off. Late, late slot. They'll be extending delivery times till midnight next. Taking the truck back now. I'll drop you home. What's in the bag?"

"Drugs."

"Well, I'm glad we made you do karate if you are taking up with dealers now. Do we need to get you a gun licence?"

It was one of her dad's most annoying qualities. No matter how deadpan your delivery, he could always, always out-deadpan you.

"I think I'm alright for now, but thanks for the offer."

They'd arrived outside their house and Kirsty shuffled across the middle seat, over to her father's side. She gave him a peck on the cheek.

"Thank you, Dad."

He glanced at her with a small smile and she could see in his eyes that he wanted to ask. About her, about what had happened, but she knew he wouldn't. He never did. One of the most endearing aspects of Paul Matthews was that he never pried. He waited for you to be ready to share. And then he would listen. Always.

She scooted back to the door, opened it and hopped out onto the pavement.

"Kirsty?" her father called after her and she turned around, holding the door open awkwardly with the wrong hand.

"Yeah?"

"You might want to hide the drugs. Nicholas is home.

Julian threw him out."

∞

*N*icholas.

Nicholas is my brother and a bit like Robbie Miller-Makambe in as much as he is not really someone who has any impact on our story other than that he is part of the reason your share of the lasagne didn't make it past midnight that night because he and I comfort gorged ourselves in the kitchen until two o'clock in the morning.

In between dancing to Herman's Hermits' No Milk Today.

Normally Nicholas hates my taste in music but he's appropriated that one.

Not that it mattered, the untimely demise of your lasagne I mean, since I don't think I would have had the guts to give it to you at school the next day anyway. Your father really knows how to stick the knife in.

But my brother's amazing capacity for devouring food in times of crisis aside, his existence falls firmly into the 'Jake and I don't actually know each other,' category of evidence.

You had no idea I had a sibling, right?

That would be because Nicholas is eight years older than me, so we never went to the same schools at the same time. There was a baby in between the two of us but he was stillborn and after that it took mum a long time to get up the nerve to become pregnant again.

I love my brother to distraction. He is the sweetest guy. And kind of pretty, too. Takes after mum with his big grey eyes and super dark lashes. Makes the dull as dishwater colour hair we share instantly look better, although he tends to dye his black. And he works stupidly hard at not being overweight whenever he is not eating away his sorrows. So he's the only skinny member of the family. Theoretically you might even have met him, but you would never put the two of us down as brother and sister. Nicholas would have just been leaving Gull Cove when you were in year seven. Back then he filled the role of token openly gay boy, but he is infinitely nicer than Ronan. Unfortunately, he has a thing for real bruisers. Enter Julian. They've been on-off-on-and-off-again for about, I don't know, seems like forever. Far too long at any rate. I hope Nicholas doesn't do the doormat thing again and goes back once Julian whistles for his lap dog. At the point of writing this, they are still split up and that's the longest that has ever lasted. It helped that Nicholas only came home for a couple of days then went up to Yorkshire to wallow in self pity at some friend's house. He's still up there, doing shifts in a pub. So there is hope. I want my brother to have a nice boyfriend for once. Stupid boy.

So why am I telling you all this? Even if it isn't really anything to do with you or us? I guess it is because it is all part of the stuff I want you to know about me one day.

If there is a one day.

Your mum and Sophia still haven't come back yet. It makes me nervous.

Surely, if your mum had something to be here for she would be back by now?

I feel faint.

∞

"**A**nd where have *you* been all week?"

Jake looked at Kirsty reproachfully to match the tone in his voice. He'd managed to make it sound as if they regularly prowled the hallways of Gull Cove together or

64

met up outside school like proper friends, and she had suddenly disappeared on him. Kirsty, robbed of any chance of a quick-witted response by a spoonful of chocolate spread on her tongue, sucked on it a bit harder, twirled the teaspoon it sat on around in her mouth and wondered why exactly he was standing on her doorstep.

Sure, it was Thursday, sure Phoebe had left about half an hour ago, sure it was cooking time soon but still she hadn't really expected him to pick her up after last week. She could feel heat creeping up her neckline and towards her jaw when she realised that the question meant he had actually noticed her subtle absence in his life over the past seven days.

She'd avoided him, plain and simple.

Whereas before her encounter with Deacon senior they'd started nodding at each other with a quick 'Hey,' whenever their paths crossed at school, she had made a point of not running into him in the first place after last Thursday. It had been an easy exercise since steering clear of a Deacon was practically programmed into her DNA following the years of abuse by the twins. All she had had to do was to adjust the programming to add a third object of avoidance to her sixth sense.

Nevertheless, the reliability with which she could feel Jake approach long before he rounded a corner, exited a classroom or entered the cafeteria had surprised her. Her twins radar had never been that accurate. The Jake sensor was so strong, she had doubted herself as paranoid a few times over the last week, hesitating in her change of course, only to then catch a glimpse of lime green and white in the distance and having to leg it faster. Now she was suddenly really glad to see that stupid jacket. Clearly, whatever J.C.

Deacon's take on her was, his eldest son didn't share it or, more likely, was oblivious to it.

They were still a team.

Girlfriend or not.

She popped the spoon out of her mouth and smiled at him.

"Been busy. Give me one second. I need to get my stuff together."

"One," he counted.

"Really?" She raised her eyebrows at him over her shoulder as she moved away to take the spoon back to the kitchen. "As my friend Phoebe would say, you need a new scriptwriter: your jokes are tired."

"Phoebe's got fangs. I don't trust things with fangs. They have no sense of humour. And never mind how tired my jokes are," he shouted after her. "Ask me how tired *I* am."

Kirsty didn't react but once she had returned to the door to put her shoes on, she stopped midway between lacing up her boots in order to scrutinise him from below. From this angle, he actually did look like he hadn't had a lot of sleep. He looked pale and spotty, with shadows under his eyes. She even thought she could see him stifle a yawn.

"Are you alright?" she asked, while returning to loop laces around little hooks with nimble fingers.

"Hmmm," he answered noncommittally. "That's kinda hot."

"What is?"

By the time he answered, she had straightened up and grabbed her jacket, stepped outside the house to join him on the doorstep and pulled the front door shut. He indicated her boots with a tilt of the head as they started walking.

"Those boots. That they are for real. Shannon's got some

similar to that. Not calf high like yours, thigh length. So they should be a real turn on, right? But they are kind of fake 'cause they got a zip at the side. So I've never seen her fingers do what yours just did. So, yeah, hers look good, you know what people call them, but they are just a prop. A fake. Yours, they are real. Proper old school. They are cool. And sexy. Old school is sexy."

"Jake?" She could barely suppress the amusement in her voice. This was turning into one of the most surreal conversations she'd ever had.

"Yeah?"

"Are you seriously talking kinky footwear at me?"

She could see him look down like a naughty child who'd been caught with a hand in the biscuit tin.

"Sorry." It sounded sincere. "I'm really tired. And when I'm tired I have no filter. I'll shut up now."

She nudged him.

"Don't be silly. I'll take it as the compliment that it is. My footwear is not a fake. Hurray. Who is Shannon?"

Not that she didn't know already but she wanted to hear it from him. She watched him shake his head in dismay before he answered.

"Wrong question. The question is not who Shannon is, but what Shannon wants."

"What?"

In the brief glance he shot her, she could see allsorts of warring emotions on his face, as if he was about to go into confession, but then he suddenly straightened his spine and hooked his arm through hers.

"Forget it. I don't want to talk about it. Let's talk about something else. Let's talk about the moon and the stars. Tell me, Kirsty Matthews, what's your favourite moon phase and why?"

∞

Everyone had already piled into the kitchen, and was looking around, a little disconcerted due to the distinct absence of their chef. When Caroline finally appeared among them, she looked slightly dishevelled but in a good way, her eyes sparkling with enthusiasm when her eyes fell on her students.

"Ah, wonderful, you're all here tonight," she said as she sailed through them to hop onto the kitchen counter in one smooth move, parking her behind in exactly the same spot where Kirsty had plonked hers on soup night, only taking up a lot less space. "So, children, tell me, what have you cooked this week?"

The silence that followed, Kirsty noticed, was distinctly different from the absence of chatter just a moment before. For the first time in her life, she truly appreciated that a silence during which every person in the room was thinking exactly the same thing was an entirely different kettle of fish from the kind that ensued when people were just idly pondering their own, individual ideas. It didn't take a genius to work out that not a single one of them had gone and cooked anything at home that week. She saw Caroline's face fall just in time with Aimee hesitantly raising her hand.

"Beans on toast?" the girl offered with a comedy smile.

"Hah. But did you have salad with that?" Maisy blurted out.

Kirsty had to bite her lips in order not to laugh out loud. She had to hand it to Maisy, the girl was quick. She'd do brilliantly in one of those ugly debating matches in the

House of Commons.

Caroline, on the other hand, seemed not to have heard the snidey remark. She looked into the round with a puzzled frown on her face.

"Why?" she asked finally, managing to make brief eye contact with each and every one of them in turn during the one, slightly drawn out syllable.

She got a communal shrug back, followed by some lame excuse mutterings. Noel and Zach mumbled something about an art project, Catalina about joining a dance class, Maisy about some committee meeting or another. Jake whispered cryptically how it was difficult to cook when you felt like the walking dead, making Caroline focus in on him for a second to give him an excusing nod. Kirsty kept her mouth firmly shut. So did Aimee, who clearly felt she had already spoken, and Poppy, no surprise there. In the end, it was Ronan who cut to the chase and really answered the question for all of them, in his customary accusatory whine but also correctly so.

"Because there wasn't anything in the cupboard to cook?"

If ever Kirsty had witnessed somebody have a light bulb moment, then this was it. In an instant, Caroline's face changed back from scowling to its earlier enthusiasm.

"Of course!" she exclaimed. "Right, I was going to teach you enchiladas tonight but that can wait. Change of plan. Grab your stuff — we are going to the supermarket."

She jumped off the counter and headed for the door, turning in the frame when she realised that they had shuffled around into the right direction but weren't making any moves to follow.

"What? Come on," she demanded.

"You serious?" Kirsty asked.

Caroline cocked her head and did that thing again where her eyes briefly met every other pair of eyes in the room. There was anger in them now, and when she answered her voice had sunk an octave.

"Damn right, I'm serious. It didn't occur to me that not a single one of you has the faintest idea how to hunt the food before cooking the food, but since that is clearly the case, that's exactly what tonight's lesson is going to be about. Maisy, keep your hand down, *I'm* paying. I'll give every one of you cash, and a list of things to get that will help you cook at least one meal over the next week. It's not like I can't afford it. I just have to think about what it is you'll be cooking. But I tell you now, come next Thursday anyone who hasn't cooked *at least* that one dinner in the interim is out. And I mean *anyone*." She threw a glance in Jake's direction. "No discussion, no excuses. Even if your grandmother dies, I want you to cook for her funeral. I'm not doing this thing for the money, of which there is none, I am doing this thing for the love, and I can't be bothered if you can't be bothered. Are we clear?"

"Crystal," Jake muttered just above Kirsty's ear then added even more quietly, "She's scary when she's angry, isn't she?"

"Very," Kirsty murmured back.

After the quiet hubbub of agreement died down, they silently collected their belongings and followed Caroline through the school, heads hanging and moving so closely together that their shoulders were nearly touching. Caroline stopped abruptly outside the caretaker's office, turned to them and put a finger to her lips with an extra sharp look at Maisy. They watched the chef fumble in her pocket for a key and insert it into the keyhole. Kirsty could see on the woman's tense face that she wasn't sure if it would turn. A satisfied smirk appeared around the corners of her mouth when it did and the door opened. Caroline signalled for them to stay put, then slipped from view. A few minutes later she appeared again, the smirk having transformed into a wide grin. She locked the door again and gestured for them to carry on.

"Talk, people, you're acting suspicious," she added to the move-along wave of her right arm.

"Where are we going, Miss?" Poppy asked almost inaudibly as they headed for the exit.

"You know what the best thing about this school is?" Caroline answered the question with a question, graciously not reprimanding Poppy for the misdemeanour of using the title 'Miss'. She pushed the door open and held it for them.

"What's the best thing about this school, Chef? Other than me, of course?" Jake asked as he passed her by.

"Disappointingly unoriginal, Jake," Caroline said dryly.

"Couldn't agree more," Kirsty tossed out as she followed behind him out into the car park. "I think the word you were looking for is lame, Chef."

"Back-stabber," Jake said without turning around.

Kirsty contemplated the lime green hump in front of her.

"I wish. Couldn't get through that stupid body armour if I tried."

He swerved around to face her off as the others piled around them onto the forecourt.

"Are you calling my jacket stupid?"

Humour and challenge sparkled equally in his eyes.

"Yes, I am."

"This jacket? The jacket I'm wearing? This jacket, my

71

poor tasteless youngling, this jacket started its jacket-life as Obi-Wan Kenobi's jacket. The force is strong with this jacket, so shut it."

"What?"

"I think you'll find that you mean 'pardon, Master'. Ewan McGregor wore this jacket. When he was in motorcycle racing. I … "

"Could you two shut up for a second?" Ronan interrupted. "Stop trying to steal the show, Deacon."

"Yeah," Noel agreed, pretend boredom seeping from his voice as he tried to catch Kirsty's eye. "Nobody's interested in your stupid jacket story."

"You were ripped off, Deacon," Zach chipped in scathingly. "Just accept it. You were a gullible little boy falling for the oldest trick in the book. Even wearing it for another decade won't make it the real deal. I researched it. Couldn't find a single picture of Ewan McGregor in a jacket like that on the web. So zip it, and let Caroline finish telling us what the best thing about this school is. Cause it's definitely *not* you."

"It's real," Jake whispered vehemently to Kirsty only, while to all other intents and purposes he conceded defeat and turned to stand shoulder to shoulder with her, facing Caroline who'd come out to join them. Kirsty suddenly realised that her heart was racing with anger. What had started off as some light-hearted banter between the two of them had somehow turned into a Jake-bashing session in the middle of the car park, all hands on deck. She didn't like it. At all. She knew he could handle it, that it would wash off him like water off a duck's back. He was Jake Deacon. Still, she wanted to reach for his hand and squeeze it reassuringly, the way she would have done with Phoebe or

72

Nicholas to show support. But they weren't on those terms yet. Instead, she sidled up closer to him and nudged his upper arm with her shoulder. With her eyes focused on Caroline, she didn't see Jake's next move coming as he abruptly put his arm around her, drew her close and kissed her temple then let her go just as suddenly as he had pulled her in. In the process, she nearly missed how Caroline's face had lit up once everyone's attention was back on her.

"The best thing about this school, children, is that everything is still kept exactly where it was kept thirty years ago."

The chef extended her arm, wielding a set of car keys. She pushed a button on the key fob, and the indicator lights of the middle of the three Gull Cove minibuses which were parked up to the right of them flashed a couple of times.

"That'll be ours, then," Caroline chuckled. "Come along, people, we're going on a school trip."

When they'd reached the side of the bus, Caroline opened the door and ushered them in. Zach and Noel got on first, after a moment's hesitation and a sharp nod of encouragement from the chef, followed by Jake and Kirsty. Kirsty already had one foot on the step that led inside when she caught Maisy right behind her in the corner of her eye. The future prime minister was stalling. Kirsty turned to see the girl raise her hand to about ear height.

"Chef?"

"Yes, Maisy?" Caroline enquired, making no attempt to mask the exasperation in her voice.

"Do you even have a licence to drive this?"

Caroline sighed deeply before she answered.

"How did my generation give birth to such a bunch of squares? Maisy, I'm so old, my licence allows me to drive anything from a horse and cart to a seven-and-a-half-ton truck. Now get in, or get out of my class."

After that there were no more hold ups.

∞

To Kirsty's surprise, Caroline didn't take them to one of the posh big players in the supermarket wars, but to one of the smaller, cheaper discount outfits, where the choice was limited, transport boxes served as shelves, and the middle aisle was full of wondrous random items from bolt cutters, hair curlers and paper diaries to body forming underwear and computers.

The chef went to the cash point next to the entrance, then returned to where the group was huddled just inside the door between pallets of special offer barbeque coals and special offer compost bags.

She handed each of them a couple of banknotes.

"That should more than cover it. Keep the change, buy some other ingredients with it as and when you need to over the week," she said as she dished out the money. "Salad, for example," she added with a saccharine smile when she got to Maisy, then carried on without missing a beat, "Grab yourselves a basket each, and let's shop."

They hit the vegetable aisle first, where Caroline made each one of them gather potatoes suitable for mashing, carrots, celery sticks, garlic, and onions. Then she ushered them on to dairy for milk, eggs and butter. After dairy came flour, Worcestershire sauce, tomato purée and beef stock cubes. The baskets were getting heavy, and for once Kirsty didn't begrudge Ronan his whingeing when it inevitably started up, although it did make her bite her lip when

Aimee slapped him on the arm.

"You're such a lady's handbag, Ro!" the Goth girl said.

"Hear, hear!" Caroline agreed. "Ronan, if you don't control your compulsion to have a moan at regular intervals, I'm going to make you put the stock cubes back and you'll have to make your beef stock from scratch."

Poppy, who'd been carrying her basket with both hands, put her load down and looked at Caroline wide-eyed.

"Could you?" she asked timidly.

As Caroline answered, all of them stopped, taking a leaf out of Poppy's book and resting their arms for a while.

"What? Make beef stock from scratch? Of course. How do you think stock cubes are made? They're dehydrated stock, formed into cubes. If you really wanted to make it yourself, you'd need to go to the butcher's first, and ask them for bones. Then you'd lightly roast those in the oven, and then boil them up with veg, salt and herbs, the way you did with the chicken carcasses. Same process, same ingredients, really. But, you know, that's restaurant level stuff. I don't expect you to go to that length. Unless you are Ronan and you don't stop whining like a three-year-old. Stock cubes are perfectly fine, provided you get good ones. Now, pick up your baskets again, ladies and gents, and let's go for the finale."

The finale, it turned out, was a stop in the meat aisle.

"So," Caroline said, grinning at them. "Shepherd or cottage? Your individual choice. The recipe is the same, at least if you believe the *Cooking with Caroline* website that you will be consulting for your homework. Make a choice. Cows to the left, lambykins to the right. Pick up the mince for your pies, and let's get out of here." She paused to aim a devilish smile at Maisy. "Before anyone realises I've nicked the minibus."

∞

And if I live to a hundred, and let's face it with a good diet and provided we, the human race, don't blow up the planet first, that's not so far fetched for our generation, I will never forget Maisy's face when Caroline said that.

Or Simm standing in the car park like an avenging angel when we got back, for that matter.

Man, was he pissed off with her.

I mean, I've seen him dress down a lot of students before but this was fury of another dimension. I think you were right with what you said on the way home that night. That you only get that angry with people you really care about. There is something about those two, Simm and Caroline.

Proper friendship, I guess.

I know she said as much but there is more.

Love.

You know, long-term love as opposed to the hot burning kind that people write books and songs and poetry about.

Actually, I don't think people write poetry about love anymore. I'm not sure people write poetry about anything anymore. It's been superseded by the spoken word song, to quote my dad. You have to say it in a derogatory tone, though. He hates rap. Says he was around when it was invented and that was the day the music truly died. When that plane came down with Buddy Holly, Richie Valens and the Big Bopper? That was just the death of three decent musicians, but when rap stopped being a spoken word competition and became 'music' that was the end of music. According to my dad.

We are very similar, my dad and I.

76

I wonder if I'll get hairy arms when I get older.

Sorry, I'm rambling again.

It's because I just bumped into your mum coming back and it made me all jittery. I can't concentrate. I'm trying not to even think about what just happened. What the implications are. I'm trying to stick with my programme here. Until somebody tells me otherwise.

See, I had to go in there. I couldn't hold it any longer. My bladder had actually started hurting. And lo and behold, just as I walked back out, your mum came back in. I must have guessed right, she went to change Sophia and get some stuff from home. She was carrying a bag, and Sophia was in a different babygrow from this morning. The one this morning was pink with purple things. Amazing the amount of detail one registers without registering that it has registered. This one was lime green with white flowers on. Daisies, I think. Oh God, I think I'm going to choke. I just realised the colour scheme.

Anyway, I really didn't know what to say or do. There was no way of ducking out of sight or anything. But then I reminded myself that your mum doesn't know me. Or so I thought. Because the thing is, the thing that really spun me out was that she stopped right in front of me and then this happened:

"Kirsty?" she asks, while she keeps stroking the back of Sophia's head as Sophia keeps snuggling into the crook of her neck, and my heart nearly stops. For a split second, I'm stunned that she knows my name. Then I realise that, of course, the police must have told your parents who I am.

"Yeah?"

"You were with Jake yesterday, right?"

"Yeah?"

There are tears in her eyes, same green as yours, and she extends the arm that isn't propping up Sophia and squeezes my shoulder.

"Thank you," her voice cracks, and then she shuffles off.

And I just stand there, petrified. Until some guy practically shoves me out of the way.

I mean, what does that mean, 'Thank you?'

Thank you for what exactly?

For coming with you?

For making sure Sophia was okay?

Or for being the last friendly face you ever saw?

Oh no.

No.

Just no.

Keep writing, Kirsty, keep writing!

∞

"This is suspiciously similar to making Bolognese," Kirsty said, tipping the lamb mince onto the onion, carrot and garlic pieces she had been frying up for the last five minutes. She started hacking vigorously at the rectangle of meat in the pot with a wooden spoon as it sizzled.

"Your point being?" Phoebe asked from the Matthews' kitchen table, which was shoved up against the wall opposite the hob. Rather than use one of the three chairs around it, she was sitting on top, back leaning against the wall, legs crossed and phone in hand.

"Oh, no, I forgot about that." Kirsty picked the sheet of paper that had separated the meat from its plastic tray off the lumps she was splitting the lamb into. She held it up before she discarded it onto the kitchen counter. "Hm. Corner missing. Darn. Oh, hang on, there is it is." She successfully retrieved the tiny missing piece, burning her fingertips in the process. "Ouch. My point being, that I detect a pattern. Caroline does this. First it was all chicken based, now it's all mince."

She didn't need to turn around to know Phoebe was shrugging when she answered.

"Clever woman. Why move on before you've explored in depth what you have in front of you?"

"Somehow I doubt you are talking food at me right now."

"Yeah, I'm not. I think I'm getting a bit bored of Norman."

"Phoebe!"

"I know. What can I say? I'm a serial monogamist."

"So how does that tally with exploring in depth what's in front of you before moving on to the next thing?"

"It doesn't. I didn't say *I* was a clever woman, did I? Just making conversation. Talking of which, word on the street has it that a certain purple-haired comic freak's taken a shine to my best friend. Care to elaborate?"

"Aimee talks too much."

"You're evading the question."

"Not sure. But, yeah, maybe he likes me. I'm not interested though. What's next on my list?"

"Tomato puree and Worcestershire sauce, stir both in, then top the whole thing up with your stock," Phoebe read out, scrolling down the phone's display.

"Oh, no, the stock! Can you boil the kettle for me?"

"Sure." Phoebe left her station and joined Kirsty at the kitchen counter to flick the switch on the kettle. "But only if you tell me about Noel. Why on earth are you not interested? He's cute. And he's a good kisser."

"How would *you* know? No, wait." Kirsty held the

wooden spoon up sideways to hover by Phoebe's cheek. "Don't answer that."

"So I've heard," Phoebe reassured her with a grin. "From—"

"Zip it. I don't want to know," Kirsty interrupted her. "Just in case I change my mind. Although I don't think I will." She retracted the spoon, returned to stirring her mince and nodded in the direction of the kettle. "Can you make me up some stock with about half of the water in there? Cubes are just there, next to the tomato purée, and there's a jug in the cupboard by your feet."

"Yes, Chef."

"Funny."

"Not really," Phoebe retorted, bending down to rummage in the cupboard, while the kettle started steaming up the kitchen. "So why don't you think you'll change your mind?"

Kirsty thought about it for a moment as she waited for Phoebe to re-emerge with the jug. It was a good question. Despite the fact that there hadn't really been any more interaction between Noel and her since soup day, the way the prettier of the two geeks looked at her hadn't escaped Kirsty's notice. And he had nice eyes to look at her with.

But.

"They weren't very nice to Jake last time."

"Jake?"

"Jake."

"Hm."

"There is no 'Hm' here, Phoe. I just saw a side to Noel and Zach that I didn't like. That's it. No cause for 'Hm'-ing. Also, Noel's a feeder. That's the last thing I need."

"What's a feeder?" Phoebe asked, genuinely intrigued, as

80

she crumbled a stock cube into the jug and topped it up with boiling water. Kirsty waited for her to finish and hand the jug over before she rolled her eyes at her.

"You really don't watch enough of those crappy late night documentaries on the depravity of the human mind, Phoe. A 'feeder' is a guy who finds himself a fat woman to feed. They get off on stuffing food in your mouth."

"And you know Noel is one of those because … ?"

"Well, firstly he likes me, and secondly he tried to feed me lentil soup for an entire night. Case closed."

"You're not fat, Kirsty."

"Tell it to my scales."

There had been more snarl in the comeback than Kirsty had intended, and she felt truly saved by the bell when her phone chose that precise moment to buzz on the table. She shoved the wooden spoon into Phoebe's hand, and stepped away from the hob to take the call. She hesitated for a moment when she saw that it was an unknown number, then shrugged and picked up.

"Hello?"

"Hey, Kirsty. It's Jake."

"I can hear that. How did you get my number?"

"Trade secret."

It was dumb, but it made her smile. She sat down at the table, leaving Phoebe to tend to the meat.

"And what trade would that be?"

"Couldn't tell you. That's the secret bit."

"Anything about this phone call you would like to share then? Like, why you are calling for instance?"

"That's not how it's supposed to go."

"How is it supposed to go?"

"You have to ask me what I want."

"What do you want?"

"A kitchen. Tonight."

"Come again?"

"Have you done your homework yet?"

"Funny you should ask. I've just finished making the Bolognese part."

"I thought we were supposed to make shepherd's pie."

"We are. Unless you went for the beef option, in which case it would be cottage."

"I didn't. I chose lamb."

"There you go then."

"But what's it got to do with Bolognese?"

"You haven't done it yet, have you?"

"No. That's why I'm calling. I need to borrow someone's kitchen. My mum won't let me use ours tonight 'cause it's Saturday and they've got guests. And tomorrow I've got … I can't do it tomorrow. My meat goes off on Monday, but even if it didn't, I've got stuff on all week. Important stuff. I've only really got tonight to do it. I need a kitchen. And I guess I was hoping you hadn't done it yet and might want to do it together."

"Here?"

"Yeah?"

"I'm halfway through already."

"Yeah, never mind, I'll figure something out."

He sounded deflated.

"There's no reason why you couldn't borrow the hob once I've finished. We could have a pie off. Phoebe is here. She could be the judge."

"Really?" The sudden hope in his voice danced across the air waves. "What about your parents? Would they mind?"

"They're not here. Dad's working and mum's over at my nan's. But even if they were, they wouldn't care. They only ever use the microwave, and occasionally the oven. Besides they are getting home-cooked pie out of this, they're well excited."

"I'll be there in twenty."

"No rush. Kitchen's open all night. And I still got to make my mash."

"You're a life saver."

"We do try."

They rang off at the same time.

Kirsty laid her phone on the table and stared at it for a minute or so. How was it that he was so easy to talk to? How did he do this? Make her feel like a valuable person. Like a face even. Someone who mattered in the pond of Gull Cove. She looked up to see Phoebe grinning at her over her shoulder.

"Jake?"

"Jake."

"Hm."

∞

Kirsty had known that Jake would win hands down as soon as he had walked through the door with a sprig of rosemary in his hand.

Lamb and rosemary. It was obvious.

Whereas Kirsty had stuck to the basic recipe, he'd let his palate decide what else should go in.

He moved around her parents' shabby, beige-brown tiled kitchen-that-time-forgot with ease and without a shred of judgement. Kirsty could only imagine how it would compare to his at home. She and Phoebe sat on opposite chairs at the kitchen table, watching him as he prepared his food at the counter. He chatted to both of them equally as he cooked, every action smooth and practised.

"So, how come you two ladies are not out and about on this beautiful Saturday night?" he asked, frying his mince.

The patter was bull, the curiosity was genuine. The day had been one of the finest this year so far, and most of Gull Cove would be gathered down by the town's tiny beach, flanked by the hole-ridden cliffs that provided nesting sites for all sorts of sea birds and had given the place its name.

"Homework to cook," Kirsty answered.

"What about you, Phoebe?"

"She's avoiding her boyfriend, so she decided to keep me company," Kirsty answered for her friend.

"Not true," Phoebe protested. "I'm not *that* bored of him. I just wanted to spend some time with you."

"Pull the other one." Kirsty grinned good-naturedly.

"Okay, I'm avoiding my boyfriend," Phoebe admitted.

"Norman, isn't it?" Jake asked with his back to them, pouring his stock into the pot. "Why?"

"I'm trying to see if absence will make the heart grow fonder."

"Ah. And? Is it working?"

"Not yet. Having too much fun here."

"Poor Norman."

Kirsty loved listening to them. She felt a sense of relief wash over her and only then realised that she'd been nervous it wouldn't work. Phoebe and Jake. Phoebe, Jake and her. But it did.

"You know him?" Kirsty asked.

"He's the only six foot four giant Goth called Norman in

84

town: of course I know him."

"Fair point," Kirsty admitted, and then turned to Phoebe. "So what *is* wrong with Norman?"

"Let me guess," Jake answered instead. "He's more interested in keeping his core THC level up than exploring his girlfriend."

Phoebe snorted.

"You know him well, I see."

Jake glanced at her over his shoulder.

"No, just the type. And I don't mean the outfit."

"Your potatoes are boiling over."

"No, my potatoes are *about* to boil over. But they won't," he replied, turning the heat down a little.

It all seemed so effortless for him, and Kirsty couldn't help but wonder.

"You could cook already, couldn't you?" she asked on a whim.

"What?"

"Before joining Caroline's class. You could cook already."

"To a point, yeah."

"Who taught you?"

"Nobody, really. My mum's a good cook. Cooks every night. She was barely out of school when she was already sous-chefing in a pub. Then she met my dad. I think she could have been really good if I hadn't happened. She was nineteen when she had me. She could have gone places with her cooking." He paused to taste his meat base, half turning towards Kirsty and Phoebe. "Hm. This is good lamb." He shuffled back around to face his pots again, added a bit more salt to the meat and stirred it in. "Mum says if you're brought up on good food and you know what it should taste like, then you know how to cook. I guess she's right. At least where I'm concerned. Completely lost on the twins and my dad though. They'd be just as happy eating out of a box. Mum went into hospital for a couple of weeks last year. After the fourth night of ready crap, I started making the meals. I don't think the idiots even realised."

Kirsty sniffed at the air, infused now with a delicious scent of rosemary, garlic and thyme, another ingredient Jake had decided to add to the mix. It beat the hell out of the smell Kirsty's cooking had produced earlier. He was definitely good at this.

"Is that why Caroline keeps you back? Are you like her secret protégé or something?" It had slipped out before Kirsty could stop it, and she knew it was a mistake as soon as it did.

He scowled at her over his shoulder.

"I thought you weren't going to ask."

"I'm not. Just putting out a theory."

He turned his back on her again.

"Hm. I guess it's better than the theory Ronan is putting out."

An uncomfortable quality settled over the room as he worked on his food in silence. Phoebe frowned at Kirsty inquisitively across the table, but Kirsty waved the question off.

"I know what we need," Phoebe said after a few minutes. She jumped up and went to open the fridge. "Cider!"

Jake, who'd been testing his potatoes with a fork with one hand, and gently stirring his meat base with the other, spun around, wielding the spoon at Phoebe's cheek in a manner uncannily reminiscent of the one Kirsty had employed earlier that evening. Only he was deadly serious when he spoke.

"No! Absolutely not. I can't have you two drinking on my watch."

"Excuse me?" Phoebe was glowering at him, the how-very-dare-you in her tone bright and clear. "Who made you Scout leader?"

He turned to face her fully.

"I'm eighteen. You're not."

"Yeah. Right. Pot? Kettle? Black?" Phoebe turned to look over at Kirsty. "When was that Halloween with Jake Deacon ending in hospital with vodka poisoning and having his stomach pumped, again, Kirsty? Let me think. Oh yes, I remember now. We—" she pointed back and forth between Kirsty at the table and herself, "were in year eight, I believe. That would have made you—" She focused back on Jake with a snarl. "What? Hang on, hang on, I got this. Fourteen. That's right. So, with all due respect, Mister, eff off."

Jake shut his eyes for a split second before he answered with barely feigned patience.

"I mean it. If we get caught with you two drinking, I'll get the shit for it. I can't afford that. End of. If you want to drink, fine, you're right, I'm the last person to judge, but please let me finish my pie first. Then I'll sod off and you two can do whatever." He let the spoon sink and looked back and forth between her and Kirsty with true desperation.

"Please," he said again after a moment, softer this time, more imploring, catching first Kirsty's then Phoebe's eye.

Kirsty looked away quickly. This was not a match she fancied refereeing. Whatever she said, she'd piss off one of them. She held her breath. Out of the corner of her eye she saw Phoebe cock her head first to the left then to the right, like a bird looking at a worm from all angles prior to descending upon it, before she seemed to change her mind. She straightened up, shook herself with raised eyebrows and finally shut the fridge door.

"Fine," she muttered as she went back to her seat at the table. "Have it your way."

"Thank you," Jake said quietly, then turned to take his potatoes off the hob and drain them.

"You're on probation, aren't you?" Kirsty suddenly burst out over the noise of the gushing water as he tipped it out of the pot, holding the potatoes back with the lid.

She stared at his back as he slowly set the pot down in the stainless steel sink, and his shoulders started shaking inside his t-shirt. For a fleeting moment, she thought he was crying, ludicrous though the idea was, but then she realised the opposite was true. He was laughing to himself, and when he turned around he was grinning. But it wasn't a good grin. It was pained, cynical.

"Yeah," he said evenly. "Something like that. Now, where is your masher?"

Kirsty pointed at the utensil sticking out from the draining rack just by his elbow. He clocked it, nodded sharply then went about his business without another word. Kirsty observed every move he made with growing dread, knowing full well that if she didn't manage to turn the evening around again, he would do exactly as he had said. He'd bolt his pie together and leave. No sitting together sampling the food, no losing to his superior culinary skills, no more fun. The atmosphere had slipped beyond recoverable. She looked across to Phoebe in the hope of help, but her friend had pointedly withdrawn herself from the interaction, disappearing behind a curtain of sleek black hair to play on her phone. Great.

Once Jake had finished composing his mash, which again involved adding things Kirsty wouldn't have dreamed of, such as warmed milk and nutmeg, Kirsty watched him take something flat and oval wrapped in a hand towel out of the backpack that had carried all his ingredients. He uncovered two ceramic pie dishes, one large, one smaller sitting inside the first.

"You brought two?" Kirsty asked, not being able to stand the silence any longer.

He looked across, startled, almost as if he'd forgotten he was not alone.

"Yeah. I figured Caroline would want proof I'd done it, so I thought I'd make a small one and freeze it till Thursday."

"Oh." Kirsty's face fell. "I didn't think of that. I just made one big dish. I thought we'd eat some and leave some for my parents, but I didn't think I had to bring some in for Caroline."

"*You* don't, *I* do. Well, she didn't say that, but I want to make sure she knows I've done it. That's all. I'm sure she'll take your word for it when you say you did your homework. I don't come with that reputation."

He smiled.

"Heaven help, you're dumb," Phoebe's head came up sharply as she said it. "You've got two witnesses. You don't need a pie."

And then, just like that, just on the inflection of the word 'pie' and with the reassurance that Phoebe would back him up if need be, the strained vibe of the last ten minutes disappeared in an instant.

"So we're still eating?" Jake asked hopefully. "Even without the booze?"

Kirsty and Phoebe looked at each other. Boys could be so dim.

"Of course!"

∞

You know, that evening was one of my favourite ones ever. I could probably write an entire book just about that one evening. Reason I had to cut it short here is that Phoebe turned up. I mean in actual, real life. The here and now.

She comes up just as I get to 'Of course' and sits down next to me on this stupid bench. Doesn't say anything, just takes my hand, so I can't carry on typing, and holds it. For about an hour. Then she gives it a squeeze, gets up, says, 'I leave you to it,' and does just that. One hell of a trek, if you think about it, just to hold my hand for a bit. But that's Phoe for ya.

So yeah, here we are again.

Just you and me. Kind of.

I can't go back to that evening now, though. I guess I just won't put the rest of that night down for posterity. I'll just keep it in my heart. Or on my tongue, really.

Your pie was fantastic. I mean, it really was.

So was the company, once we got over that little glitch. We did have fun, right? I know we only sat around the kitchen table playing 'Who am I?' with stupid yellow post it notes stuck to our foreheads until my parents came home, and that's not exactly rock 'n roll. But for dull girl here, it was a good night. The best. Although the next Saturday was a pretty good contender, too, foot in mouth disease not withstanding. But there was a Thursday in between. Linearity of time and all that. I guess that's where I should pick it up next, despite the fact you're hardly in it. Although on another level you were all over it, of course.

'Next' needs to wait until tomorrow though.

An orange grocery delivery truck has just pulled up on the double yellow lines by the bus stop.

My pumpkin's arrived

.

∞

*D*ay three.

What can I say?

Same old.

Slept.

Kind of.

Woke up at dawn.

Packed jukebox (and a bottle of water this time).

Got on the train.

Parked arse on bench.

Saw the Deacon tribe arrive.

Nodded at them, got nods back.

Started typing.

∞

"**H**ey, Kirsty, wait up." Jake's muffled voice reached her eardrums through the horns of *Ring of Fire* at the same time as his palm touched her shoulder. She stopped, turned to face him, took the ear buds out and buried them in her fist. It was Thursday afternoon, school was out and people were spilling out of the building around them in droves. The noise should have more than drowned out the unmistakable Mariachi intro to the song's chorus that was escaping faintly through her fingers, but it didn't. She could see Jake picking up the tune. He stared at her fist for a second before his face lit up.

"You like Cash?"

It was more amazed statement than question and Kirsty answered with a shrug. She didn't have particularly strong feelings about The Man in Black but she liked a couple of his songs.

"It's a good song," she stated defensively.

"Hey, nothing wrong with a bit of Cash," Jake said vehemently. "Good songwriter. Good man. Fantastic love story. I mean, what a life! I want a June. Minus the teeth though. I'd prefer the Reese Witherspoon version. Have you seen *Walk the Line*?"

Kirsty shook her head.

"One of my favourite films ever. I've seen it about a million times. Anyway — " He raised both his hands and ran them through his hair. "I just wanted to let you know I can't pick you up tonight. I'm sorry. I'm … I'm not going to make cooking tonight." He held up a hand when Kirsty drew a long breath, his other hand still clinging to his scalp. "Caroline knows. I bribed her with pie and she let me off the hook. But under one condition."

He smiled the cocky smile she had seen him use over the years just for talking himself out of trouble with teachers and Simm.

And once on her.

To coax her into walking into the first Caroline class with him.

"Why do I think this involves me?" Kirsty asked dryly.

"'Cause it does?"

"Go on then."

"She says I need to meet up with my cooking partner over half term to catch up and make whatever you're making tonight. Otherwise not to bother coming back."

"Harsh."

"And?"

"Okay."

"Okay?" He breathed a sigh of relief.

"Yeah, okay. When?"

She could see him mentally go through his options. His face fell.

"I'm … oh, crap. I can't. Unless … "

"Unless, what, Jake?"

Kirsty was getting annoyed now. He hadn't even had the courtesy to ask back, what days would be good for *her*. There was an underlying presumption here of her not having a life, which she despised. Not that she did, other than studying, cooking on Thursdays and karate on Fridays, but it was still galling to have it rubbed in like that. In her annoyance, she almost missed how difficult getting out the next sentence seemed to be for him.

"Unless you just happen to be free on Saturday again. This one coming, I mean. And you don't mind cooking and babysitting at the same time."

It had come out in a big rush, followed by another one of those charming, toothy grins of his, but the way he'd phrased it didn't sound like he thought she'd actually be free at all. Her anger dissolved into astonishment.

"Babysitting? You?" She had to bite her lips before she could carry on. "How old is the baby? Oh no, please don't tell me there are two of them."

"What? No! Not the twins. I grant you they could do

with babysitting, but sadly my parents disagree. No, they'll all be out. Sailing club do. I'm staying at home with Sophia."

"Sophia's the baby?"

"Yes." He smiled softly. "She's five months old and she's nothing like the twins, I promise. She rocks. You'll like her."

"She might rock but can she cook?"

"What?"

Kirsty laughed.

"Forget it. Yes, I'll come and cook with you on Saturday, no worries. I'm not going to do any of the babysitting though. Forget it. Not my thing. But I'll happily watch you do that part. What time?"

"Six?"

"Works for me. See you later, Jake."

She started walking. He fell into step with her.

"Where are you going?"

"Home?"

"I'll walk with you."

"Why?"

He stuffed his hands into his pockets and shrugged.

"I want my Thursday-Kirsty walk. So if I can't have it later, I'll have it now."

He'd said it so totally matter-of-factly it didn't even register as strange with her. Besides, they had more important things to talk about.

Like music.

Turned out there was another person at Gull Cove who knew music had been invented long before even their parents had been born.

∞

She caught a lift with her mum that evening, since it had started raining sheets around half an hour before cooking started. But despite the fact that she was grateful for not having to drown with the rest of the world outside the windscreen, and despite the fact that she'd already had a Thursday-Jake walk it just didn't feel right.

She was dreading going into class alone and wondered who she'd be teamed up with.

"You're very quiet, baby," her mum said, while they waited at a red light.

"Hm. Not looking forward to it tonight."

Her mum turned her attention away from the road to look at Kirsty's profile.

"That's unusual. You haven't fallen out with Jake, have you?"

Kirsty's head spun around to look at her mum in record speed.

"No. Why would you think that?"

The lights changed and her mum pulled away as she answered.

"He's not picked you up tonight. He always picks you up."

"He's picked me up three times, Mum. Three is hardly always."

"You wait till you are in a long-term relationship, babe. In a long-term relationship *once* can be *always*. Or never. Sometimes once can be *never*."

Her mum sighed deeply.

"You're rambling, Mum. Everything alright between you and Dad?"

"Hm."

"What's up?"

"I want him to stop working so much. He's going to drive himself to an early grave. Literally. He sits in that bloody truck of his all day, eating crisps and drinking coffee. Then he kids himself into thinking he's doing exercise because he unloads the groceries. I worry about him. I worry about his heart. I bloody well want him to cut back on shifts but he says we can't afford it."

Kirsty remained quiet for a minute. There was always a note of true desperation to it when her normally softly spoken mum started swearing, which happened about once in a blue moon. It never failed to focus Kirsty away from whatever else might be going on to hone in purely on the matter at hand.

"Can we?" she asked soberly, after a moment.

"I don't give a crap." Her mum's voice trembled a little. "I know I can't afford to lose him. So we just eat less. Would do all of us a load of good. Or not go to Spain. We could stay home instead. We live by the sea. There are some gorgeous walks around here. Or we could rent Nicholas' room out to foreign students. You know, language holiday kids. We constantly get flyers through the door trying to recruit host families. I don't think Nicholas is coming back any time soon. I think Julian is finally over. And about time, too. Never liked that man. Or I could go part-time in a salon somewhere. Part-time hairdressing jobs are easy to find. The paper is full of them."

"But you've always hated working for other people. You like being your own boss."

"See, just like I said. I worked for somebody else *once* and didn't like it. Not always, no, *once*."

Kirsty chuckled.

"Point taken," she said as they arrived at the entrance to

the school's car park. "You don't need to drive in. Just pull up here." Her mum did as requested, and Kirsty unbuckled her seat belt. "You know, if you are seriously worried about Dad, we should actually talk about it. I'll back you up. I don't want to lose him either, thank you very much. I don't mind having students in the house or not going to Spain or any of that. Or, you know, *I* could get a job."

"Oh no, you won't," her mum said resolutely. "I'm not making the same mistake twice. That's exactly where we went wrong with Nicholas. Let him start working when he should have been concentrating on his education. And you are the smartest of the lot of us, Kirsty. I'm not letting you go the same way."

Kirsty grunted softly in protest but knew too well that there was no point arguing the issue. They'd been here before.

"Okay. But, you know—" She hesitated. "If you are worried about Dad's health, there is definitely one thing you could do already."

"What's that, baby?"

Kirsty could feel her heart speeding up with anxiety before she answered. She didn't like challenging her mum. Elise Matthews was one of the nicest, gentlest people on the planet, and as far as her daughter was concerned deserved never ever to have to endure criticism. But needs must. She took a deep breath, and then thought of something to soften the blow.

"You enjoyed the pie I made on Saturday, right?"

"Yeah, it was very nice."

"And you liked the lasagne I made, right?"

"Yeah?"

"Cook, Mum. Stop eating the crud Dad brings home.

Even if it's cheaper. Even if it's *free*. Let's just stop eating it. Let's start eating *actual* food."

To her great relief, her mum started laughing, a hearty belly laugh.

"Would you like a soap box with that? Get out of my car, child."

Kirsty was already out on the pavement, and had slammed the door shut when her mum let the passenger window go down.

"Oh, and Kirsty?" she shouted across to her daughter, who was rapidly getting drenched. "Be careful what you wish for."

The window went up again and she pulled away, leaving Kirsty to fend for herself.

∞

"**A**h, Kirsty, fabulous, just in time."

Caroline beamed at her when she entered the kitchen. The rest were already gathered, though Maisy was missing, and Kirsty could see the surprise in their eyes when she walked in alone. Or maybe she was just imagining it. She felt oddly naked without Jake by her side. There was no time to dwell on it though, as Caroline carried on talking without so much as taking a breath while Kirsty shed her sodden coat and found a place to stand next to Poppy.

"So, did everyone do their homework?" Caroline asked into the round.

A cacophony of mutterings replied that they had.

"And did anyone cook anything other than pie this week?"

Aimee's, Noel's, Zach's, Poppy's and Catalina's hands all

went up.

Kirsty looked around, astounded and mildly ashamed at the same time. For all the high and mighty speech that she had just given her mum, somehow the week had snuck by again without her standing at the hob for anything other than her homework.

"Excellent," Caroline said, clearly deeply pleased with the result. "That's great, people. Tell me more. Aimee, what did you make?"

"Cottage pie on Friday. Roast on Sunday. Soup on Monday. Macaroni cheese yesterday," Aimee counted off proudly.

"Teacher's pet," Ronan whispered, not entirely amiably, next to her.

Caroline ignored the remark and questioned Noel and Zach next.

"What about you two? I'm hazarding a guess it was a shared effort?"

"Nachos," they answered in one voice.

"That's not a meal. That's melting cheese over some crisps," Aimee said dryly.

"Ah," Zach answered with a wink at Kirsty, who happened to be standing behind Aimee. "But not if you make the salsa and the guacamole from scratch. Right, Chef?"

He'd turned to face Caroline again, and she nodded her reluctant approval.

"I suppose so," the chef agreed. "What about you, Poppy?"

"Just pasta and sauce," the girl answered quietly.

"What kind of sauce?"

"Carbonara," came the almost whispered reply.

"That's great, Poppy!" Caroline said, encouragingly. "Carbonara is tricky and I think it's great if you do things we haven't done here. Good on you. Now, Catalina, last but not least."

"Paella," the Spanish girl answered with an undertone that suggested embarrassment for being a cliché. "My parents came to visit at the weekend and I made paella for them and my host family."

"Again, brilliant. To be honest, I don't know why you are here. Anyone who can make paella is a genius. Paella is a nightmare. I've never managed to make a decent one. I'll get you to show us at some point. Now, as you may have noticed, we are short of both Maisy and Jake tonight. So, who would like to adopt Kirsty into their team for the time being?"

Kirsty saw Zach nudge Noel in the ribs. Both their hands shot up in the air at the same time as Aimee declaring an interest, a gesture which made Ronan frown, and Kirsty's heart warm.

"Right. Looks like you get to cook with Batman and Robin tonight, Batgirl," Caroline decided, then added in a mildly threatening tone, "So, does anyone here have fish issues? And when I say fish, I mean that in the loosest possible sense. Almost fish finger territory. So?"

She scanned her little crowd. Nobody lifted a finger. Kirsty wasn't the greatest fan of seafood but there was no way in hell she was going to expose herself. She wondered for a moment if anyone would have dared unless their life was at stake. In an anaphylactic shock kind of way.

"Good." Caroline grinned. "That's my baby chefs. And as a reward you'll even get a choice of salmon, tuna, mackerel or pollock. Now, get peeling your King

Edwards—" She paused to indicate a sack of potatoes on the counter with a jerk of her head. "And start on making mash. Welcome to the wonderful world of fish cakes."

∞

To be fair, Kirsty had fun that night. Close up, Zach and Noel were genuinely hilarious, the kind of friends who finished each other's sentences while constantly mocking and taunting each other in the best possible way. Yet somehow, they managed to include Kirsty from the off, ensconcing her firmly between them while putting her to work and making her laugh all at once. They imparted on her a sense of belonging that made her feel almost disloyal to Jake. The thought occurred when they were in the middle of forming patties out of their mash, salmon, egg and seasoning. Sadness seeped through her. She wondered what he was up to tonight. They hadn't spoken about it any more earlier that day, too wrapped up in a fierce discussion of fifties versus sixties tunes. The boy might have had knowledge of the old vinylverse but his decade of preference needed working on.

Noel elbowed her gently.

"Missing your co-pilot, huh?"

She nodded without looking at him, intent on making the perfect patty.

"What's the deal with you and Deacon anyway?" Zach asked smoothly while re-dusting the counter they were working at with flour.

She shrugged, laying the fish cake she'd just finished onto the plate in front of her. She pressed her hands into the flour on the counter surface and rubbed them lightly together to coat them all over, then scooped out another handful of fish-mash mix from the bowl in front of Noel.

"No deal. We're just doing this together."

She didn't look up but could feel the look Zach and Noel exchanged above her head nevertheless. She could practically hear the unspoken communication whizz back and forth between them across the frizz on the top of her head. She had to bite her lips when half a minute later Noel seemed to be a lot closer by her side, all of a sudden. It made her skin sing. There was something exciting about being so blatantly fancied. Even if she couldn't for the life of her figure out what exactly he saw in her. He could get a lot better. She stole a glance sideways at his profile to confirm. Yup, he was pretty. No doubt about it. Clear skin, a complexion that could somehow carry off plum hair, cheek bones, those massive dark brown eyes and a ski-slope nose that sat above a well-defined mouth with a plump lower lip and a wide cupid's bow, fit for a boy band member. Maybe not the lead singer, maybe not even one of the guys directly left and right of the central ornament but definitely fit for casting as the wild card on the outer edges. She watched his hands pat a fish cake into shape and decided they were nice, too. Kind of square and wiry but long-fingered, older looking than the rest of him, with leather straps and woven friendship bracelets wound around the wrists above them. She knew she had lingered on them a little too long when she heard Zach chuckle.

"Hey, Kirsty, you still with us?"

She returned her attention to the patty in her hands.

"Uh-huh."

"So, how are you getting home tonight?" Zach asked, more badly disguised laughter in his voice. Again, Kirsty could feel the glance he was shooting Noel over the top of her head. Subtle.

"My mum said to call her if it's still chucking it down. She'll come and get me. Failing that I'll walk."

"I'll walk you home, if you want," Noel said so quietly it practically qualified as a phantom of a sentence.

For a fleeting moment, she thought he was embarrassed for offering, didn't want his interest in the fat girl to go public, but then she caught another glimpse of his hands. They were shaking ever so slightly. He was nervous. She decided to put him out of his misery.

"That would be really nice, Noel, thank you," she said with conviction, turning to him with a big smile.

The smile she got back made her feel six-feet-tall and half her current width, while somewhere right in the back of her mind some alarm bells went off that she managed to studiously ignore.

∞

The difference between the two boys and the two walks on that same day couldn't have been starker. Night and day didn't remotely cover it. Away from Zach, Noel turned out to be exceptionally quiet, and Kirsty found herself in the driving seat for most of their conversation as they walked through the fine drizzle she had deemed not bad enough to justify calling on her mum's services.

Pinballing around subjects they could talk about other than food, she'd tried music first, but as it turned out, she hadn't heard of any of the obscure, firmly contemporary Indie bands Noel favoured other than maybe as logos on t-shirts, while his knowledge of pre-millennium recording

103

artists was limited to only the most classic of the classics on her player. There were no prolonged dialogues to be had here about whose version of *'You Don't Own Me'* was the definitive, or should one be able to take only one Buddy Holly song onto a desert island would it be *Oh Boy* (Jake) or *Everyday* (Kirsty). She fared better with the subject of films for a stretch, until they'd exhausted sci-fi, which Noel liked as much as she did, and got to superheroes, which Kirsty despised. Books were even more of a catastrophic failure since Noel didn't really read, unless whatever it was came with pictures. While Kirsty inwardly wondered if Jake liked reading, a subject they'd not got around to talk about as yet, and if so what kind of books, on the surface she carried on half-humouring Noel as he finally showed some initiative and tried to discuss Youtubers with her. But that, too, fizzled out quickly due to a distinct lack of interest on her side. After that they walked in silence for a bit, which wasn't uncomfortable, as such, but felt a little odd, until Noel tried to spark up the conversation again by returning to the obvious.

"So, what did you think of the fish cakes tonight? Would you make them again at home?"

"Not sure. Maybe. I liked the mackerel ones that Catalina and Poppy made the best. I thought ours were alright, too. The tuna and the pollock ones were pointless. Not enough taste," Kirsty answered. "To be honest, I liked the caper mayonnaise Caroline made more than the actual cakes. And that really worked with the mackerel, and it kind of worked with the salmon, but I thought it totally overpowered the other two."

"I didn't really like it. Don't like tartare sauce either. Not a great capers fan. I like my mayo to be just mayo. Got any idea what you'll be cooking for your homework yet?"

They had been told to find themselves dishes that they liked the look of over half term, try them out and then bring in the recipes after the holidays.

"I don't know yet. I guess I need to talk to Jake first. Should be something we both agree on."

They'd come to a halt outside her house, and as she turned to Noel to say goodbye, she saw his face darken.

"I don't think we were necessarily meant to do it in our teams," he said.

"Aren't we? But that's what I thought. You're not going to do yours on your own, are you? You're doing yours with Zach, right?"

"Well, yeah, but—"

"No." Kirsty cut him short. "Look, I really appreciate you walking me home. It was nice. But just 'cause you get to walk me home tonight doesn't mean you get to do it next time or that I'm all of a sudden going to ditch my cooking partner because he happens to be another male of the species. Understood?"

He nodded, an apologetic, insecure smile flickering on his lips.

"I like you," he said quietly, while he looked over her shoulder into the distance.

Kirsty softened her voice.

"Yeah, I got that memo. And I didn't mean that I don't think you're nice. I think you're really good looking, and you're sweet, and you could do loads better than me, but I'm not desperate enough to ditch my friend over some cute boy who's suddenly decided to take an interest in me for whatever obscure reason."

He looked back at her then, frowned deeply and stepped

up closer, fixing her with those saucer-big eyes of his.

"It's not sudden, Kirsty. I've liked you for a quite a while."

She stared at him, aghast.

"Really? Why?"

She realised it was a bit of an idiotic question, but didn't get to think about it much further, because suddenly he had his hand on the side of her throat. His thumb stroked her jaw line and his fingers were tangling in the hair at the base of her plait. It felt just like it looked in the movies and compatibility suddenly threw itself out of the window. She leant towards him and when he kissed her, the last fleeting thought before her body dissolved into jelly was a vague wondering about where the shy boy from earlier had gone. The one who'd replaced him was sure-tongued and possessive, with hands that knew exactly where to roam, how, and when, and with what pressure. In one of the nano-seconds when rationality managed its way through her lust-addled haze, just as he spread the hand he didn't have in her neck across her butt, palming it to pull her tighter against him, Phoebe's voice boomeranged back to her ear from the recesses of her brain. Her friend was right. This boy could kiss. But it was all body, no soul.

He abruptly let go of her again and took a step back to look at her as if she was the most scrumptious dinner on earth.

"Wow," he grinned, surreptitiously adjusting his jeans. "Can I come in for a bit?"

It was tempting and technically there was no reason not to invite him in, but she found herself shaking her head.

"Not tonight, no."

"Tomorrow?"

"Sorry. Got karate."

He looked stunned at this revelation for a moment, then started grinning.

"Dangerous lady, huh? Saturday then. Go catch a film? Or go to the beach? Or we could cook something together. You know, not for Connelly. Just for us. To eat."

"I can't. Not this Saturday anyway. I'm already cooking," she replied truthfully.

"Let me guess." Noel's tone had become icy. "With Deacon."

"Yes," Kirsty replied. "With Jake. I promised I'd show him how to make the fish cakes."

"Change the date."

If the temperature between them had dropped a few degrees over the last ten seconds, it now dropped a few hundred further. Kirsty inspected him through eyes like slits. Here he was again, the third Noel. Not the shy boy, not the kissing god, but the cocky one, who along with his friend hadn't been very nice to Jake when the opportunity arose.

"Can't. Jake can't do any other day. And I wouldn't anyway. I don't blow out my friends like that. Not my style."

"You wouldn't change cooking with Deacon to hang out with me?"

"Nope."

She could see anger and disappointment on his face but to her great relief there didn't seem to be any hurt. He turned away.

"See you, Kirsty."

She didn't respond but stood watching him as he disappeared into the advancing dusk and around the corner.

He didn't look back.

∞

Before you ask: I still feel bad about that. That's why I never told you about it before. I have a hard time admitting when my morals slip. And slip they did. I know. You shouldn't play with someone's feelings like that. There is an unwritten rule somewhere that says only snog people who you either actually like exactly as much as they like you, or people who don't like you and you don't like either. Don't snog someone who is really into you when all you're after is a bit of a kick. But in my very weak defence, I didn't really buy it. That Noel was that much into me. Or that he had been for a while. Me, wallpaper. Noel, one of the faces. Like you.

To be honest, I thought the whole thing was more to do with competing with you than with liking me, and I just took the opportunity to get a little kink out of it. Beggars can't be choosers, and the last time prior to that someone looked at me twice and stuck their tongue in my mouth was a French student at the beach last summer who was way too old for me, and whose face I barely remember. That was fun for the whole afternoon that it lasted. Ten months ago.

Anyway, back to the present.

Nothing's happened on the bench front in hours. No comings or goings, at least not that I've noticed, although it appears that I am a familiar enough sight for the smoking staff by now to give me a nod as they go in and out of the building.

I'm starting to wonder what to do about tonight. I don't want to leave here again. I don't want to leave you. Each time I go home to sleep it seems like you slip further away. And then I have to write twice as hard the next day to begin feeling the connection.

What if tonight I go to sleep (and I use this term in the loosest possible sense here) and then I can't get back to you? What if the words become just that? Words, no signal.

∞

Kirsty's heart started drumming long before she got anywhere near the Deacon residence. Her last visit to this corner of Gull Cove had instilled enough aversion in her never to want to return again, and that wasn't changed by the knowledge that none of the Deacons, aside from Jake and little Sophia, would be at home. Jake had texted her when the rest of his family had left the house, and had reassured her repeatedly that sailing club dos never finished before eleven at the earliest, but somehow, she still felt as if she was trespassing. On one level, she knew it was silly, and that J.C. Deacon didn't own the street, but on another, she had started feeling like a burglar on the prowl as soon as the Deacon trucks, clogging up parking spaces along the road once again, had come into view. She still hadn't told Jake about her little encounter with his dad, and he'd taken her worry as being rooted in her history with the twins. He'd poked fun at her for it a little, but had accepted her paranoia at face value nevertheless. He was good like that.

She realised that despite her anxiety, she was really looking forward to this evening, and sped up towards her destination. When she arrived at the door, she didn't get the chance to knock or ring the bell before it opened. For a heart stopping moment she thought the Deacons might have returned for something they'd left behind, and were just heading out again, but then she saw Jake standing in the doorway, cradling a tiny baby dressed in nothing but nappies against his shoulder. He, too, was naked from the waist up, his lower half encased in his customary washed out jeans and his feet bare. It was a peculiar, vulnerable sight that touched Kirsty deep inside in a way that was oddly primeval. There was something bizarrely attractive about a boy like Jake holding a baby like that. Kirsty had to shake off the feeling the picture in front of her elicited in the pit of her stomach, while Jake crouched down and picked up the baby's blanket from the floor, where he had evidently dropped it in his effort to open the door.

"Hey," he said with a broad smile as he straightened up again, throwing the blanket over his little charge. "I saw you coming from the window upstairs. We've been looking out for you. Sophia's only just nodded off." He tipped his head gently to indicate coming inside. "Come on in, make yourself at home. I'll just put her down in her crib. Kitchen is straight ahead. I'll be back in a tick. Put the kettle on if you like, or help yourself to some lemonade. There are some cans in the fridge."

While he went upstairs to put the baby to bed, Kirsty did as she was told and headed straight for the kitchen, barely taking in the cream carpeted hallway on her way.

The kitchen was exactly how she'd imagined and then some, a catalogue dream of granite work tops, eggshell walls, blood red high gloss units and brushed steel appliances. There was a centre island breakfast bar, the entire square double meters of which was covered in open study books that surrounded a baby carrier parked right in the middle. Kirsty took a peek. There were revision guides for at least five different A-level subjects here. She nosed around them some more. Chemistry, biology, law, business

110

studies, English lit. With a start she realised that he'd been studying for his exams. She felt a pang of guilt for her own lack of study application. Exam season had started before they'd broken up and she had sailed through the first couple of papers. But there was more to come. She had just started rifling idly through some random texts on classic fairy tales, and was wondering whether all of this had anything to do with his lack of time over the holiday period, when he returned to the kitchen, in the process of pulling a t-shirt over his head. She eyed his midriff one last time before it vanished completely under the fabric. Body-wise he was a good looking example of the male human, no doubt. He caught her looking and seemed almost flustered, which was so not Jake Deacon it made her snort with giggles.

"Sorry about the lack of decorum," he said earnestly. "Sophia likes skin on skin but she doesn't get nearly enough of it." He paused for a disapproving grunt. "So I try and give her as much as I can on my watch. Oh, yeah, sorry about that, too," he added, making a beeline for the books to shut and stack them before carrying them over to the windowsill.

"Impressive," Kirsty noted. "How many A-levels are you taking exactly?"

"Seven."

"Seven?"

She had to proactively remind her jaw to shut.

"Seven. Chemistry, biology, law, business studies, psychology, English lit and maths."

"You're kidding me, right? No one sits seven A-levels. That's not even possible."

"Yeah, that's what I'm starting to think, too."

He took the baby carrier off the centre island and gave the work surface a wipe with a damp sponge cloth. As Kirsty watched, something quite fundamental about him suddenly dawned on her. He was intelligent. Not just a little on the bright side but stellar, could-change-the-world clever. And that's how he'd got away with being who he was for all those years. That's why he'd never got expelled no matter what stunts he'd pulled.

"Right," he said, putting the sponge cloth away by the sink. "Considering the list of ingredients you texted me, I'm guessing we're making fish cakes?"

"That's right."

"Brilliant. I love fish cakes. I can make those in my sleep."

He'd crouched down to open a cupboard built into the centre unit, and was taking out potatoes one by one, putting them on the counter above his head without looking.

"So what do you need me here for?" Kirsty asked the back of his head, feeling strangely deflated all of a sudden. He straightened up and turned to face her.

"Company, you donut." He'd said it with a smile but when he picked up on the flinch that went through her on the term of endearment at the end of that sentence, his lips flat-lined. He closed the space between them to grab her gently by the shoulders. "The pleasure of your company, fair lady. That's what I need you here for. Now, peel!" he demanded, letting go of her again and turning away to gather the rest of the ingredients from the fridge and cupboards.

"Potatoes?"

He looked at her over his shoulder.

"I actually meant the coat but if you're offering ... the

112

potato peeler is in the drawer next to the oven."

He looked away again, and Kirsty took the unobserved moment to straighten herself before she went shedding clothes and peeler hunting.

∞

"Go on, you know you want to," Jake was wriggling half a fish cake in front of her mouth with an encouraging smile.

"I couldn't eat another fish cake if I tried."

"It isn't. It's *half* a fish cake."

"Nope." Kirsty gently pushed his hand away. "I couldn't even if it was the last food on earth and I'd never get to eat again. I'm full."

"I guess I'll have to take one for the team, then," he said, with a dramatic sigh.

He mopped up the rest of the caper mayonnaise and the entire thing disappeared into his mouth in one fell swoop.

"How can you eat that much? Where do you put it all?"

He chewed and swallowed before he answered.

"Hollow legs. That's what my mum says. I tell you what, that sauce is inspired. Caroline is a genius. I mean I like fish cakes but with that … that's another dimension of yumtastic. I tell you—" he stopped abruptly mid-sentence to put a finger to his lips as if Kirsty had been the one talking. "I hear Sophia. I'll be back."

Kirsty hadn't heard a thing, but Jake was out of the door and up the stairs in an instant. He was up there quite a while before he came back down, and Kirsty entertained herself by doing the washing up in the meantime, of which he had once more created an extraordinary amount. She was downright grateful for the mess. Without him in the

113

same room, she had become acutely aware again of whose house she was in, and concentrating on the menial task helped her not to feel too uncomfortable in the knowledge she was occupying Deacon territory, breathing Deacon air. She was pretty much done by the time Jake reappeared, a grumpy baby head-butting his neck in regular intervals while making angry slurping noises.

"Sorry, she needed a change. That's what took so long. And now that she's leaked out of the bottom we need to refill her at the top." He grinned at Kirsty then let his eyes wander over the dishes drying on the draining board. "Oh no, you didn't have to do that. We have a dishwasher."

Kirsty shrugged.

"Yeah, I figured. But I thought I'd do it anyway."

"Well thank you, you may come and eat at this establishment again. Do you think you could hold her for a minute while I warm up a bottle for her?"

"Sure."

Kirsty held out her arms to receive the baby, but instead of handing Sophia over, Jake walked around to stand behind her, lowered Sophia over her head and positioned her arms around the baby while cradling both of them at the same time.

"Here, one arm under her bottom and a hand behind her head. You need to support her neck. That's it," he instructed, so near to Kirsty's ear she could feel his breath tickle her cheek.

With Sophia secure in her embrace, and clambering around using Kirsty's breasts as footholds, Kirsty rolled her own head around in the crook of Jake's neck to look up at him. He smelled of lemon and parsley, fried fish and baby wipes.

"Jake?"

They were so close he had to lower his eyelids to look back down at her.

"Yeah?"

"I know how to hold a baby."

"You do?" He stepped away from her and around to her front. "Sorry. I get a bit overzealous. I didn't know the first thing when she came along. Mum had to show *me* everything. She thinks this is a doddle compared to the twins."

He went about heating a bottle while Kirsty wandered up and down the kitchen mumbling nonsense to the little creature in her arms with mixed results. Occasionally Sophia would stop complaining and look at Kirsty, transfixed for a second or two, her small face honing in on Kirsty's features earnestly. But before long she'd recommence her wailing song. Kirsty didn't know much about babies, but it seemed to her that this one was particularly ickle and dainty.

"Isn't she really small for five months?"

"Hm, yeah," was the only reply she got. There seemed to be volumes of unsaid judgements between those two grunted words but he didn't elaborate. For a moment, Kirsty wondered if he disapproved of his mum having had another child. There was some funny vibe there. She'd noticed it earlier. But she didn't ask.

When Sophia's formula was ready, Jake gave the kitchen a once over, then pointed to the door.

"Let's go to my room. Are you alright to carry her up the stairs?"

"Jake?"

"Yeah?"

"I can carry a baby up the stairs."

Having said that Kirsty found herself walking on eggshells as they went up, terrified she'd drop the increasingly wriggly and irate Sophia.

Jake's room turned out to be about three times the size of Kirsty's, and surprisingly tidy, with blue walls the exact same shade as hers. The only decorations were a couple of large, starkly black and white, framed photo prints of urban landscapes, hung above a king size bed that was cradled into one corner. The navy blue covered duvet had been rolled up and pushed against the wall to provide a cushioned zone to the cold plaster. What remained was a flat mattress space, fitted with an equally navy blue sheet and devoid of anything else bar some rattle toys. Jake climbed onto the bed, sat cross-legged with his back against the duvet roll, balanced the bottle next to his knee and held out his arms for the baby. Kirsty gave her up more than willingly and a blissful silence settled over the room half a minute later.

"So, how do you like Sophia?" Jake asked, not looking at Kirsty but the object of discussion as she sucked eagerly on the bottle's nipple.

"She's alright. I wouldn't want a whole one though."

He gazed up at her, a bemused smile playing around his mouth.

"What's that supposed to mean?"

Kirsty shrugged, wandering over to the window which overlooked the street. She imagined him for a second, standing here, looking out for her arrival earlier in the evening. Now that the food part of the night was well and truly over, she felt a bit awkward. They were buddies in kitchens, and friends on walks but she wasn't quite sure how to incorporate his bedroom into their relationship. Especially not his bedroom while he was bottle feeding his baby sister.

It felt weird, almost too personal. There was a level of closeness that exuded from him and the baby and which permeated the room that she didn't even share with Nicholas or Phoebe. Or anyone. Not since she'd been a very small girl. She'd read once that the amount of physical affection a child received decreased steadily as it grew older, until the parental cuddles were replaced by the first romantic encounters with peers. It hadn't meant anything then. Suddenly it did. The intimacy in the air reminded her of something she hadn't even realised she'd lost by growing up.

"Kirsty?" he called her softly.

She shrugged.

"I didn't mean anything. Only that I wouldn't want a baby just yet. You know, like Alisha and Chantelle and Chardonnay."

"Who are Alisha and Chantelle and Chardonnay?"

"They aren't. They're just typical names for people who get pregnant at sixteen." She turned to him and leant against the windowsill. "It's long hand for idiots. Actually, that's just Chantelle and Chardonnay. Alisha was real. She was in my year till she had a baby. You must remember her. Or maybe you don't. That was around the same time you got Livingston sacked, so you were definitely the bigger news."

He looked across at her expectantly and she realised he was waiting for more.

"I mean, yeah, she —" She nodded at Sophia. "Is cute. No doubt about it. And I'm sure it's fun playing with her and

117

good on you for doing this and all that. But if I look at people like Alisha … well, I wouldn't want to do this all day every day. I don't get it. Teen parents. I mean I do get how people get pregnant accidentally and then don't want to have an abortion. If I ever did I probably wouldn't want to do that either. Seems quite brutal. Not that there is anything wrong with it as such. Each to their own and choices for all and so on and so forth. But I wouldn't want to live with that. I think I'd feel guilty. Not to mention that my mum would kill me. And I'm still not too sure about the whole soul thing and how that works to go ahead with something like that. I'd rather have the baby. But, actually, I'd rather not have one by making sure I didn't get pregnant in the first place. I mean, it's not the 18th century anymore. We have contraception. And half the time I just don't buy it. The 'accidental' thing. I think eighty percent of the Alishas, Chantelles and Chardonnays get pregnant accidentally on purpose 'cause they're idiots who want a cute little me doll to dress up, and when it happens and they realise it's an actual person that grows and that they can't just put in the cupboard if they want to go out and play, they turn into the world's top whingers."

"Wow." Jake was looking at her aghast. He clearly hadn't expected quite that much of a sermon. "Thought about this a lot, have you?"

Kirsty shrugged.

"Only in passing."

He laughed, subdued.

"What about the other twenty percent?"

"What?" Kirsty frowned at him. "Oh. Them. Right. The other twenty percent do it 'cause they want to bind some guy to them. Like throwing another person in the mix is ever going to achieve that."

"You do realise you're putting the onus entirely on the girls here, Little Miss Feminism, right? What about the babyfathers? It takes two eggs to make an omelette."

"Nice phrase. I think you missed a point in sex ed there. That wriggly thing that looks a bit like tadpole? It's not an egg." When he didn't laugh, Kirsty shrugged. "I don't know. I'd hazard a guess the kind of guy who impregnates the Alishas, Chantelles and Chardonnays of this world isn't the sharpest tool in box either, you know. I guess they're just dumb."

"You actually think people are that stupid?"

There was an edge to his voice now. A subtle dig at her for thinking she was superior somehow.

"Yeah, maybe. I don't know." Kirsty could feel herself soften her stance suddenly, remembering the fleeting thoughts of earlier. "Maybe not. Maybe I'm being unfair. Maybe it's something instinctual. That —" she made vague swirly gesture at Jake and Sophia, "kind of closeness only happens when we're little. The older we get the less snuggling there is unless it's sexual somehow. So how do we get it back once we're not the baby anymore? We get a baby. Also, we weren't really designed to live as long as we do now. Maybe we're drawn to reproducing earlier than our current life span would suggest is wise because we are still programmed that way. But that doesn't change the fact that we have a choice."

"Interesting," he said thoughtfully, looking down at the little girl in his arms again. "What do you think, Sophia? Shall we ask the baby hater here if she wants to snuggle up in a totally non-sexual way and watch a film with us?"

He took the now empty bottle away and stuck it

somewhere between mattress and wall then put Sophia up against his shoulder to rub her back. Kirsty left her spot by the window and let herself fall onto the edge of the bed.

"I'm not a baby hater! You didn't listen to a word I said, did you? I—"

"Kirsty?" he cut her short.

"Yeah?

"I'm winding you up. Now put down the talking stick, come here and watch a film with us."

He patted the space next to him. She crab-crawled awkwardly up the bed, trying not to make the mattress wobble too much under her weight, and settled where he'd indicated. A moment later she had Sophia back in her arms while he went to dim the lights, boot up the computer on the desk opposite, and start a film.

Now that she was sated, Sophia seemed quite a happy, gurgly soul, and Kirsty let herself be infused by the little girl's energy for a moment.

A small part of her envied Jake for having this in his life. She would have liked to have been a big sister, or an auntie. At this age difference, it would be more like an aunt. A really cool young one. The aunt she was in all likelihood never going to be, not even when she would be of proper auntie age. She couldn't see Nicholas ever adopting or finding a surrogate or creating any kind of construct in which he'd become a father one day. She'd never thought about that before, and when Jake returned to his space and took Sophia back from her, Kirsty suddenly wasn't so keen on letting go anymore. He smiled knowingly but snatched the baby away anyway and laid Sophia with her back onto his stomach so she faced the ceiling. He let her grab his pinkies and began absentmindedly drawing circles in the air with her little fists.

"Ready?"

"What are we watching?"

"Have a guess, June."

"You sure? I thought you'd said you'd seen this film a thousand times."

"I have." He kept his eyes on the screen as the opening shot of *Walk the Line* unfolded. "But never with my two favourite girls on the planet."

∞

You know what the single most infuriating thing about me is? The thing I will never forgive myself for if we don't come out the other side of this?

I took you for granted. I took it for granted. The affection and the words like that. They didn't even register at the time. Not even to the point where I should really have thought that we were sitting mightily close there, and that that was a seriously strange thing to say for someone with a girlfriend. It was just filed under 'this stuff that Jake comes out with', you know. Because it comes so easily for you. You bestow love on people as if there was an infinite supply of the stuff. Like it's the one natural resource that isn't running out fast on the human race. Even worse, it never even occurred to me to give some of it back. It just didn't look like you needed it. I think that's what I'm really doing here. I'm giving back. So bloody well take it, alright?

∞

The rest of Kirsty's half term went by Jake-less, and so did the first days back at school when she just about caught a fleeting glance of him every morning as they went into their respective exams. They'd had a couple of text exchanges to talk about what recipe to choose for bringing into class, and to wish each other luck, but that had been the extent of it. They'd settled on a lamb curry, which sounded easy enough, and agreed to try it out separately since Jake didn't have the time to meet up.

It didn't bother her though.

She had bigger fish to fry. Like refereeing her parents, studying, and cooking up a storm.

The morning following Fishcake-Saturday she woke up to the noise of her mum and dad arguing, a rare and disturbing sound. Scraps of sentences containing phrases such as 'early grave' and 'don't want to sleep with a tombstone' on the one side and 'unrealistic ideas' and 'can't afford' on the other side floated across the landing to make Kirsty's first waking thought a reminder that she needed to stick to her word.

She had to go and back up her mum.

At first she thought bringing them up a cup of tea might do the trick but as she heard the argument grow fiercer she decided this particular negotiation needed more than a hot beverage and a bikkie.

She got up, walked over to her parents' bedroom, knocked loudly and stuck her head around the door without waiting for an answer. Their shouting match aborted by the arrival of their daughter, both the Matthews stared up at her from their perches on the marital bed as if freeze framed in mid-action.

"Can you keep it down, please, children?" Kirsty asked wryly. "You're waking the neighbours."

It had the desired effect, making both her parents smile

apologetically, first at her, and then each other.

"Good," Kirsty continued. "Now keep it that way. We'll all sit down and talk about it over dinner tonight. Which I'm going to make if one of you drives me to the supermarket to get some ingredients. Until then, not another word out of either of you."

She went back to her room, got dressed and trawled the web for a suitable recipe. It didn't take long until she'd come up with something. Her dad was a huge fan of stew and all things moist and saucy; her mum had the sweetest tooth on the planet. Beef casserole and mash, followed by a crumble of some description, depending on what fruit she could find at the shop, was going to be the perfect negotiation menu. All of it sounded easy to make.

And when it came to it, it turned out it actually was.

It always made Kirsty cringe when chefs on screen pontificated at pretentious length about how one could feel the nutrients being absorbed by one's body, but with the first spoonful of her concoction she suddenly understood what they meant. A certain measure of pride rose in her when her parents fell silent over the food. Watching them savour a meal she'd prepared, without it being something she'd brought back from class, or being homework for Caroline and that, really, hadn't taken that much effort, was a thoroughly gratifying experience. So was the knowledge that during the long wait for dinner they had eventually come to a compromise, to do with if not fewer shifts for her father, then at least learning to say 'no' to overtime.

Kirsty dug into her plate happily, for once not feeling guilty in the slightest about her lust for all things edible.

∞

123

After the night of the peace meal, Kirsty found herself cooking every day of the holidays. Just for the hell of it. At first it was like a chefing frenzy. Binge-cooking. Anything she fancied. Then, slowly, it became a ritual to clear her head after cramming all day.

And a challenge.

Around midweek her dad stopped bringing back last-day-of-sell-by frozen meals from work and instead started hauling home real meat and veg on the date stamp cusp. Some nights what dinner to make would be obvious, other evenings the assortment he brought home was a lot trickier to work with.

But Kirsty soon found she enjoyed the absurdity of it. Squeezing a meal out of the most impossible of ingredients turned into a sport. One she excelled at if the *Cooking with Caroline* website she consulted regularly was anything to go by. The most popular forum thread was *Cooking the Cupboard*, which was home to suggestions as to what to do when one only had a dollop of ketchup and two herrings left in the house (go out and shop) and which became Kirsty's virtual home for the next few days. She learned that other people actually did always have certain things in the cupboard, that a never-depleted supply of staples wasn't just an abstract concept but a necessity, and that when people said they only had two herrings and a dollop of ketchup to work with, they actually meant two herrings, a dollop of ketchup, flour, milk, butter, a variety of oils and cheeses, eggs, onions, potatoes, rice, pasta, tomato puree, tinned tomatoes, stock cubes, paprika, salt and pepper, oregano, basil, thyme, curry powder, some stale bread and half a pot of cream or yoghurt. At the very least.

It was a good thing this realisation had already occurred

and prompted the necessary shopping trip to fill up the larder before the first Wednesday back at school, when her father came home with a box full of less than desirable vegetables. For a moment, Kirsty was stumped but then, as she carefully began carving the good bits out of browning cauliflower, yellow broccoli, runny-outer-leaf chicory, dried out leeks and bendy carrots, an idea formed in her head. Excitement struck her when she realised that she knew exactly what to do with this, without asking the internet first.

After discarding everything but the choicest pieces she blanched them, added some sliced cooked potatoes, arranged all of it in an oven dish and set out to whip up a white sauce. Without Jake to give her a drumming lesson in between, it didn't exactly go smoothly, and she had to push the result through a fine sieve a couple of times before getting an acceptable texture, but in the end, it tasted great. She poured it over her vegetables and finished the dish off by smothering the whole thing with a cheese topping. Once her vegetable bake was bubbling in the oven she felt a sense of achievement that she hadn't felt since her grading as a black belt.

Her pride doubled when the dinner turned out absolutely delicious, and even her vegetarian food despising father could not find fault with it.

∞

She was still so full of her dinner successes the following day and so happy to see Jake properly again, she didn't notice at first how withdrawn he seemed when he picked her up for class. She hardly let him get a word in edgeways, though to be fair he didn't really try. So she kept happily chewing his ear off about her cooking adventures in minute detail all the way to school. It was only when they'd already entered the building, and were nearing their destination that she suddenly stopped and nudged him.

"Are you alright? You're really quiet. How are exams going?"

"Yeah. They are going," he answered, noncommittally. "How are yours?"

"I think I'm doing alright. Starting to appreciate that Simm abolished study leave. I think if I was left to my own devices all I'd do is cook and eat."

"Hmm."

They'd arrived at the kitchen.

"Ah, my star student," Caroline exclaimed as soon as they entered and she laid eyes on Kirsty.

Kirsty pointed at herself raising her eyebrows in question, then pointed at Jake.

"No, you, Kirsty. Kirsty, ladies and gents, has been cooking for England over the last ten days, haven't you?"

Kirsty turned a dark shade of pink when she realised with a start that Caroline Connelly clearly moderated her own website. But despite feeling nicely buoyed by Caroline's unexpected praise, Kirsty found the evening that followed uncharacteristically laboured.

After the chef had collected their homework recipes off them, to be tackled the following week, she'd carried on with her pre-break fish theme, much to Kirsty's dislike. To top off cooking a dinner Kirsty didn't fancy in the slightest, the atmosphere among the group was fractured, and even Caroline's attempt at injecting an upbeat vibe into the affair by putting the kitchen radio on once they got down to business didn't work. There was a distinct divide, and the bibs for the two sides were easily allocated: those who were sitting A-levels and those who were not. Jake, Ronan, Aimee, Maisy and Poppy all had moans to share, while Zach, Noel, Kirsty and Catalina had not. And share they did. At length. Camaraderie in the face of a common pain allowed even Maisy to join in the recounting of the trials and tribulations of the week without being told to shut up, and all of a sudden, the year thirteens seemed utterly superior. Though as the only year eleven in the group Kirsty had her own examination cross to bear, the failure or success of her GCSEs seemed peanuts in comparison to the older students' results determining if and where they'd go to university. For Maisy, who had a conditional offer from Oxford, her entire life seemed to hang in the balance. Jake was the quietest when it came to talking about the exams but, still, for the first time since she'd started working with him, Kirsty felt like a hanger on, like a little dinghy trawling in the wake of a much bigger boat.

As she listened in quietly, acting as his obedient sous who followed his every growled order, she couldn't help but let herself recognise the expiry date of their arrangement. They'd do this for another five weeks, until the summer, and then he'd be off and gone. She sighed deeply while dripping a spoonful of melted butter onto beaten egg yolks, which were being furiously whisked by Jake in a bain marie. It was just her luck. It had taken her twelve years since finding Phoebe to make another friend, and soon he'd be leaving. For a moment, she also considered what would happen with Caroline. Kirsty wondered if the chef would return to Gull Cove next year, but a quick glance over at the woman made her doubt the possibility profoundly. The difference between the skeletal creature who had turned up at their school a few weeks previously, and the competent woman who was presently helping Poppy sear a filet of salmon, was staggering. Even without camera make up, and dressed down in jeans and a t-shirt beneath the obligatory black apron, Caroline looked remarkably close to the star presenter who had once inhabited her body. Lost in those thoughts, Kirsty scooped two spoonfuls of melted butter from her little dish in quick succession and let them drop onto the egg yolks.

"Kirsty!" Jake's voice was scolding and dragged her back into the room. "Stop dreaming. You need to give me enough time in between spoonfuls. You only just put one in a second ago. Give me more time. Otherwise the sauce will separate."

"Yes, Chef!"

"Funny."

"Not really," she said, fighting a distinct sense of semi déjà vu. "Do you know where you might be going yet?"

"What are you wittering on about now, woman?" He briefly stopped to furrow his brow at her then returned to the whisk action with double the effort. "More butter! This is a bitch."

She followed his command.

"I mean, what universities have you applied for?"

"Who says I'm going to university?"

"Seven A-levels? The fact that you've got the brains *and* the means?"

"What's that supposed to mean? Butter!"

"What it says on the tin? That you are clearly super intelligent and have the glorious advantage of parents who can afford to send you into higher education? What do you think it means?"

"Butter! I'm not going to university, Kirsty. I'm not going anywhere."

It should have made Kirsty jump with joy, but he'd said it in such a flat way, in a tone that signalled such complete resignation, it just left her sad. And incredulous.

"You're joking, right? So what are you going to do after school finishes?"

"Work for my dad. Butter!"

"Fencing? You are taking seven A-levels to become a *chippie*?"

"Glad to know there are still people in my generation who know what a carpenter is called." The sarcasm dripped off him like the perspiration running down his brow. "Yes," he added matter-of-factly. "Butter!"

Kirsty dropped the last spoonful of butter into their Hollandaise, then grabbed a tea towel and dabbed at the drop of sweat which had made it to the tip of his nose by now, and was threatening to fall into their sauce. For a brief moment, he flinched away from the fabric before he lent towards it and let her achieve what she'd set out to do. He glanced at her with an apologetic smile.

"I'm sorry. I know I've been an arse tonight."

Kirsty put the tea towel down and made the sign for so-so.

"It's alright. But next week we switch. I'll be head and you'll be sous," she said decisively. "And, boy, am I going to give you a hard time."

"That's right, baby. You go all dominatrix on me. I like it."

He grinned for the first time that evening, and took the sauce bowl out of its waterbed to add a bit of the lemon juice he'd had her squeeze for him earlier. He stirred it then dived in with a crooked index finger to try it.

"Hm," he murmured happily, before dipping his pinkie into the sauce and holding it in front of Kirsty's mouth. "Try it. Tell me if it needs more lemon."

It didn't occur to Kirsty until just after she'd sucked his finger clean what a sensual thing that was supposed to be.

If one believed the literature.

For a moment, she thought she could feel the others' eyes, most of all Noel's, burning into her back but when she took a quick scan of the room, everyone appeared busy with their own stuff. When her eyes returned to Jake, he was looking at her intensely, his entire face sparkling with anticipation.

"And?" he asked.

She clicked her tongue against her palate appreciatively. "It's perfect."

He beamed.

"Bring on the asparagus and the salmon!" He nodded in the direction of the pan where the items in question were being kept warm before his eyes found hers again, a serious expression lingering beyond the ever-present mischief. "And I'm truly sorry, Kirsty, it's been a rough week. But that really shouldn't mean I get to take it out on you, of all people."

"It's alright. I guess you just haven't nicked enough fork lifts lately," she answered nonchalantly, while plating up their food.

"What?" He laughed.

"No outlet," she said gravely. "I've figured you out now."

"You have, have you?"

"Yup. You have this energy, Jake Deacon. This bursting at the seams lust for life. You know, as opposed to my bursting at the seams lust for food. And if it doesn't get to have an outlet every now and then you go sour. Terribly, terribly sour. Curdling. And I suggest that you've been treading the straight and narrow for too long. It's like me trying to diet. It's just a no go. I go super-grumpy. Absolutely grumptastic. And the thing is, there hasn't been a Jake Deacon story to make the rounds since before Christmas. That's absolutely friggin' ages. Can't be healthy. You need an outlet. You need to do something seriously crazy soon or you'll lose it."

She'd turned to him during her little speech, holding their plates up in front of her chest. Around them the other teams were also plating up now, and it was time to find their places at the table, but he was holding her on the spot with his stare, mesmerized. The narrowing of his eyes told her that what had started out as a light-hearted dig had somehow hit home.

Really, really deep home.

He leant over the plates and whispered into her ear with a hoarse voice.

"Any suggestions?"

She knew he hadn't intended for it to be sexual, and if he had she would never in a million years have suggested what came out of her mouth then. But it was rough, full of desperation and longing and the only thing she could come up with to cure that was what slipped out.

"Moon Pool."

His eyes were big and shiny when he drew back.

"You and me? Tonight?"

She couldn't believe herself when she answered.

131

"You and me. Tonight."

Day four.

Hi. Guess where I am?

Oh, yeah. It's bench time.

Just waved at the Deacons rolling in. Got greetings back, George even started coming towards me, then changed his mind.

Appears I'm not the only Gull Cove student bunking off this Monday. I wonder if they are missing any exams. I am. I'm missing Spanish. Shame. I quite like Spanish. My parents weren't happy. Understatement of the century. They wanted me to sit it anyway. But in the end, they gave up arguing with me. My dad even drove me here and mum packed me a lunch bag.

So, really, we're good to go.

Another day's praying, Kirsty style, coming up now.

So, where were we?

Like I don't know.

Ha!

You know, according to my parents, the Moon Pool challenge is as old as the hills. Isn't that funny? We think we invent this stuff and it turns out the last seven hundred generations before us have been there, done it, dropped the t-shirt. Or camisole. Or whatever. You know what? I don't even know what a camisole is. My nan's favourite reading material is full of them though.

Anyway, when I told my dad about it back when I first heard the rumours that people in my year had started doing it, he barely looked up from his paper, just mumbled, 'I'm glad you kids are still doing that. Good to know it's not all technology and gadgets for you. When it's your turn, just make sure you do it with the right person. The first time is magical, a one-time only thing. And don't ever go in anywhere else. The Moon Pool is special. No undercurrents, natural barriers, not deep. You know the drill, anywhere else and the sea will probably claim you in two seconds flat. Never forget that.'

That's my dad for you. Not all 'Don't you dare,' and 'If ever I catch you,' but just pragmatic to a fault. Love him to distraction, that man. I also remember feeling chuffed that he thought anyone would ever want to go with me. I mean, to quote one of my mum's favourite films of all time: who would want to see this naked?

∞

It was not until Kirsty came out of class and into the balmy June evening, still full of daylight, to sit down on the little wall that separated the car park from the forecourt and wait for Jake that the gravity of her suggestion really hit her.

What on earth had she been *thinking*?

The bizarre thing was that although her throat went dry at the idea, she didn't want to chicken out. She wondered if he'd done it before but the light in his eyes when she'd suggested it made her think that maybe he hadn't. Although considering who he was, that was almost impossible. She'd ask him later, on the way there. Or maybe she wouldn't. Maybe she would just hang on to the fantasy that this was going to be a first for both of them.

She didn't get much further in her reflections, because just then he stepped through the double doors, smiling widely, and walked over to sit down next to her.

"Second thoughts?"

She shook her head without looking at him.

"No, not really. Although—" She stopped herself abruptly.

133

"Although what?"

She shut her eyes.

"Although I would fully understand if you'd rather not see this—" She ran her hands up and down the air surrounding the sides of her body. "In its natural state."

She opened her eyes in time to see him get up and face her with arms crossed in front of his chest to berate her for a whole minute without uttering a single word.

"I'm not even going to respond to that," he finally said, offering his hand to pull her up. "If you're in, I'm in."

"I'm in," she said quietly and slipped her palm into his.

∞

The night was still too young for the stipulations of the challenge. It needed to be dark for the pool, but Kirsty and Jake didn't want to part until then. They knew they needed to stick together to go through with it, so they followed the rest of the crowd who had been lingering outside the school gates down to the beach. Every one of their little group went, even Maisy. As uncomfortable as Kirsty still felt around Noel, she was glad they were all going. It felt good. Even more so when she watched Noel, who was walking ahead of her, sidling up suspiciously close to Catalina.

Butts, Kirsty decided, *the boy must have a big butt fetish.*

She was glad he'd found another tree to bark up, and wished them luck. As if he could hear her thoughts, he turned around to look at her over his shoulder. She held her right thumb up with a big grin and he smirked back at her, tipping his head.

"What's that about?" Jake asked suspiciously from beside her.

"Nothing," she responded, pushing down the relieved smile that wanted to form on her lips.

"Be careful with that guy. I don't trust him as far as I can throw him. He's classic dickbrain. And I mean that exactly as it sounds. In its individual components. One brain. And it's not situated between his ears."

She refrained from telling him that she'd already figured that much out herself, and changed the subject.

"Any idea how we are going to sneak away once it's dark?"

"Hadn't planned on being sneaky. We'll just up and leave. And if they ask silly questions, they'll get silly answers."

∞

When it came to it though, there were no questions. One by one, the others had slipped away from the little bonfire they'd inherited from a bunch of tourists, leaving behind a feverish discussion about what had really driven Caroline Connelly to come to Gull Cove. Nobody, Kirsty found after a little poking, really believed the obesity story as a sole driving force. They all thought there was more to it. Theories flew around wildly, ranging from some sort of mystery illness having befallen the chef, via the pregnancy theory, despite her advancing years, to a family tragedy calling her home, and all the way to speculation that there was more between Simm and Connelly than age old friendship.

Some of them grilled Jake as if he knew the answer.

"Go on, Deacon, spill it," Ronan said, as nicely as he could muster, in between swigging from a bottle of rum, the top of which he carefully wiped each time it circled around to him. "We all know you know more. That's what you talk to her about when she keeps you back, isn't it?"

"I thought you thought I was showing her a good time in the store cupboard," Jake answered dryly, declining the drink as Ronan held it out to him.

"Yeah. Right. As if."

"Can I have that in writing?"

"What's that supposed to mean?" Ronan seemed to be genuinely struggling with the concept, but before Kirsty could step in to clarify, Maisy got up to leave, wrapping it up in a crisp parting shot.

"It means, Ronan," she said, in her best running the country voice, "that that sort of gossip gets good people into bad messes, and unless you are willing to put it in writing, never to spread that kind of crap. Have a nice night, everyone."

Her exit, and the stunned silence that followed the fact that Maisy Miller Makambe had openly used the word 'crap' in public without hell freezing over and pigs dancing La Cucaracha in the sky, signalled the end of the evening for most of the remaining stragglers.

By the time the last buses had been and gone, only Jake, Kirsty, Aimee and Phoebe, who'd come out to join them after rehearsal with two older guys from the Badminton Gardens crowd in tow, were left at the beach. It was nearing midnight, the fat half crescent of a waxing moon hung low in the clear sky, and while the people around them were getting notably tired, Kirsty's nerves were increasingly becoming like live wires. The senior of the Badminton Gardens boys, a surfer who went by the name of Gray and chain-smoked away his time out of the water in ultra-thin roll ups, yet never drank or got stoned, rose to his feet.

"Right, that's me done. I've got to go to work tomorrow. If anyone wants a lift, now is the time."

Phoebe, Aimee and Gray's hanger-on, a waster called Silas with jet black, wild hair and equally jet black eyes, who had been steadily drinking himself into a near stupor all night, all jumped up. Some with more success than others.

Phoebe and Aimee both steadied Silas between them while Gray collected up their belongings, roll up hanging from his lips. Phoebe looked down at Kirsty expectantly, at the same time wobbling expertly back and forth in tune with the drunken boy. When Kirsty didn't move, Phoebe cocked her head at her.

"Are you not coming?"

Kirsty shook her head.

"No. Jake will walk me home later."

She could barely suppress an embarrassed smile when she said it.

"It's a three-mile walk, Kirst!"

"I know."

"Hm."

Kirsty doubted Phoebe would have said anything else, even if Silas had allowed it, but as it was, the boy suddenly started staggering forward and Phoebe and Aimee were dragged along with him.

Gray hung back for a second.

"You certain?" he asked both of them. "It's a bus. I got space for all."

They shook their heads in unison, and Gray smiled.

"Well, in that case, have fun. Be safe. Especially you, Deacon."

Then he walked after his passengers, who'd disappeared into the distance already.

Jake and Kirsty waited until he, too, had been swallowed by the night before they got to their feet. They collected their things and walked silently towards the smaller cove that adjoined the main body of Gull Cove's beach. It was so well hidden behind a large rock formation which jutted out majestically into the ocean that tourists rarely found it. Only the initiated knew where the entrance was, a short little passageway hewn into the rock by pirates some centuries prior, according to the local lore that was carefully kept out of the guide books. This bit of the coast belonged only to the people who lived here, and Kirsty felt as if she was entering something sacred every time she snuck into the little cove.

She'd gone there countless times before, learned to swim there under the careful guidance of her father and Nicholas, but never at night, never to do what she was about to do.

The tunnel was so narrow that they had to go single file and Kirsty slipped in behind Jake. For a moment, as the rock encased them, it was pitch black and dead quiet. Kirsty's left hand found the small of Jake's back in front of her and they let themselves be guided only by their knowledge and their fingertips scuttling along the wall.

When they came out the other side, the sight took her breath away. She exhaled slowly as she beheld what lay before them.

She walks in beauty like the night, of cloudless climes and starry nights.

From out of nowhere Byron's words ricocheted through the centuries, sending a quiver of enchantment from Kirsty's scalp all the way down to her toes.

What in daylight was merely a nice little pool, almost

entirely surrounded by a natural circle of rocks with only a small opening to the sea to let the tide in and out, appeared like a magic portal to the sky at night. The moon and the stars were reflected perfectly in the black mirror of the water, only the occasional gentle ripple of waves giving a clue as to where was up and where was down.

"Oh wow," Kirsty whispered, while in the face of all this beauty, the thoughts of unworthiness and shame that she'd been nursing in the background all evening fell away.

Without hesitation, she began peeling herself out of her clothes.

Jake was still standing motionless, staring at the water, when she had already shed her jacket, shoes and socks, and she halted for a moment.

"Have you ever …?"

"No," he answered, almost inaudibly.

"Are you …?"

"Yes." His voice was shaky but certain. "Oh, yes, I am."

He shook himself out of his reverie and out of his jacket and they carried on undressing together, neither looking too closely, nor not looking at all. For a fleeting moment Kirsty noted that this was the first time in real life she'd seen a grown-up boy other than her brother entirely naked. She was also acutely aware that for Jake the opposite most definitely wasn't true. But somehow it didn't matter. None of it mattered as he took her hand, and they waded into the freezing cold water side by side. The pebbles beneath their feet were smooth and round, and seemed smaller than Kirsty remembered from her childhood excursions. Back then they had been like cobblestones under her tiny toes.

They stopped to acclimatise for a second when the water reached half way up their calves.

Kirsty shivered violently.

"I so want to squeal," she whispered. "It's freezing."

Jake chuckled.

"Go on. I won't tell."

"Nope. You squeal, the merfolk come."

"Right." He smirked. "I always knew you had a fin loose."

"Haha. Finny."

"Hilarious. Come."

He tugged at her hand and they went in more quickly, deeper, until he gently slid down into the water, dragging her with him. And then they sat, the sea to their necks, waiting for the ripples they had caused to die down. Once everything had stilled, they looked at the reflections of the stars around them.

They were floating in the Milky Way.

"This is amazing," Jake said, in a reverent tone.

"Uh-huh." Kirsty barely managed to form the sound in her throat.

He looked over at her and squinted at her tightly clenched jaw.

"Are you okay there, buddy? You don't look okay."

"Fr-fr-freezing," Kirsty answered, through chattering teeth.

"Come here." His arm found her waist under the water and pulled her closer.

A second later, he'd wrapped her from behind, his legs around hers, his chest pressed against her back, exuding impossible warmth, and his arms slung tightly around her front. She could feel all of him, skin on skin, bits against other bits and still there was nothing sexual about it.

Well, mostly.

Maybe she was a little excited and maybe he was, too.

Kirsty squirmed with embarrassment, only to feel Jake's embrace become even surer.

"Stay," he whispered into her ear. "Ignore that, it's not important."

It should have hurt, the dismissal. But it didn't.

Because she understood what he meant.

This was beyond the vanities of attraction.

It was as real and as magnificent as life ever got.

∞

I'm welling up here. I knew this was going to be one of the hardest things to write down. That's why I procrastinated for so long around the whole Noel episode, and around how I discovered cooking with the internet, neither of which was even remotely important in the grand scheme of things.

Purely because it prevented me from getting here. To this. The night of a lifetime.

I'm so glad I did the challenge with you and nobody else.

It means I have something of yours forever, no matter what happens next.

You're the boy I did the Moon Pool with.

In the universe of Kirsty, you are legend.

∞

Kirsty couldn't remember ever having been hit harder with cold than when they came out of the water that night. Almost entirely incapacitated by her chattering teeth and the shivers shaking her body, she could hardly manage to pick up her shirt. Her fingers kept missing the target. She marvelled at Jake, who didn't seem to feel the cold at all, and who was back in his boxers and jeans in two seconds flat.

"You need to hurry up, Kirsty, you're going to catch hypothermia. Here, use this as a towel," he said, pushing his t-shirt into her hand.

She began rubbing herself dry frantically.

"Th-th-thanks. T-t-technically I d-d-don't think hy-hy-hypo-thermia is something you c-can catch."

The shakes were slowly dying down now and once she'd put her clothes back on she felt comfortably hot in her skin. She could feel water dripping from the end of her plait down the back of her jacket and decided to free the beast. She untangled the braid, took the tee from in between her knees where she'd been storing it, and rubbed her hair from wet to seriously damp with the last element of absorbing powers the cotton had to offer. She raked the mass of curls with her fingers, ripping at them to spread them out, and only then looked guiltily at the soggy t-shirt in her hand.

"Oh crap. I'm sorry. What are you going to wear now?"

He stared at her for a moment before he shrugged, picked up his jacket and put it on over his naked torso. He took the t-shirt from her, scrunched it up and stuffed it in his pocket, his eyes still not leaving her face. Suddenly uncomfortable under his stare, Kirsty dipped her eye lashes and divided her hair back into sections in order to replait it. In a flash his hand was over hers.

"Don't."

His hand sunk away and she let go of the strands, squinting at him inquisitively.

He smiled.

"Leave it." He stepped back to scrutinise her with arms

folded in front of his chest. "Wow. That's impressive. I don't think I've ever seen *impressive* hair before. Now I know why you know so much about merfolk. Come, Ariel, let's go find a petrol station that sells hot chocolate and rubbish donuts."

"Technically, Ariel has really straight red hair," she argued as they made their way back to the stone passage.

"What are you? Five? Only in the Disney version." He laughed, then stopped to turn around to her for a second. "If I read *The Little Mermaid* to Sophia one day, although I'm not sure I will because Andersen's original is depressing as hell, *my* Ariel is going to look *exactly* like you."

∞

There you go again, bestowing love and affection on people as if it was nothing. You know, nobody's ever said anything sweeter to me, and, yeah, I admit it, my heart skipped a beat. Of course it did. It would have to have been dead not to.

Funny that, isn't it?

How words can do you in so much more than the obvious. It's ridiculous, really, if you think about the whole thing. So there we were, about ten minutes before all that, huddled naked together in the water, so close it felt like our skins were grafted together and there was no 'it'. Well, maybe a little body-'it' but not any real 'it'. And ten minutes later, you go and say something like this, and I a) seriously understand why you are so bloody successful with the double-x-chromosomes and b) contemplate asking you to consider taking my virginity.

Yup. I admit it. I have thought about you in that way. On occasion. Maybe even at length. But would it be worth it? I'm sure you wouldn't laugh in my face or anything. Not your style.

143

But it's that old chestnut. I don't want to lose you. And lose you I would. I mean even if we turned out to be these star-crossed lovers, excuse me while I go laugh my head off, how many couples do you know who got together at our age and then stayed together, forever and ever, till death does them part, amen? Yeah, exactly. There is a reason all those romantic teen flicks end with the first kiss, because, realistically that is the end. Or the beginning thereof. I totally believe in true, all-consuming, endless love, don't get me wrong. But I have this theory. Basically, once again, it's that increased life span of the modern age that comes and bites us in the arse. I know, I know, first world problems, I can hear you say it, but bear with me while we carry on waiting for the day it's our turn to be third world – I'm sure it'll come soon enough – and let's just run with it for the moment. So, where was I? Ah yes. Increased life span versus endless love. You see, when those happy-ever-after fairy tales were written, the ever after was only ever roughly fifteen years long, right? They meet at 15(ish), get married, live happily ever after. Until they die of natural causes at 30. So that's a hell of a lot less than the sixty, seventy years of living together we'd be looking at these days. And people wonder why divorce rates are so high??? It amazes me every day that my folks have made it as far as they have. But I think it's precisely because they were not teen sweethearts that they are still together. Admittedly they were cutting it fine with pairing off at twenty-four, and I'm sure having Nicholas pretty much immediately didn't help, but somehow, they've made it. So far, anyway. And I think that's because they weren't each other's first big love. More like the third. I'm pretty sure that each of them had already gone through that whole cycle of being in love and then not being in love a couple of times before they met. So expectations were probably not that high. They knew from the beginning that they could live without each other. And that's what made them stick.

Sod's law.

Anyway, what I'm trying to say is, I've thought about it and I'm almost certain you wouldn't refuse me, and I'm sure you'd be loving and kind and not all about self-gratification, and altogether fantastic, and a great choice for doing the do, but I'd rather be your friend for the next seventy years than your girlfriend for the next seven seconds. Figuratively speaking, of course. My pride tells me we would probably last quite a long time. For our age and circumstances. But not forever.

And you, my friend, I want to keep forever.

∞

It was well past one o'clock in the morning when her phone buzzed for the last time. Kirsty took it out of her pocket, smiled at the text and put it away again. Jake looked at her enquiringly over the cardboard rim of his hot chocolate cup.

They were sitting on a couple of rickety barstools, nursing their second round of drinks and donuts at the coffee counter of the one and only petrol station in Gull Cove where the night attendants didn't shut the door at midnight to serve through a hatch.

"My dad again," Kirsty explained. "He's going to bed now."

"Is he not pissed off with you for staying out this late?"

Kirsty shrugged.

"I often stay at Phoe's till dawn comes up."

His eyes went big.

"On a school night?"

The almost believable tone of upset in his voice made Kirsty splatter her latte all over the front of his jacket, which he had zipped up before they'd entered the shop. She picked up a wad of napkins from a stack by his elbow and started dabbing at him. He took them from her and wiped himself, looking at the splashes and shaking his head in disapproval.

"If you were my daughter, no way," he muttered fervently.

Kirsty laughed and hopped off her stool.

"Right, I'm off then."

His head flipped up.

"What?"

"Well, I'm clearly out past the Jake Deacon curfew, so I'd better run, huh?"

He grabbed her wrist.

"Point taken. Sit."

She clambered back up onto her chair.

"Yes, Master, Sir."

"Don't be like that."

"Okay. I won't."

"Are you eating the rest of that donut?"

He eyed the remnant of her chocolate and salty caramel crunch ring. She grinned.

"A really nasty part of me wants to say yes, just to see you suffer, but the girl who's got an ongoing relationship with her bathroom scales says have it."

He picked up the piece in question and ripped it in two. He gobbled up the bigger bit then held the other in front of her mouth.

"Go on, have it both ways."

"And there was me saying Noel was the feeder," she mumbled.

Jake's features instantly darkened.

"What's that guy got to do with anything?"

146

"Nothing. Just saying you do an awful lot of feeding me," she answered, just before her mouth snaked forward and sucked the remaining piece of donut out of his pincer grip. "Hm. Bless the empty calories," she carried on with her mouth full, trying to distract him from the subject of purple haired butt-fetishists.

"Don't give me that crap." Jake frowned. "That's the kind of idiotic statement Shannon comes out with. Empty calories. What a load of bull. Empty of nutrition, maybe, but not empty of joy, are they? Donuts are stalwarts of stress relief. They deserve reverence, adulation, daily fan mail. Raw celery, now there is an empty calorie, if ever there was one. Devoid of nutrition *and* of joy. Double whammy. Shannon had this phase when she munched on those silly sticks all friggin' day. Like she was some stupid super model or something. Just 'cause some newspaper told her to. And I'm using the word newspaper in the loosest possible sense here. 'Cause, like, allegedly, digesting raw celery uses up more energy than it gives you. Did you know that? A vampiristic vegetable that eats you from the inside. Halle-frickin-lujah."

"Down boy," Kirsty said, suppressing a laughter fit. "That's between you and your girlfriend."

"Between me and who?" he snapped.

"Shannon? Your girlfriend?"

If Kirsty had thought the mentioning of Noel had somehow blackened Jake's mood, she hadn't seen anything yet. It was as if the door to the shop had opened and a personalised little thunder cloud with the name 'Jake' written across it had wandered in and made its way over specifically to hover above his head. He stared at her with an icy glare for a good half a minute before a string of

147

growled words left his mouth.

"Do you really think," he asked darkly, "that I would have done that—" he pointed through the glass front of the shop into the night, "—with you, if I had a *girlfriend*?"

Now that he'd asked it so bluntly Kirsty realised that it was a pretty far stretch. Nevertheless, she could never have imagined how angry and hurt he would be at the suggestion. He got off his stool.

"No matter what, huh? I'll always just be Jake Deacon," he said, disappointed, more to himself than to her, then shot her a look that told her in no uncertain terms not to even bother trying to pedal back from that one. "Come," he added flatly, "I'll take you home."

∞

When she woke up the next morning, Kirsty really wished she could have been a less robust specimen of the human species. How could she possibly not have at least a little bit of a cold after skinny dipping in the North Sea at midnight? Although she would have preferred full blown pneumonia, if she was honest. She swallowed a few times, hoping to trace a touch of a sore throat but, nada, nothing, nix. She would have no choice but to confront the day. Physically, at least, she was bright of eye and bushy of tail even with only four hours' sleep. Emotionally was quite another matter. It was a good thing she had no exams today. She would have flunked even English lit.

Jake had left her on the doorstep, without so much as a goodbye, at around quarter past two. She'd tried a couple of times on the way from the petrol station to her house to talk to him, to explain, but his stony silence had proved impenetrable. He'd stopped and turned to watch her make her way safely into the house once he'd put some distance between them, but it was little consolation. On the contrary, their eyes had met briefly in the dark across the gulf between them, and Kirsty had felt his disappointment like a dagger piercing her heart. It had been a painful ending to what should have been one of the most amazing nights of her life.

Thinking about the Moon Pool made tears well up in her eyes. It had been so wonderful. And she'd so royally messed it up.

Thou shalt not make assumptions.

Of course, now, in the stark light of day, she realised another side to her misconception. Not only had she assumed the worst of him, she hadn't exactly painted the best picture of her own moral compass there. It took two eggs to make an omelette. If she had believed he was taken, and that hadn't stopped her from frolicking naked in the sea with him, not that frolicking was the right word for what they'd done, more like decidedly-not-frolicking-in-the-face-of-magnificence, whereas he had known he was free to do whatever he pleased … that made her the 'Jake Deacon' in this scenario, really. Especially considering who had suggested the whole thing. Despite feeling like she'd just lost a limb, the thought made her laugh out loud into the emptiness of her room. Kirsty Matthews, the hussy. The ruthless, ruthless hussy.

She got up to get dressed, go to class, and face his wrath some more.

∞

I just caught Caroline in the corner of my eye.

With Simm. They arrived together.

For a heart stopping moment, I thought they'd come to drag me to school. But they are not here for me. They are here for you. Or rather your parents, I guess.

They've just gone inside. They didn't see me, I don't think. Which is just as well. I don't think I could handle Caroline right now. Unless she came out with good news. But ever since our little encounter, I reckon that your mum would let me know now if there were any new developments. I think she knows I'll be here till the bitter end. And I'm sure she'd come and tell me if there was something to tell. If Caroline came over it would be a bit like when Phoe came to squeeze my hand. To share in my vigil. This is what this is, isn't it? That's the word for what I've been doing here. Vigil. Only difference being, if Caroline came to sit with me I'm pretty sure I'd dissolve. So hopefully, once she and Simm are finished doing whatever it is they are doing in there, they'll just leave.

There's hoping.

∞

Jake's anger was infinitely worse than she'd expected. Kirsty had hoped that after a few hours' rest, he would have cooled off, and he'd let her apologise, maybe make him laugh with her analysis of Kirsty Matthews, the shameless harlot. But no such luck. He wouldn't let her get near enough to talk to him, wouldn't answer her texts. Not that day or the whole of the next week. She even caught him changing direction in the school corridor as she headed towards him a couple of times.

So she knuckled down, and got on with her exams

instead. At some point between the last two papers of the week, she decided that she'd have a major row with a friend *every* time she had to pass something from now on. There seemed no better way of making her concentrate than as an avoidance tactic to feelings of regret. On the downside, she feared she'd actually lost Jake's friendship.

"I feel like I'm in some stupid Hollywood romdram without the rom," Kirsty said to Phoebe as Thursday rolled around again. "And it's the really crappy part of the film when you are sitting there shouting at the screen, 'Just *talk* to each other, you idiots!'"

They were lying on their sides, opposite one another on the floor in Kirsty's room, comparing notes and eating banana bread cupcakes, which Kirsty had been baking all night from the half a ton of black bananas her dad had brought home the day before.

"See, that's why I never go to the cinema with you anymore. Too much shouting. People don't like it. Romdram? Is that even a thing?" Phoebe asked, looking up briefly in between her finger eeny-meeny-miny-moe-ing back and forth between a full-on chocolate butter icing cake and a smiley face royal icing one.

"I don't know. Pretty sure it is. It's basically a romcom that's not funny," Kirsty answered, then jerked her chin at the tray between them. "You know it's always the one you start with, right?"

"That depends on how long you string out the rhyme for."

Phoebe grinned and picked up the one with chocolate icing.

"Fair point. I really don't want to go tonight."

Kirsty let her head sink into the crook of her arm and

they stayed silent for a while, the only sound being Phoebe's molars making short work of the cake. She took a sip of tea from the mug in front of her to wash it down then fixed Kirsty with serious eyes, all flippancy put on hold.

"Look, it would probably help this viewer here with the whole shouting thing if I knew what the problem was."

"We've been over this."

"No, actually, we haven't. All we've managed to establish so far over the last few days, and a very painful process of word extraction it was, if I may add, is that nothing happened between you."

"That's right."

"So what's happened between you?"

"It's complicated."

"No shit," Phoebe answered, rubbing her face violently with both her hands.

Kirsty was always amazed how her friend could do that without smudging the ton of eye makeup she wore.

"I'm sorry, Phoe, I'd tell you if I could. But it really is between me and Jake. Although I don't think there'll ever be a 'me and Jake' again."

Phoebe got to her feet and Kirsty flipped over onto her back to look up at her friend who was nodding disapprovingly.

"Well, I agree, *grammatically* speaking, I sincerely hope there will never be a 'me and Jake' again," Phoebe said in her finest Mrs Dodson voice. When the impression of their English teacher didn't rouse a chuckle from Kirsty, Phoebe sighed resignedly and scrunched up her nose. "Look, I've got to go. If you don't think he's coming to pick you up today anyway —"

"Yeah. Fat chance," Kirsty interrupted.

"Then why don't you walk with me now?" Phoebe offered. "Hang in the hall for half an hour, watch the rehearsal. Or go to the library or something."

Kirsty rolled her head from side to side, feeling the carpet load up her hair with static electricity. Great, to add insult to injury she'd walk into class with a plus size frizz halo tonight.

"Okay." Phoebe sighed. "Suit yourself. But you *are* going to class, right? You ain't quitting on cooking with Caroline over some idiot boy, right?"

"No way."

"Atta girl." Phoebe stepped over Kirsty and headed for the door. "*Arrivederci, bella amica.*"

Despite the quasi promise she'd just made, Kirsty began debating whether she could maybe pull a sickie even before she heard Phoebe shout a goodbye at her mum and slam the front door shut. She was Caroline's star student after all, and really, the mass of banana bread she'd eaten in the last twelve hours was starting to make her feel a bit queasy now. Maybe there was such a thing as potassium overload. She'd look it up later. She went to find her phone, sat back down on the floor with her back against the bed, and scrolled down to the number Caroline had told them to call if they ever needed to miss a class for any reason.

Kirsty was still staring at it undecidedly half an hour later, when a loud knock on the front door made her jump out of her skin and her heart race for the Olympics. For a fraction of a second, she kidded herself into thinking it had to be a parcel delivery service, despite the fact she knew this particular knock well by now. She listened, immobile, holding her breath, as her mum opened the door. There were some murmured words and then heavy footsteps up

153

the stairs. The rush in her veins was making her truly nauseous now, and her throat tightened so much when the same pattern of knocks was repeated on her bedroom door that she hardly got the words out to let him in. But somehow, she managed and, even more amazingly, somehow he heard her. Jake opened the door and took a step in before suddenly stopping to take a look at the walls. In the half a second before he spoke, Kirsty realised he hadn't been up here before and she smiled weakly, knowing exactly what he was thinking.

"Wow. That's my blue." His eyes focused on the clock for a moment. "Cool clock."

Only then did he make eye contact. And suddenly she couldn't hold back the tears any longer. The river of sadness and regret she'd been damming all week broke through in slow, silent, continuous trickles.

Jake stared at her for a minute then closed the distance between them and crouched down in front of her, his jacket squeaking like a bunch of mice in the process.

"Stupid jacket," Kirsty said helplessly, in between snuffles.

It made him smile, just a little.

"Hey, you need to mop that spillage up before we can go to class. I have a reputation to protect, you know."

She looked at him apologetically before drying her cheeks on the sleeves of her shirt.

"I'm sorry, Jake. When we … the girlfriend thing … it didn't even occur to me at the time. I really don't think … "

"Shh," he interrupted, steadying himself with a hand on the floor. "Forget it. We're alright. It's taken me a little while, but I've figured something out."

"What's that?"

"You won't like it."

"If it means you're still cooking with me, and you'll stop giving me the brush off, whatever it is, I'll like it."

"You won't."

"Try me."

"On your head be it."

"Go on already."

He grinned then, a proper wide Jake Deacon smile, and she suddenly knew what was coming. Great minds and all that.

"Well *I* knew I was free to go bathing in the stars with whoever I fancied. You, however, are a bad, bad girl, Kirsty Matthews."

"So how badly do you think of me now?" she asked, trying not to give away in the face of his lightness that, actually, she was hanging on his answer with bated breath.

He jumped to his feet and extended a hand to pull her up.

"Not at all badly. I think that when you and I do stuff, we just do stuff and it's right, whatever the circumstances. And that's that. I'm just sorry it's taken me this long to figure it out. I've never met a girl, never met *anyone*, like you. Clearly, here—" the extended hand stopped offering its services for a moment to brush back and forth through the air between them, "different rules apply."

The hand aborted its weaving thing and Kirsty grabbed it to let him help her to her feet. She indicated the tray on the floor with a tilt of the head.

"Do you want some banana bread cupcakes? I have about a gazillion."

He didn't answer immediately, smiling at her in a way that made her not able to meet his eyes. So she missed his

155

arm sneak out to wrap itself around her shoulder and pull her in. He nuzzled a kiss onto her forehead and let his lips linger by her hairline for a second to mumble against her skin.

"Banana bread cupcakes sound great. Missed you, Kirsty Matthews. Let's not do that again."

∞

See? Exactly my point.

You said it yourself. Let's not do that again. So let's not do that again.

You're not allowed to leave.

I keep having the lyrics to Pink's 'Great Escape' going round and round in my mind now. It's on my player but the thing is so friggin' cheap that you can either listen to music or use the word processing function but you can't do both at the same time. I suppose I could use my phone instead but then I'd have to go through the whole palaver of youtubing it first. And if I get really unlucky I have to sit through a dishwasher tablet ad first and then the moment is truly gone. I think I'd rather stick with listening to it in my head.

And yes, you heard right. Pink.

I have my contemporary vices and she is one of them. Love, love, love that woman. You didn't know that, huh? I think she is great. In every single respect.

Uh-oh. I just saw Caroline and Simm.

Yup, they're out. She's spotted me. She's squishing his hand. She is making a beeline for me.

∞

*O*kay. Well. That was neither here nor there, really. I thought I could finally get some actual intel but there isn't any. According to Caroline, four of your five vital organs are all hunky dory (not least thanks to the best jacket in the world) but your head still not so much. I did get a bit more detail on that than I already knew. Not sure it is detail I wanted to know though. Your arm wasn't that big a deal, apparently: they fixed that. Wasn't even broken. Popped out of its socket, they popped it back in, job done, no biggie. The concussion is the killer. Literally. Your brain started swelling on the way here and they discussed drilling your skull to let some of the fluid out (lovely) but then didn't because the swelling stopped. As in, stagnated rather than miraculously disappeared. So, that's the status quo: your brain's swollen, you're comatose and the prognosis changes depending on if the doctor is more of a glass half full or a glass half empty person. Although each day that passes without significant improvement is a point for the half empty brigade.

Caroline really didn't pull any punches when she gave me the low down.

But, honestly, I'd already figured that there hadn't been any change, due to the fact that your parents and the twins seem to be pretty much camping out here. I don't know what the policy is, but I'm pretty sure you can't have each patient's whole tribe hanging around for days on end unless it's a proper life-in-the-balance scenario. I mean, our hospitals have standing room only for half the patients, let alone their entourage.

You know what? I know I said if Caroline came out and sat with me I'd dissolve, but in reality, the opposite happened. There is something about that woman, about her delivery, that makes things somehow instantly better. Like when you have a pilot on a plane with that deep reassuring voice that makes even the worst turbulence sound like just a little pothole in the sky. She was very *matter of fact about it. She also tried to get me to go home, of course. Rumour has it that I'm slowly gathering legendary status with the hospital staff. If I'm not careful I'll become 'The Girl on the Bench' or something. Anyway, when Caroline realised she couldn't convince me, she gestured Simm over so he could try his luck. And you know what?*

That man is so cool.

As of about five minutes ago, I am the first president of the Gull Cove Anthony Simm fan club.

So there I was, fully braced for a headmaster type lecture. You know, something along the lines of 'You know you can't do anything for Jake sitting here, you might as well go home, come back to school, carry on with your exams, blah blah,' but you know what actually happened?

This:

Simm walks over reluctantly and Caroline looks up at him from her perch by my side, sighing rather exasperatedly at my stubbornness.

"Anti, could you please tell her she needs to go home? She's sat here all weekend, apparently."

But he just frowns at her and looks back and forth between me and the building a couple of times.

"No," he says. Then he points at the building behind him while looking at her. "If that was me and she was you, no force on earth could make you leave, Caz. Let her do her thing." He swings his arm back around to offer her a hand up and nods at me sharply with approval at the same time. She lets him pull her up and drag her into a hug.

I have to look away when he briefly presses his lips to her hairline.

∞

Kirsty and Jake were the last to arrive, once again, and Kirsty noticed the change in the air straight away. The whole group seemed to be standing tighter together, although that seemed impossible since the limited space in the kitchen had never allowed for any extra elbow space in the first place, while Caroline was bustling around in full on presenter mode.

"Ah, the terrible two," she greeted them with a gorgeous smile, in between emptying the contents of half a dozen bags-for-life onto the counter. "Come in, come in: we have been waiting for you. You'll be cooking the recipes you brought in last week. I bought all the necessary ingredients, even some lettuce—" She held up a Romaine before carrying on unpacking more salad related items. "Tomatoes, cucumbers, et cetera for Maisy's salad." She threw a wicked glance in the direction of the girl in question. "We should end up with a great buffet."

The chef seemed greatly amused with some private joke as she said it, and when it came to it, the variety of food they ended up cooking went a long way to explaining her mood. Beside Maisy's salad, Jake's and Kirsty's lamb curry stood next to a chicken curry, courtesy of Zach and Noel, a mixed vegetable curry brought to the dinner plan by Catalina and Poppy, and another chicken curry that Aimee and Ronan had chosen. When they had laid a table in the cafeteria and put their dishes out, they looked down at the spread and Caroline started laughing, loud and clear. It echoed around the cafeteria and startled the lot of them.

"And this, children, is what happens if you tell a bunch of British kids to go find something to cook. You couldn't make it up. It's a shame half of you are not allowed to drink yet. This cries out for a few rounds of lager. Let's eat, people."

She was about to sit down, when a male voice came from the walkway looking down onto the canteen floor and interrupted her, mid-process.

"Did someone mention lager?" Anthony Simms asked, bemused, from his position by the railings above them.

"Anti!" Caroline all but squealed, smiling up at him. "Perfect timing. Come have a bite. See what's been cooking in your house."

Simm smiled back at her and came down the stairs to join them. When he arrived at the table, Caroline ushered him on into the kitchen.

"Go get yourself a plate and some cutlery and join us," she said while putting little bites of each dish onto plates for her students.

Kirsty loved her in that moment, for the fact she didn't send one of them to fetch the implements for Simm, but told him to get them himself. She watched their headmaster proceed without protest and tentatively stick his head into the kitchen as if he was expecting to get it chopped off by the kitchen manager, then tread carefully inside, almost in a carbon copy style of Kirsty's first ever steps onto the hallowed ground. It made her chuckle to herself. She was still grinning when she put her hands out to receive the plate Caroline was holding out for her.

"Are you alright there, Kirsty?" the chef asked amused.

"Yup. Never been better."

"Good."

Caroline started preparing the next plate.

"What was he like when you were at school?" Kirsty seized the opportunity to ask.

The question had been burning in the back of her mind

ever since Caroline had first told them about always working with Simm when they'd been at school together, and even more so since the minibus incident when he'd completely lost his rag with her.

"Exactly the same. Straight-laced and square as a cube for the most part and then the complete opposite for the remaining ten percent. If there had been an opportunity to wear a three-piece suit then, I'm sure he would have done. It surprises me that he didn't make that an actual uniform option when he took over the joint," Caroline answered, handing Jake his plate and starting to dish up for Aimee now.

"Was he always going to be a teacher?" Jake asked.

"Heavens, no." Caroline looked up with a dead pan expression then lost it as a whole army of smirks started battling around the corners of her mouth. "He was never going to be *a* teacher. He was always going to be the head teacher. Of *Gull Cove*. You should have seen him strut around this place back in the day. As if he owned it, even back then. Like a young James T. Kirk as a cadet on the Enterprise. He was always certain he'd run this ship one day. Well, once he came out of his shell, that is."

"You're a trekkie?" Zack and Noel asked in the same breath, and with identically raised eyebrows.

"Well, obviously not, otherwise I'd know that James T. Kirk never did serve as a cadet on the Enterprise but in actual fact started his career as an ensign on the Republic. But that's not the point at discussion here, the point at discussion is Anthony Simm, back in the day when he was an annoying little git," she answered breezily to a round of agape faces.

"Are you calling me little, Caroline Connelly?" Simm

had reappeared by her side carrying a plate and cutlery. He set them down on the table and dragged another chair over.

"Not anymore, no." She grinned up at the distinctly taller and distinctly broader man just before he sat down next to her. "Years later and you're only marginally scrawny now, rather than all the way scrawny. But back then, children," she carried on, while handing Aimee her food, "This man here was so skinny he could fit through the railings outside the school."

"Until I couldn't," Simm answered ominously.

"Until you couldn't." Caroline echoed while handing Ronan, last in the round, his plate. "He got stuck one day. School had to call the fire brigade to cut him out."

"Did you get into trouble?" Poppy asked the head, breathlessly.

"No, I did," Caroline answered for Simm, having measured out his portion and finally served herself.

"Why is that, Chef?" Catalina's thick Spanish accent made the wonder in her question even more defined.

Caroline sat down and picked up a forkful of curry, letting it hover in front of her mouth while she answered.

"Because I was the one taking bets on whether he'd make it through. *Bon appétit*, people."

All the curries were good, although Kirsty soon regretted having started with the hottest. It packed a punch, and after its all-consuming taste, none of the other variations on the theme really had a chance to break through to her taste buds. She made a mental note never again to eat the hottest thing on the menu first.

"So, Sir," Ronan asked after a few minutes, "What was Caroline like?"

Simm looked up, still chewing, swallowed and pulled a

face.

"Hellraiser. Complete nightmare."

"What did you do?" Aimee asked with a respectful look over to the chef, who chose to shrug off the question.

"It would probably be easier to ask what she didn't do," Simm said, wryly, with a slight shake of the head. "She didn't manage to burn the building down while taking one of her cigarette breaks in the toilet, but that's about all she *didn't* do."

Kirsty could feel, more than see, Jake sit up straighter next to her, cock his head and stare at Connelly. The chef, who'd been scrutinising her plate for most of this recent exchange, suddenly looked up and met Jake's eyes. Kirsty could practically read the unspoken words between them in the air, as if their thought bubbles were colliding.

You?

Me.

Like me?

Like you.

Kirsty looked over to the head. It was obvious that he, too, could clearly see the captions in the air.

"I'm officially intrigued," Aimee said into the round. She pushed her empty plate away and folded her arms on the table to lean forward, commanding Simm's eye contact. "If you two were so different, how could you be friends? Are you related somehow? Or did your mothers meet while they were pregnant or something?"

Simm and Caroline looked at each other and something passed between them to do with who was going to tell what, before Simm finally took a breath.

"No. We met here. We were in the same year. But we didn't really have anything to do with each other. Then, at

163

the beginning of year eight, my little sister died. It wasn't unexpected. She was born with a gene defect, which meant her reaching puberty had always been unlikely, but it still threw my family sideways. Even if you know, you don't really believe it is going to happen. Even when they are already in palliative care, you still don't think they're actually going to die. Everyone knew about Lucy, but aside from one teacher and the school counsellor, nobody would say anything. It was all business as usual. I took a day out for the funeral and that was all there was to it. The other kids just carried on around me, and nobody said a word. That one teacher, Mrs Mantle her name was, asked me if I wanted to talk about it in class but, honestly, I'd rather have gouged my eyes out. I told her as much, and she accepted that, which was sympathetic, but it didn't help. I was like a ghost kid. Until one day this girl corners me in the corridor. It was about a week and a half after we buried Lucy. 'I heard about your sister,' she says as if it was the most normal conversation starter in the world. 'I'm really sorry. That must be awful.' And that was enough. I completely broke down. Cried like a baby. But the most amazing thing happened. This girl, she didn't run. She just put her arms around me and gave me a hug."

They could have heard a needle drop at the other end of the cafeteria, such was the complete silence that had fallen over them. This man had been in charge of their school, of their everyday lives, for the entire time they'd been at Gull Cove, and they'd always taken his curiosity about them, his compassion and his phenomenal memory for each and every student's background story, right down to the names of siblings who weren't even at the same school, for granted, maybe even a bit obsessive and over-intrusive.

Now it dawned on them that his interest in them had been forged by personal experience rather than a general predilection for sticking his nose in.

"Yeah." Caroline said into the lingering silent awe and grinned. "And then I made you bunk off school for the rest of the day, took you home and got you pissed on my mum's Tia Maria."

"At twelve?" Maisy exclaimed in shock.

Caroline shrugged.

"I call that extenuating circumstances, don't you? Anyway, from that day onwards, Anthony Simm and Caroline Connelly became best friends forever and ever and ever. Amen."

"Awh, how cute," Ronan said semi-sarcastically and Caroline focused on him with a sharp eye from which all humour had drained.

"Don't knock it, Ronan. It's good to have someone who watches your back. You'll never know when you need it," she said in a low voice, looking pointedly at Aimee next to him.

"Why are you here, Chef?" Kirsty asked into the quiet that ensued, slowly dragging her eyes away from the swirls of curry sauce on the empty plate in front of her to glance up at the woman.

"Perceptive," Caroline stated, meeting her gaze. "I'm here, Kirsty, because I had a nervous breakdown. One day I woke up and I was terrified of leaving my bed. So when I finally did manage to get up, I ran all the way home."

"What? And it happened just like that?" Aimee asked, snapping her fingers.

"Well, no. There was a certain amount of working so much I was burning the candle both ends, and my partner

165

of twenty years, who also happened to be my producer, leaving me for another, much younger woman to have the children with her that he had said he never wanted while we were together, preceding that particular morning, but other than that, yes, just like that." Caroline mimicked the finger snap. "But trust me, you really don't want to hear the sordid details in all their clichéd glory."

"Hm. But why this?" Kirsty asked quietly, letting her chin indicate the round.

During Caroline's little speech, Simm's hand had come up to rest on her shoulder and he was gently, reassuringly massaging the side of her neck now. The chef crossed her opposing arm over her body and laced her fingers with his before she answered.

"Because a very clever and kind man thought working with you lot could be therapeutic for me."

Caroline's and Simm's hands squeezed each other lightly then parted and they both stood up at the same time. Caroline smiled down at her students.

"Time to break up the party, folks."

PART II : BED

I've moved.

I'm in your bed.

In your home.

The blue of my own walls surrounds me, without being my actual own walls, which is both mindboggling and reassuring, and everything smells like you. I kind of don't want to touch the sheets, really, for fear my own smell will mask and eventually obliterate yours. The thought alone makes me want to pick up the pillow and inhale until your scent is burned into my nose forever. But it doesn't work like that, does it? You can no sooner tattoo a smell into your nostrils than you can burn a taste into your taste buds. Now there is an aphorism for you. By Kirsty Matthews™. I know, I'm just drivelling now. I can really feel the extreme sleep deprivation of the last few days. You know, that state when you think you're still forming coherent thoughts but, actually, all that comes out is nonsense. The funny thing is it's not actually that late. It's only just going on ten o'clock and I've been here around an hour and a half, a spectre in your life.

My dad dropped my stuff off, including my laptop, which is what I'm writing this on since my little jukebox well and truly

*went to sleep on the way here. I'd exhausted it, the poor little mite.
I tell you, I didn't even think it was possible to write as much as I
did today. Had a mild panic attack when I got here and the screen
was pitch and there was nothing doing. Wasn't sure if it would
automatically save what I'd written or if I'd lost everything. Not
that it would really matter all that much. No amount of words
will ever do you justice, no amount of words will ever feel like
walking next to Jake Deacon into a kitchen, no amount of words
will ever taste like the food you cook, sound like your laughter, or
feel like the warmth of your body in the cold of the Moon Pool.
What use are memories if the other person isn't there to share
them with? But I still wanted them to cling to in times of need.*

*So the good news is, my dad brought me the charger cable and
once it had regained a little charge, I found it was all still there.
I've backed it up now. Didn't occur to me to do that before. The
whole thing is on cloud storage now. And you know what?
Absurd though it may sound, as soon as I did that, I felt better
than I have in days. Suddenly I feel like you can hear me all the
time, not just when I'm on the bench. Isn't that weird? The power
of the net. The true deity of our age. Afterlife assured. Although if
I'm honest, this feeling is probably equally to do with where I am
now, thanks to your mum.*

*I was still on my bench when they all came out. Your dad,
your mum, Sophia and the twins. Only this time they all saw me,
of course. I watched from afar as your mum spoke to your dad and
then watched him look at me, frowning. Not in a horrid way, just
in a 'Really?' kind of way. But I guess she is persuasive, your
mum, or maybe she just wears the trousers in this house – what
do I know? Point being that he nodded after a couple of minutes
then indicated to the twins to follow him. Presumably to get the
car because then your mum came over on her own, well, with
Sophia in her arms, and sat down next to me.*

169

"You're coming with us," she says. Doesn't ask me, tells me. But nicely. I know where you get it from now, this gift of making me feel comfortable.

"Where are we going?" I ask, which is really code for 'What about Jake? Any news?'

"Home," she replies, really calmly. "Visiting hours are over, and they are strict about that in the ICU. Really, we shouldn't have got under their feet with the five of us again all day. Officially it's only two relatives per patient but we've been doing a relay up and down between intensive care and the cafeteria. Honestly, if I never see another hospital coffee again it's too soon." She laughs and that gives me hope. Sophia wriggles against her chest and she asks me with a look if I want to hold her. I realise I want nothing more in the world. Well, I do, I'd prefer to hold you, but beggars can't be choosers, and Sophia is the next best thing. Your mum passes her over and I sling my arms around her and pretend not to draw in a deep breath of baby smell, which of course I do. It grounds me and I finally get the question out.

"How is he doing? Caroline said his brain's still swollen."

"Yeah," she says slowly exhaling the word without turning to look at me. "But what else is new?" She smiles sadly and nudges my upper arm in a gesture so much like you it makes my heart contract. Then suddenly she takes her gaze away from the distance and looks down at her folded hands on her knees, her thumbs taking turns in kneading the insides of their opposing palms. "Actually, the swelling's gone down quite bit today. The doctors just told us. But he's still in a coma. Otherwise I would have come and got you."

She turns to look at me. Sophia has started doing that thing again where she rock climbs up my body using my boobs as footholds and I half hide my face behind her.

"It's strange." Your mum's breath hitches. "It's not at all like

170

you suspect. You look at him and it's like he's just lightly asleep. I always thought a person in a coma would be dead still until they wake up, completely limp. You know, off until they switch on again. Silly idea, really. But it's not like that. Not at all. He flinches and groans and if it wasn't for the machines he's hooked up to, you could think he was just snoozing. But then you try and wake him up and nothing happens. Nothing." She takes a couple of deep breaths, suppressing tears, then changes the subject abruptly. "It was nice of them to come by, Caroline Connelly and Simm. Jake's been raving about her at home. And Anthony Simm is a good man. Always looks out for Jake. In a different school that boy would have been expelled a long time ago. But Simm has always understood that Jake's not defiant for defiance's sake. He just gets so bored. His brain needs constant stimulation and if he doesn't get it, he gets reckless …"

She is crying at this point, tears dripping down the side of her nose. I'd dig around in my pocket for some of the stolen loo roll that I've got in there but my hands are still full of Sophia, who's started sucking on my neck, which really tickles. Turns out I don't have to anyway because your mum comes equipped with her own wad of pilfered hospital issue tissue. She dabs at her tears, and I seize the opportunity to remind her of a vital fact. I want to start the sentence with her name but suddenly realise that she doesn't have one other than 'Jake's mum' and 'Mrs Deacon' which sounds too formal for the huddle we're in.

"But he's not here because he was reckless," I tell her softly.

"No." She straightens up. "He's here because, when all is said and done, he does what's right. Because he's my Jake." She breaks down and cries in silence for a couple more minutes, then straightens, wipes the tears away and takes Sophia back off me. "We need to get you kids home. You have school in the morning. This can't go on. Nobody knows how long this will take. You kids

171

need to go back to school."

She gets up and nods at the road beyond the railings, where I notice a stupidly long Mercedes parked on the double yellow lines with its hazard lights on. I look up at her.

"I'm alright," I say. "I'll stay till my dad comes and drags me home. I don't want to leave him just yet. And I will be back tomorrow. I'm not done here." I manage a half smile at her. "And I have a headmaster's pass."

She cocks her head and looks at me. Really looks at me.

"Do you think your dad would mind if you came to stay with us tonight instead?" she asks.

And that's pretty much how I got here.

Well, no, I got here in that stupidly long, seven-seater Mercedes, sitting next to Sophia in her baby seat with George and James behind me. I've never seen them so quiet. It's like somebody's taken the Deacon out of the Deacons. I hate it. I want them to call me names and be rude and inconsiderate and horrible to me. Instead they made me toast when we arrived, and showed me how to work the shower, then kind of hovered in the door to your room, not wanting to leave. I get it though. They want to be in here as much as I do. But in the end, they left. George came back after about two minutes, and stuck his head around the door.

"Kirsty?"

"Yeah?"

"I'm glad you're here."

Then he disappeared, and quarter of an hour later my dad arrived with my stuff. Once your mum and I had established that I was staying here, I called home. My parents were reluctant, but ultimately, they agreed. I think mum feels a bit rejected. But I'm sure she also gets why I want to be here. Despite the fact it feels weird. Even weirder if I think that a couple of walls away are your folks and they're going through what must be the hardest time of

172

their lives, and they still don't really know me, yet they let me into their home, which frankly is the only place I want to be other than on my bench.

I like my bench.

I think I might have a slat pattern permanently engraved on my butt now.

∞

The night Simm joined them at dinner, the whole group walked out of the building together. It was Catalina, of all people, who commented on it as they passed through the school gates and spilled out into the road.

"What?" she asked, half-turning to Jake under the arm Noel had loosely wrapped around her shoulder. "No private talk with the boss tonight?"

Jake shrugged with a small, tight smile.

"I guess she has someone better to chew the fat with for once."

Catalina looked at him, puzzled, and Kirsty translated.

"Chewing the fat means to talk to someone."

"Ah." Catalina's face lit up. "I like it. It is apt, no?"

"Talking of, is anyone interested in a bit of a barbeque on the beach Saturday night?" Aimee asked, just as the theatre group emerged, hot on their heels. Aimee waved them over. "I think we should celebrate the end of exam week two." Aimee focused on Kirsty for a moment while she waited for the Little Horror Shoppers to catch up. "How are *you* doing? Aren't you sitting your GCSEs right now?"

"It's going. Thanks for asking."

Most of their group had already seconded the beach barbeque idea when Phoebe and the rest of the musical cast arrived, and Aimee repeated the invitation.

"I'm in," Phoebe said, hooking her arm into Kirsty's. She looked back and forth between Jake and Kirsty as the others carried on making arrangements. "I take it, someone shouted loudly enough?"

"Uh-huh," Kirsty answered, marginally distracted by Jake's lack of enthusiasm for the weekend plans. He appeared deeply contemplative, standing with his head hanging slightly, examining the toe part of his shoes and seemingly waiting for the general communion to dissipate. "You're out early tonight," Kirsty added for Phoebe's benefit while not taking her eyes off him.

"Yeah, apparently Elliot got her wrists slapped by Simm last week about rehearsing past bedtime. He's imposed a strict nine o'clock kick out time on her now. You lot are out later than normal, aren't you? You're usually long gone."

"We had Simm come for dinner tonight."

"I see. Well, good for him." Phoebe looked around at the thinning ranks. "Are we walking, or what?"

"Sure." Jake nodded, and the three of them started heading homewards.

They walked in silence for a while, Phoebe and Kirsty with arms linked and Jake escorting them on Kirsty's other side.

"There is something really nice about you two," Jake finally said.

"Thanks," Phoebe replied across Kirsty's front. "You want to elaborate on that at all?"

He shrugged.

"You don't have this constant nattering thing going on like other girls. You know, the vacuous waste of oxygen."

It should have been offensive, but the girls both

174

appreciated the sentiment. They covered another stretch of road while none of them said a word. It really *was* nice. Companionable. But Kirsty couldn't shake the feeling that Jake was mulling.

"So, are you coming on Saturday?" she asked, hoping to get him into a more talkative mood.

"Can't. Got Sophia."

"Again?"

"Yup."

"What's a Sophia?" Phoebe enquired.

"A baby," Kirsty answered for him.

Phoebe stopped in her tracks, halting Kirsty with her and by default also Jake, who half turned to them.

"What?" Phoebe raised her eyebrows at him. "*You?* Looking after a *baby?* That's hilarious. How much is that info worth?"

"Don't be a cow, Phoe," Kirsty intervened.

Phoebe uttered a hearty 'Meh' and then they were moving again.

"So bring the kid," Phoebe said, earnestly, after a couple of minutes. "It's a barbeque, not a funeral. There is no reason not to bring her, is there? We're starting early anyway. Five, Aimee said. That's a perfectly respectable time to take a baby for a stroll on the beach. And make a rest stop. At least for a bit."

Though he carried on looking into the direction of travel, Kirsty saw a smile creep onto Jake's face when she stole a glance. She elbowed him.

"She's got a point, you know. Come, bring Sophia. I'll even hold her while you have a hot dog or something."

Phoebe raised a hand.

"Dibs. I wanna have a go on the baby, too. I love babies.

175

I'd just never manage a whole one."

It was only when she heard Jake laugh then that Kirsty realised just how serious he'd been for most of the evening.

∞

They dropped Phoebe off first.

"Night, people," she said, with her back to them as she turned the key to her apartment. She threw them a last look over her shoulder. "I'd invite you in but I have a feeling you have stuff to talk about that doesn't need my input."

And with that she slunk away into her place.

"She doesn't mince her words, does she?" Jake asked, as they turned away from Phoebe's doorstep.

"Nope. The Phoebe Faulkner word-mincing function died a long time ago."

"You think she meant it?"

"What?"

"About bringing Sophia?"

"Yeah, why the hell not?"

"Hm. I'll think about it. I'm not sure how compatible the beach is with a buggy."

"Doesn't your mum have one of those sling things?"

"No." He drew out the word a little. "But I could buy one." There was another pause. "Fancy going into big town Saturday morning?"

'Big town' was Gull Cove's euphemism for the next stop along the coastal rail line, which was only marginally bigger, but contrasted their town's quaintness with modern facilities such as retail outlets spreading over more than one meagre high street, clubs, pubs, a small multipurpose venue, a hospital, more than two secondary schools, and even a campus of the County university, although the real thing was located twenty miles further west.

"What? To the Mall?" Kirsty asked.

"Kirsty Matthews! We're not in America! Yet. It's called a shopping centre."

"Not on the door it isn't. It says 'Mall Opening Times'," she retorted dryly.

"Really?" He sighed.

"Really."

"Man." He shook his head in dismay.

"Don't be Americanist. It's rude."

"To whom?"

"Ninety percent of the people in your music collection, from what I've heard."

"They're all dead."

"Even worse then." Kirsty grinned. "Ever heard of not speaking ill of the departed?"

He grunted at that.

"Okay. I admit, they do make exceedingly good music."

"And good films."

He made another grumbling noise in his throat.

"And good TV."

"And good books."

He sighed defeatedly.

"Okay. They make a lot of good stuff."

"But we make the exceedingly better cakes."

"We definitely make the exceedingly better cakes. Back to the beginning— so would you want to come shopping with me on Saturday?"

"Hm. Honestly? I'm not sure I can afford bringing something for the barbeque as well as the train fare."

"I'll drive us."

He seemed a little too eager. Kirsty stopped abruptly and turned towards him, waiting for him to do the same and face her. She narrowed her eyes at him.

"Hand on heart, are you asking because you want my company, or because you don't want to walk into Mothercare on your own?"

He scrunched up his face and ran a hand through his hair.

"Can it be a bit of both?"

Kirsty laughed and started walking again.

"Yeah, it can be a bit of both. How good a driver are you?"

"When I'm transporting valuable cargo? I drive like an old lady."

"I'd rather you drove like an intelligent young man."

"Huh? Isn't that a bit sexist?"

"No, not unless underneath that male exterior of yours really beats the heart of an old woman. But you don't come across terribly transgender to me."

He had to think about that one for a moment, then laughed.

"Man, you are quick. So are you coming?"

"Okay."

"Okay?" He'd made it sound more like an ecstatically happy 'Really?'

"Okay."

After that he seemed to lose himself in his thoughts again, and Kirsty didn't interrupt, content to just walk beside him. They were already nearing Kirsty's house when he suddenly opened his mouth.

"I had no idea why Caroline kept asking me to hang back, you know," he said, out of the blue. "Not until tonight, anyhow. She never seemed to want anything specific. Just asked me how I was doing and stuff. I thought Simm had put her up to it. That he'd told her to keep an extra special eye on me or something. But if I think about it now, I think, actually, she might consider me a, I know it sounds stupid, but like a kindred spirit, you know?"

He appeared almost shy about his analysis and it made Kirsty snort a laugh.

"No shit, Sherlock," she said.

He glanced at her sideways.

"You reckon?"

"Yeah, I reckon. I reckon she's taken a shine to you because she sees herself in you. Her, before life turned her into the shell of a person she was when she hit Gull Cove. And because you stood up for her when she needed it the most."

"I did what?"

They had stopped only a couple of houses from Kirsty's home, and faced each other. Kirsty found herself frowning deeply at him.

"You don't even remember, do you?"

"Remember what?"

"The day she first came to Gull Cove, when your brothers started heckling her, you rescued her, you cut them short."

She watched his eyes grow big in comprehension, and for an instant he looked a whole heap younger than his eighteen years. More around eight.

"But that was nothing."

"Maybe not for you but for her, in that moment, it was *everything*." Kirsty slipped her fingers inside the open flap of his jacket and rested her hands lightly on his waist, the way she'd always do with Nicholas before saying good-bye, and looked up at him with a smile. She let her voice gather a mocking edge. "Whether you like it or not, Jake Deacon, you're one of the good guys. Deal with it."

Then she lunged herself at him, half-nestling into his jacket to give him a fierce hug. Her head landed sideways somewhere in the crook of his neck and the serrated edge of the zip that went all the way up to the stiff collar pushed painfully into her jaw line. She didn't care though.

He had to balance himself before he could return the hug and when he did he immediately started spitting at her hair, which had evidently got in his mouth and up his nostrils. It was a familiar sensation, although usually it was Nicholas or her dad making the *ph-ph-ph* sound above her head. Kirsty chuckled.

"Sorry about the tendrils of doom." She stepped out of his arms and smiled at him. "I'll see you Saturday if I don't catch you tomorrow. What time?"

"Eleven?"

"Eleven is good for me."

She turned and walked the last fifty yards on her own. She looked over at him one last time before she turned the key and opened the door. He still stood where she'd left him and she knew he wouldn't move until the door was firmly shut behind her.

Yep, this boy watched her back.

∞

*W*hoa. *That was freaky.*

I fell asleep. I'd switched the light out to type that last bit on the laptop one-handed, with my head resting sideways on my arm, already drifting off. My eyes shut on the last full stop. Then, suddenly, I woke up again because there was a noise. And there you were, standing in the doorframe, your silhouette backlit from the hallway, a Sophia shaped bundle asleep against your shoulder. And for a second, one gorgeous, perfect second, I thought I'd dreamt it all, that none of it was real, that we were having a film night and I'd just dozed off into this epic nightmare. That's before I recognised that the shape in the door was shorter and squatter than you. More thick set. Older. And then there was that shitty moment of realisation. That it's all real, all happening and that it's not you but your dad standing there.

"Hey," he whispers into the room. "I didn't mean to wake you. I just wanted to check if you had everything you needed before we go to bed. Not that I think anyone is actually going to do any sleeping, but do you need some water or something?"

"No, I'm fine. Thank you, Mr Deacon."

My voice sounds groggier than my mind feels.

"Call me Jude." He pauses. "You need to switch your computer off. It'll overheat sitting on the mattress like that."

"Okay."

He's still not moving, and there is a part of me pondering the fact that in any other set of circumstances, and if he wasn't holding Sophia, this would be majorly creepy.

"Erm, Kirsty?"

He's gone back to hushed tones and I match him.

"Yeah?"

"You're the girl who came to the door that night, aren't you?"

"Uh-huh," I answer, bracing myself.

He sighs, a deep sound rich with sorrow and regret.

"My wife told me to apologise. I'm sorry if I was stand offish. I was still hoping then … I guess I just wanted him to try and do the right thing. Children should always come first. He … he tried

to tell me that Shannon was no good. I didn't listen. I'm an idiot. Do you ... do you ever have song lyrics pop into your head? I mean repetitively, as if they were a comment on your life?" He sounds forlorn, exhausted, nothing like the timber tycoon who turned me away that day, nothing like the big boss business man he is. "Never mind," he adds and half turns away.

"No, I get it. I get that a lot, actually," I say hastily.

I can hear him breathe a sigh of relief in the dark before he clears his throat and goes on.

"Ever since the police came to the door, I keep having this line go round and round in my head, you know. It's from an old song. From before you were born. From before even I was born. I doubt you'd know it, it's by Cat ..."

"Stevens," I interrupt him softly, suddenly wide awake and knowing exactly which song it is, what line is haunting him. "From Father and Son.*"*

"Yeah," he answers ever so faintly. "I can see why he likes you. Night, Kirsty."

He curls around the baby in his arms and then quietly shuts the door.

And I can't go back to sleep now.

Kirsty didn't particularly like going shopping at the Mall on a good day, let alone on a day when she felt like every pair of eyes she passed had an opinion of her, unfounded or not. Jake seemed impervious to the stares that they had started collecting from the moment he, Kirsty and Sophia had got out of the *J.C. Deacon* company car that Jake had borrowed for their trip. They had crossed the car park and entered the elevator to ascend to the temple of consumerism above them under a constant stream of furtive and not so furtive glances. Nonchalantly pushing Sophia in her buggy out into the sea of shoppers cluttering up shopping level one, Jake had kept his cool perfectly, right until the judgemental gawping from one particular lady with lilac hair and huge crystal earrings had finally got his goat. The woman had been glaring at Kirsty as if she was the symbol of everything that had gone wrong with the country, and Jake had stopped to stare back at her, eyeballing her until she fled up an escalator. Kirsty couldn't help but snigger.

Jake touched her shoulder, concern written across his face.

"Are you okay? I'm sorry. It didn't occur to me how this would look."

Kirsty shrugged, grinning at him reassuringly.

"It's okay. Let them make their assumptions. I tell you what's bothered me most so far, though. Not the older people giving me the evils. Them I get. But did you see those girlies outside the bear making shop? They were maybe thirteen, tops, but did you see how they looked at us? Like I'd hit the ultimate jackpot with the fit guy pushing the pram. Shudder." She performed the action that went with the word then caught the gleam in his eye and added, "Yeah, yeah, save it, buddy."

He started walking again in long, confident strides. Glancing at his profile, she could see a grin tugging at his lips but he didn't say anything else until they'd reached the entrance to Mothercare. As Kirsty held the door for him so he could push Sophia inside, he stopped mid-motion, leant right into her face and smiled broadly.

"You really reckon I'm fit?"

Kirsty rolled her eyes.

"What do you think?"

Suddenly the mischief went out of his face and he looked at her seriously.

"I think," he responded quietly, "I've hit jackpot with the mermaid who lets me push a pram beside her."

He searched her eyes for a moment longer until Kirsty couldn't bear the intensity anymore and looked away. There seemed something vaguely triumphant in his movement when he finally entered the shop but Kirsty didn't get time to analyse it as a matronly shop assistant descended upon them with all the professionalism of someone who knew how to make a sale.

Exactly twelve minutes later they were about to leave the shop with their newly purchased baby sling, no questions asked. While Kirsty pushed the now empty buggy, Jake kept nuzzling the back of Sophia's head as she dangled in front of him, looking at the world with bright, recently woken eyes.

"This is brilliant. Top idea, Matthews. I love it," Jake managed to say in between nuzzles. "What do you say? Can I buy you an ice cream for your brilliance?" he asked, opening the door for her. Kirsty weighed up the idea of an all singing, all dancing sundae at Millie's Ice Cream Parlour on the top level, against the fact that her jeans had started pinching at the waist recently, but before she could answer, Jake suddenly let the door go again and dragged her back into the shop.

"Shit. Stay here for a sec."

Kirsty frowned.

"Why?"

"Shannon is out there."

"And?"

"And she and her bitches are going to have us for breakfast if they see us."

"I thought you weren't with her anymore."

"Am not."

"So?"

"Just trust me on this. Better all around if she doesn't see us."

"Huh," Kirsty agreed reluctantly then stepped up to the door to look out through the glass.

"Kirsty," he said warningly.

"Chill." She grinned at him over her shoulder. "You go hide in the cotton nappies or something, but I'm taking a look. It's not like she knows *me*." She turned back to spy on the shoppers outside and felt a spike of adrenaline course through her veins. This was not her life. This wasn't like her. Spying. This was movie stuff. Dangerous. Cool. Like sitting on the school kitchen counter.

Though there was a throng of people on the other side of the glass, Kirsty's eyes settled instinctively on a group of three girls in their late teens, embalmed in makeup and marching alongside each other as if they owned the place. There were two blondes, one honey with a plastic cleavage, one bleached with deliberate roots showing, and a black haired one with extensions down to her waist, all sporting long fake talons, terrible handbags and permanently dissatisfied expressions under look-at-us, exaggerated laughter.

"Wow," Kirsty commented without turning around, "It's the plastic fantastic trio, isn't it? So which one is Shannon?"

"The blonde," came the muffled reply from behind a rack of babygrows.

"There are two."

"The bleach blonde."

"Huh," Kirsty muttered in surprise. Her initial money had been on the high priestess of black extensions since she was the only one out of the trio who underneath the veneer seemed genuinely pretty, if somewhat hardnosed. She had a ghetto charm that Kirsty could understand a boy falling for. Her second choice would have been the honey blonde, who despite the silicone balcony area seemed the most natural of the three. The bleach blonde she'd instantly dismissed. She focused in on Shannon now, and something she hadn't even realised had been tight inside her for some weeks suddenly relaxed. The woman, because on second examination Kirsty realised she was looking at someone who had definitely passed the twenty barrier, and probably had a good five years on her, was reassuringly plain with a mild case of hamster cheeks, quite a bit of extra weight around the hips and tummy and bad skin glued down patchily with foundation. Regardless of her body's shortcomings though, Shannon had squeezed herself into a schoolgirl outfit, complete with patent leather sandals, knee high socks, blazer and tie, and a small part of Kirsty admired the woman for her confidence. That's what she had on her side, Kirsty thought, *confidence*. The walk wasn't laboured. Shannon really believed she was something, deserved to be looked at.

Kirsty watched the three of them produce themselves on their imaginary catwalk until they disappeared up an escalator, and then turned to tell Jake they were safe to leave. Gone from where he'd been perusing, she found him back at the till, in the process of purchasing a pack of fruit themed babygrows. She sidled up to him.

"The coast is clear. But maybe we should give Millie's a

miss. They went in that general direction. I guess we'd better get out of here, huh?"

"Sorry," he mumbled with a small nod, half hiding behind Sophia's head, as they started for the exit again.

Kirsty elbowed him gently.

"Forget it. My scales say thank you kindly for bypassing Millie's and not collecting 2000 calories. And I don't need a bitch fest to complete my Saturday morning. Anyway, you didn't promise ice cream, the only thing you promised was that we'd drive to the supermarket and get something for the barbeque. So let's go meat shopping."

∞

Good morning. I've just woken up in your bed and I can smell fresh coffee wafting through the house, so I guess I'm not the only one awake in the Deacon residence. I wonder how much sleep everyone else got? Once I finally did crash out, I think I was more unconscious than actually asleep. No dreams. Which may well be a blessing.

Right, I better get up.

Not sure where I'll be tonight or when I'll get a chance to write any more down. But I will, I promise. I'm not going to just leave you hanging. It doesn't feel as urgent today though, which is weird. Not sure if that's a good thing or not.

Ah, a knock on the door.

Laters.

∞

Hi. I'm back. Full to the brim with Ava Deacon's heavenly chicken fricassee, and in your bed again. Don't ask. Your mum's decided that as long as she can hold on to me, you are going to be alright. She also seems to believe that cooking what she says is your favourite dish of all time helps. No more preposterous than me believing that as long as I carry on writing us down I can keep you alive, I suppose. Although right now it might not seem like that's what I've been doing today, but I have. On paper, no less. With a pen. I forgot to take any hardware on my travels.

After stopping by at home to hug mum and reassure her that I'm alright (which is a complete lie) but need to be with your family, I spent the rest of the day at the hospital, where I am now another official resident of the cafeteria and where I jotted more of our story down on actual paper. Well, depends on how you define actual paper, I suppose. I went to the little hospital shop and asked if they sold any note pads and guess what the only kind of writing paper they had was? Airmail paper! You know that blue stuff that is so thin you can use it for tracing or wrapping food in. I mean, really? Why? Because so many people while away their time in hospital writing to their loved ones in those parts of the world where there is no email but plane mail delivery? The mind boggles. Between you and me though, it didn't half appeal to my anachronistic heart.

Moving on.

Today I stuck exclusively with the third person narrative. I guess there wasn't any solitude for 'me' time because when I wasn't writing I was talking to your folks or helping your mum with Sophia, or answering messages from the cooking club asking how you were. So right now is the first time I've been truly on my own all day. That's how thoroughly I've been adopted by Ava Deacon. She is amazing, your mum. And what an immensely cool name. I want to be an Ava. Anyway, she struck exactly the right balance between asking questions about me (well, really about you and me — subtle!) and letting me get on with writing while cups of hot chocolate, cookies, bad hospital sarnies and fresh bottles of sparkling water regularly appeared in front of me as if by magic. I'm warming greatly to your dad, too. He tried to get the hospital to let me see you but they really are very strict. It was a no go. I don't know if I feel more annoyed or more relieved about that. I'm not sure I could cope with seeing you like this. Not knowing if you're actually still in there or not.

The twins didn't come with us today. Your parents actually sent them into school. I think they preferred it. I don't think they wanted to come to the hospital again or even stay at home. It's strange, because despite the fact we are the same age I now feel like they are babies in comparison to me. I can't even imagine how they could ever have got to me with their relentless taunting. When your mum, your dad, Sophia and I came back to the house they greeted us at the door like lost puppies. It was a good thing I was carrying Sophia at the time because each twin picked a parent and just sank into their arms and then they started sobbing. I don't think I've ever seen either George or James cry before.

It really hit home.

In case you are wondering, at this point there has still been no real change as such, medically speaking, although your brain's swelling has gone down more and rather than just grunt and move involuntarily, you've started withdrawing from pain. No, make that <u>correctly</u> withdrawing from pain. Who knew there was a difference? Means when they pinch your shoulder, you don't just flinch away, your arm actually comes up and tries to bat away at whatever is pinching you. This, believe it or not, is not actually as good a piece of news as it sounds. It puts you barely a notch up on the Glasgow coma scale (I'm learning things I never wanted to know about) from practically all dead to more in direction mostly dead. (If, against all odds, you read this one day and you don't know where that distinction comes from, let me know. You're in for a treat.) But make no mistake, your chances of *survival are still infinitely slimmer than your chances of not making it. Your brain is still a mess, like a bruised fruit on the inside, and if you do make it, they're talking about serious lasting damage. I can't bear to think about it. Honestly? I don't know what would be worse: losing you or losing you.*

Okay, not good, welling up, panic mode.

I tell you what, I'll shut up now and start typing up what I wrote today instead. That might help. It's not as much as the last couple of days, firstly because when I handwrite I can do about an inch per hour as opposed to the light year I can do on any keyboard no matter how ridiculously small (evolved thumbs, my mum says) and secondly because I didn't spend today in a solitary confinement bubble.

So, here goes.

∞

There was something almost mythical about the figure Caroline Connelly cut against the light of the evening sun as she crouched down on the rocks, long thin coat fluttering behind her in the wind, her hands searching the crevices for something Kirsty couldn't define from this distance, and placing her spoils in a bag whenever she was successful. The image reminded Kirsty of a pen-and-ink drawing from a vintage graphic novel, sharp in stroke yet blurry around the features.

She had been watching the chef for a good ten minutes now, from the cosy shelter of the lively thirty or forty strong group that had gathered around the mosaic of disposable barbeque trays half a mile away. Nobody else seemed to have noticed the woman, so it startled Kirsty when Jake's legs suddenly appeared by her side and his voice travelled down from somewhere above her.

"What do you think she's foraging for?"

He'd been gone a while to retrieve Sophia from the far end of the party where the baby had spent the last quarter of an hour being peek-a-booed and tickled to her heart's content by Phoebe and most of the rest of the *Little Shop of Horrors* cast. He was cradling her in his arms now, belly down, head nestled sideways in the crook of his arm and swishing her gently left and right while his eyes were fixed on the woman on the rocks.

"No idea," Kirsty replied. "It's not oyster season."

"They wouldn't be that high up anyway. She looks lonely."

"I was thinking mythical but, yeah, lonely will do, too."

"We should ask her over."

"Off you go then."

She looked up to meet his eyes. He caught her gaze with raised eyebrows.

"I'd rather you went," he said then threw a meaningful glance around the crowd. "Besides I need to make up a feed for Sophia."

As if on cue, Sophia started making hungry noises, and he changed her position so he could lower himself onto his haunches. Kirsty got up. She didn't leave immediately but watched him for a few minutes as he put the mewling baby gently down on the thick blanket he'd spread out for her earlier, and started getting a thermos flask with boiled water, formula and a clean bottle in a sealed plastic bag out of his backpack. His movements were practised and easy, his actions mindful of where the baby was in relation to the hot water without it seeming conscious.

A sneaking suspicion that had been nagging at Kirsty all

day with ever increasing volume became too loud to ignore any longer. It had started around about the time she had watched him pay for the babygrows in Mothercare, and had gathered intensity over the course of the afternoon as they'd left big town to drive back to Gull Cove and take a stroll through the supermarket. There had been a peculiar naturalness about the way he had worn Sophia during the rest of their shopping trip, an amount of tenderness in his handling of her that way exceeded the care of a big brother, however loving. That bond Kirsty had noticed during their film night together seemed to shine more brightly, more obviously, outside the intimacy of his bedroom and against the backdrop of the world at large. She wondered for a moment how she could voice the question without falling through the very thin ice she'd be treading on. There was, after all, still a slight possibility that she *hadn't* got it wrong initially, that Sophia really was his little sister and Jake just an unusually affectionate big brother, and that her long monologue about the idiocy of teenage parents hadn't been one humungous exercise in putting her foot in it. Part of her still doubted her new theory. After all, surely this would have constituted the ultimate Jake Deacon story. Uncontainable. She would have known. Everyone would have known. But then again, Kirsty was sure that if J.C. Deacon wanted to keep something under wraps, the man had the means. Especially with Shannon not living in Gull Cove. So if the shoe fit...

Her thoughts raged on and stumbled over themselves as she lingered, observing Jake prepare Sophia's feed, shake the formula in the bottle, test the warmth against the thin skin on the inside of his wrist and then pick the baby up to pop the teat in her mouth. Sophia started sucking greedily and he leant over to kiss her forehead.

"There you go," he murmured against her skin, then looked up at Kirsty. "You still here?"

"You know," she answered steadily, but with her heart racing in her throat and her lip trembling, "You make a great father."

She could, she figured, always pretend that she hadn't said, 'You make,' but, 'You'd make.'

What a difference a *d* made.

She needn't have worried. At least not about this part.

His response was instant and the smile he sent her beamed with the glory of a thousand suns. If suns were sea green.

"Thank you." His face quickly took on a worried expression as he turned away and gazed at Sophia. "Now," he added quietly, "If I could have that as a character reference for my next custody hearing that would be great. As they say, every little helps."

Kirsty didn't enquire any further.

She couldn't.

Her knees had gone wobbly and she needed to go process.

She turned on her heels and focused on soldiering towards the solitary figure in the distance until the whirlpool in her brain had stilled a bit.

Sophia was Jake's daughter.

Of course.

She'd mouthed off at length about teen parents to a teen parent.

She was an idiot.

Kirsty felt embarrassed.

And dumb.

Immensely dumb.

Really, really stupid.

"Hello, Kirsty. Nice to see you."

Caroline's voice dragged her out of her marching tune. Lost in berating herself, Kirsty hadn't noticed that Caroline had come down from the rocks and had evidently started walking towards her.

"Good evening, Chef." Kirsty's voice sounded croaky, and she cleared her throat. "What's in the bag?"

"Ahhh," Caroline's face lit up and she opened up the bag so Kirsty could take a look. There were stalks of a green succulent plant inside that Kirsty knew grew between the rocks of the cove from spring all the way through to autumn. She'd never paid it much attention before, other than when she'd built pebble castles as a child and used it to make forests around her fortifications.

"It's edible?" Kirsty asked the obvious. "I never knew. What is it?"

"Rock samphire," Caroline answered. "It's delicious when lightly steamed in butter, but you could also roast it quickly on your barbeque and use it as seasoning between a burger and bun, for example. It's quite salty even if you give it a good wash first, which of course you always should." While Caroline had been talking, she had extracted a handful of stalks from the bag and was holding them out to Kirsty now. "Here, take some back with you. Try it."

"I've got a better idea," Kirsty answered, not taking the offering. "Why don't you come and cook it for us. Join the party. That's what I came over to ask you."

Caroline looked sceptically over at the crowd.

"I don't know. I don't want to spoil your fun. Is there anyone there who isn't a third of my age?"

"Yes, actually." Kirsty grinned. "There is at least one who is a fortyninth of your age."

Caroline's face scrunched into a puzzled expression, then it lit up.

"Oh! Clever!" she exclaimed as her eyes focused in on Jake at the edge of the crowd. "You're one quick-witted cookie, aren't you? So Jake has brought his baby, has he?"

Kirsty had to admit it came with a stab of jealousy to find out that Caroline already knew about Sophia when Kirsty had only just figured it out. But, to be fair, it wasn't as if Jake had ever deliberately deceived her. She'd just been a little slow on the uptake. Very, very slow.

"Trust me," she replied to the first half of Caroline's statement, "Mostly I'm more of a really thick cookie. Oatmeal, I think. A thick, fat oatmeal cookie." She could see in Caroline's expression that she'd lost the chef. "Nevermind. Come on, it's a food party and you are the goddess of food, so you can't not come if you're invited. And, yes, Jake's brought his daughter."

It felt strange saying it out loud.

"Splendid," Caroline replied, hooking her arm into Kirsty's and dragging her back towards the gathering. "If there's a baby to cuddle, I'm always game. Let's go cook some samphire."

Around halfway back to the party Kirsty stopped debating with herself where exactly prying ended and righteous curiosity started, and asked the question that was burning on her lips.

"Chef?"

"Kirsty?"

"How long have you known about Sophia?"

"Sophia? Who's Sophia? Oh, yes, Jake's baby, right. From

the start. He wrote about her in his application letter. He was very honest about it. Figured joining my little club would help him prove to the judge that he's managed to turn his life around and makes the better parent. I had reservations about letting him in, to be honest. It seemed to me as if he was clutching at straws, even if the Deacons have money on their side. As far as I understand it the baby's mother is older than him, doesn't have a record and, well, she's the mother, you know. If there had been more applications I would have moved him to the bottom of the pile. But back then I didn't know how genuinely talented he is. He's a good little chef, that boy. And photogenic. Without being too pretty. Shame, really. The camera would have loved him, I'm sure. We could have done something with that." She sighed wistfully. "He's a good kid. I wish I could do more for him. Here we are."

They'd arrived back at the party to enthusiastic greetings, and Caroline took a couple of comedy bows.

Despite her misgivings, the chef fit in effortlessly, sitting among them as if she belonged, taking swigs from the beer someone had handed her, and regaling them with stories of her school days while roasting the samphire, which turned out to be a lot like the crispy seaweed Kirsty liked to order with her Chinese takeaway. After everyone had eaten obscene amounts of burgers, sausages, chops and drum sticks, the chef quietened down a bit, begging to hold Sophia who'd drowsed off after her feed, and who hadn't roused since, despite the raucous surroundings. It seemed the more vibrant the life around her, the more contented the infant had become in her sleep. Jake gently transferred the baby from his arms into Caroline's and the grateful look on the woman's face didn't escape Kirsty's attention. Jake got to his feet for the first time since he'd settled down with Sophia and shook out his limbs before holding a hand out to Kirsty who had been sitting next to him.

"Walk?" he asked, then turned to Caroline. "Are you happy to keep hold of Sophia for bit?"

Kirsty took his hand, let him pull her up and dusted crumbs off herself while Caroline answered with a happy nod.

"Sure. You go for a stroll, kids."

They walked silently to where the sea lapped gently at the shore, then took their shoes off and let the waves flow around their feet as they proceeded along the water edge. Only when they were way out of earshot did Jake nudge Kirsty's shoulder gently.

"What's up, Matthews? You've been really subdued all evening. I don't like it. What's bothering you?"

Kirsty didn't know how to answer him. She still felt like a complete idiot.

"Honesty is usually the best policy," Jake egged her on when she didn't reply.

"I feel dumb," she finally said.

"What? Where did that come from? Why?"

Kirsty sighed.

"Because I only just realised tonight that Sophia is your daughter."

"What? Really?" He laughed. "Who did you think she was?"

"Little sister?"

"That would explain it," he said, in between chuckles.

"Explain what?"

"Your refreshingly honest opinion of parenthood at my age."

197

"Thanks for reminding me," she snarled.

"Hey," he stepped around to stand in front of her and grab her by the shoulders, "I mean it. I like it when people are honest. I like that you have an opinion. And you were right. It is dumb to have a kid at my age. I was dumb. I was dumb when I believed Shannon when she said she was on the pill, but in my dumb-dumb defence I was a bit starry-eyed because I got picked up by this older chick and felt like the man. But, honestly, now that she's here, I wouldn't swap Sophia for the world. I just wish Shannon wasn't her mother."

"Harsh," Kirsty commented, just as he let go of her and swivelled back to be by her side.

"You don't know the half of it," he said flatly as they started moving again, but he didn't elaborate, and Kirsty didn't push it.

For the rest of the walk, they talked about samphire and cockles, crème caramel versus crème brûlée, and what year The Beatles had stopped being samey and had become good before spiralling into the weird and unpalatable. Kirsty didn't recall when exactly it had started, but by the time they returned to the party, she realised that they'd been walking hand in hand for the better part of their constitutional.

And she didn't quite feel like a complete idiot anymore.

∞

I just finished typing this up. When I think about the fact that that was ten days ago, it just doesn't compute. I can't get my head around it. It seems more like ten centuries ago. How can that be?

If I look out of your bedroom window I can see the same stupid

198

sun doing the same stupid sunset routine but nothing feels good, nothing is right, everything is wrong.

The worst thing is that I know I'm going to have to write down what happened eventually. Not to keep you here necessarily but for my own sanity. I'm scared though. I'm scared that if I put it into words, then on some plane of existence it will happen all over again and that this time it will actually kill you. I felt the same at the police station when I was giving my statement. That was probably the shortest, most tight-lipped witness account they've ever taken. I felt like any extra word could tip you over the edge into eternal oblivion.

Crazy? Insane?

Sure.

You try staying rational when you watch while one of your only two friends gets half killed and there is bugger all you can do about it. I'm scared that if I repeat the story again you are going to veer from mostly dead back to practically all dead.

But 'we' are not complete until the bitter end, I guess.

So let's get it over and done with.

Let's fast forward to the Thursday after the barbeque.

∞

It was the end of exam week three, and they felt well and truly zombified.

Phoebe and Kirsty had been sitting on Kirsty's bed all afternoon, staring vacantly at the laptop screen, which was playing mindless fodder at them, while communicating strictly in grunting code and only when absolutely necessary, such as when the nachos were out of reach or the dip jar was threatening to fall off the mattress. They were utterly spent, and even the prospects of a dress rehearsal

199

and cooking with Caroline respectively couldn't rouse any interest in either of them. So it was no wonder that when there was a knock on the bedroom door, Kirsty simply forgot to react.

Phoebe nudged her in the ribs.

"Huh-huh-huh-huh."

"Huh?"

"Huuuuuuuuuuuh."

"Huh! Come in," Kirsty finally managed to say.

Her mum opened the door and stepped into the room, bringing with her a steaming bowl and the smell of freshly cooked vegetable soup. Over the last few days she'd taken up Kirsty's baton and was trying hard to emulate her daughter's endeavours in making meals out of the reject groceries her husband brought home. She'd got quite good at it, much to Kirsty's relief. What had been fun and a distraction for a while had turned into a serious chore once the novelty had worn off.

"Hi girls, could you do me a favour, and try this? Tell me if it needs anything else in terms of seasoning."

Both Kirsty and Phoebe dutifully tried a spoon of the mostly green concoction which seemed to revolve around asparagus and potato, while barely taking their eyes off the screen. The soup was good but it lacked depth.

"Bacon," Kirsty said absent-mindedly, handing the bowl back. "It needs bacon. A handful of crispy fried lardons and it'll be perfect."

Her mum stared into the liquid.

"Yeah, I can see that. Thank you." She made towards the door, then asked over her shoulder with a nod at the clock, "Are you not rehearsing tonight, Phoebe?"

Phoebe suddenly woke from her daze, looked above her

head at the time piece and erupted in a plethora of expletives.

Five minutes later she'd collected her belongings, put her shoes on, had half opened the door and was leaving with a hearty, "*Au revoir, Mademoiselle Matthews.*"

Before Kirsty could search her extremely limited French for a fitting reply, the door opened wider, and Jake passed Phoebe in the door frame.

"One in, one out," he commented.

"Hi Deacon, bye Deacon," Phoebe responded and then she was out of the room, racing down the stairs.

Kirsty shut the laptop down, got up with a sigh, stretched to the ceiling and broke into a yawn. The sudden flurry of activity had made her even more aware of how lethargic she felt.

"I fancy this like a hole in the head tonight."

"Yeah," Jake responded, seating himself on the floor. "I don't think you're the only one. I'm fried."

"Got anything tomorrow?"

"Yep. Second maths. In the afternoon. How about you?"

"Done and dusted. For this week anyway. Last one was English this morning. I'm exhausted. I just want to slouch around in my jammies for the rest of eternity now. Eat junk food. Get fat. Not think. If I think about going to school tomorrow, I feel numb. Simm and his revision classes. Trust us to have a headmaster who insists on keeping you to your schedule till the bitter end. Still not sure of he's actually gonna let us go once exams are *over*."

"Hmmm."

Kirsty wasn't quite sure what he'd responded to. He seemed to be only half listening, but under the circumstances he was just as entitled as she was not to be fully present in the moment.

"You okay?" she asked anyway.

He shrugged.

"Hmmm."

"You think you messed up the exam?"

His head snapped up.

"What? No. I'm sure it was fine. And even if it wasn't, it's not like I couldn't retake it. No." He made a dismissive gesture. "Forget it. Get your shoes on, we need to get out of here if we don't want to incur Caroline's wrath."

Kirsty looked down at herself, examining her thin black slack pants and the skimpy tank top that did nothing to cover her huge arms or flatter her belly.

"I need to get dressed first," she answered matter-of-factly.

He squinted at her.

"You look dressed to me. It's boiling outside."

She laughed as she opened her wardrobe.

"And that, my friend, is why I love you," she said flippantly as she started pulling more appropriate attire off the shelves. She nearly missed his soft reply in the rustle of fabrics.

"I love you, too, Matthews."

∞

In hindsight, I really wish you hadn't said that.

Or that I hadn't said it.

That we hadn't said those words.

I really wish we could take them back.

I know it wasn't like this big confession thing or anything, just banter, but nevertheless now it's like, we told each other that we love each other so, really, it's perfectly fine if you go and die on me.

Those are the rules, right?

Either 'I love you,' brings the person back from the brink of death, or the words act as the final release form: 'I love you.' Croak.

I think it would have been fine if there had been a substantial amount of time between those words and what happened. For example, if what happened had happened next week rather than only a few hours later.

Then those words wouldn't feel so significant.

Who am I kidding?

They are always significant.

The kitchen was already in full swing when Kirsty and Jake arrived, despite the fact that out of the other seven, only Maisy had got there before them. But Caroline's energy easily accounted for the rest and then some. By the state of the counters and the smell of perfect roast beef that infused the air, it was obvious that the chef had been at it for at least a couple of hours already. She was just in the process of taking a lump of perfectly browned beef out of the oven to rest it on a wooden board when she spotted Kirsty and Jake.

"Ah, fabulous. Remoulade or horseradish sauce, you two? Your choice."

"Erm. Remoulade?" Jake answered.

"Good choice. More fiddly but kinder on the hands. All the recipe cards are on the counter. Probably under the eggs or thereabouts." Her eyes wandered over to Maisy. "Why are you still standing around, Maisy? Salad? Get washing. See those beautiful little purple and yellow flowers over there? They are for the salad, too. Viola tricolor, Johnny-jump-ups. Delicious. And pretty. Wild forefather of the pansy. Also, today I'd like the tomato seeds discarded, the cucumber peeled and the olives halved, *s'il vous plait*. That'll keep you occupied. And then you can actually try to make a honey and mustard dressing, so help us all. Ahh, excellent," she commented as Aimee, Ronan, Catalina and Noel entered the kitchen. "Aimee, Ronan, you're on horseradish sauce detail. You'll find frozen horseradish roots already peeled and wrapped in cling film on the top shelf in the freezer. I grew them myself last year. On a balcony. In London. Wear gloves when you grate them, they pack a punch. Recipe cards are where Jake is rummaging right now. Catalina, do you reckon you could make us a proper Spanish tortilla tonight? I'm assuming you don't need instructions for that. And if you could smuggle in the extra egg whites that the others will have left over from their mayonnaise bases that would be great. The less waste the better. I already cooked the potatoes for you: they are in the pot over there. Noel?" Caroline suddenly frowned. "Where is Zach?"

"He had him surgically removed, Chef," Aimee answered dryly.

"To make space for Catalina," Ronan added.

"Funny." Noel glared at them before he answered the chef. "In the loo, chef, coming in a minute."

"That's great. You two are making two sauces. Aïoli, as in a garlic mayonnaise made with olive oil, but go easy on the garlic, otherwise it'll overpower all the other dips and flavours. Give the leftover egg whites to Catalina. Secondly, a vinaigrette with little cubed boiled eggs. Paper, scissor, stone for who does which sauce for all I care, but make them good, they are the dips for our artichokes. The artichokes depend on you and these are the first of the new season. I hope they turn out tasty. Poppy?" Caroline looked around.

"Here, Chef," a quiet voice came from the door.

"Good, glad you're here. You're boiling them. Not the most difficult job in the world but someone's got to do it. Put some lemon slices in the water to prevent them from going brown. And be generous when adding your pinch of salt, otherwise they'll end up lacklustre. Once you've put them on, you could also be a darling and make some coffee — in the cafetière, please, then decant it into a jug and put the jug on ice. I'm dreaming of iced coffees for afters. I made some vanilla ice cream last night. It's in the freezer. It's divine. To die for. You've never tasted anything like it, I promise. Once you've dealt with the coffee, check on your artichokes. They shouldn't need more than twenty minutes at the most. You know they're done when you can pluck away a leaf from the middle easily. Don't burn your fingers. Drain them, leave them to cool. Tonight, children, everything will be served lukewarm to room temperature or ice cold. It's too hot out there for anything else. And that's where we are eating. *Al fresco*, in the fresh air." She took a breath and laughed at the round of faces staring at her, then clapped her hands twice. "Come on, get to it, people."

They scattered on her command and the whole group worked in full concentration for the next hour until all sauces were made and all the individual components of the meal were ready to be served. Caroline walked among them like the culinary queen they knew from TV, argus-eyed and vigilant, always at hand with comments and help, funny and critical, all rolled into one. Completely different from the Caroline of the last few weeks, Kirsty thought, even from the already improved version. Stricter. Self-assured. Happy. In her element.

Kirsty couldn't suppress a grin when the chef circled by and criticised the size of Kirsty's chopped herbs in the remoulade. The woman cocked her head at the girl.

"I fail to see what you have to smile about," Caroline said, earnestly.

"You, Chef," Kirsty answered her, as she wiped her brow with the back of her forearm. "You're back. Really back. Caroline Connelly is back."

∞

It was a great evening, wasn't it? Such a beautiful spread. When I close my eyes (and ignore the ghosting loop, which is still running, by the way, more erratic and not as constant as it was initially, but ready to pounce at any point in time) I can still recall the table so vividly. The blue of the table cloth (only Caroline would think to bring a table cloth to a grotty school playground), the delicate pink of the sliced beef, the deep green of the artichokes, the yellow and succulent brown of Catalina's omelette cut into neat wedges and the little dishes with the sauces — those delicious, beautiful sauces, worth every drop of sweat — and finally the red and green and black and purple of Maisy's salad. I never told her, but she did actually make a lovely honey and mustard dressing, didn't she? All of it was absolutely delicious, wasn't it? Such beautiful food. And festive, somehow, if you ignore the plastic school crockery and cheap steel cutlery.

Special. Really, really special.

Fit for a last meal.

I mean, I'm not sure if you would have chosen it exactly, and I'm still hoping that's not what it turns out to be, but if it does, or if from now on all your food comes through a tube then you went out on a high, right?

Culinarily speaking at least.

Well, provided you didn't eat anything else between the most sensational iced coffee known to man and ringing me at two o'clock in the morning.

Who knows.

It really is time now.

The last leg of the journey.

Tomorrow.

I'll deal with it tomorrow.

For now, I'm going to snuggle deep into your pillow and chase the last of your scent.

Whoa.

What was that?

Something's just changed.

It's the middle of the night, my phone says it's just before 3am but I'm not sure that's accurate. (Did you know you have no actual clock in your room? You need a clock!) I feel way too wide awake for 3am, although when I woke up a few minutes ago, I was so disorientated, I didn't know where I was, who I was, where was up, where was down. Once I had a little grip on reality I pulled the curtains back just to check the world was still out there. It's pitch black outside and it's raining. There are drops on the window pane and now I can hear a quiet pitter-patter on the roof. First rain we've had in weeks. Oh wow — that's what woke me up!

Thunder. Ah, and here comes the lightning.

Okay, just took five to watch the storm. Impressive. So impressive. I love thunderstorms. They never fail to remind me how in the great scheme of things everything that is Kirsty is really totally insignificant. I know some people wouldn't find that a happy thought, but for me it's tonic for the soul. It greatly reassures me. That nothing I do or say is really all that important. Gives me breathing space to just be me. Preferably while dancing in the elements. But I had to give that one a miss just now. I don't have a key to this house. I really wish I had. I'd be soaked to the bones by now and happy as Larry, whoever Larry is. I know, I know, how can I even think like this? Here? Now? Under the circumstances? But I feel totally different from the last few days. Amazing what a bit of electricity in the sky can do.

So, I guess I'm awake now.

And like I said, something's changed.

Fundamentally.

I can do this.

I can do this now.

∞

At first Kirsty thought it was the typical after garlic thirst that had roused her in the middle of the night. Disorientated and slightly lost between the dream she'd been having and reality, she grappled around for the bottle of water she habitually kept by the side of her bed, unscrewed the cap and took a few gulps, then glanced groggily at the station clock. The hands on its face, illuminated by an insipid streak of yellow light that had snuck through a gap in the curtains courtesy of the street lamp outside her window, showed four minutes to two.

Kirsty screwed the cap back onto the bottle, let it sink to the floor and was about to let her head rejoin the pillow when her mobile rang. It insistently rattled along on the nightstand, and she realised with a start that it had been this sound that had woken her, not her dry throat. She reached for the phone, fully expecting to hear Phoebe's voice, mid-anxiety attack because her mother was not home in the house above her and she'd got the creeps alone in her granny flat, as sometimes happened — not often, but often enough. Instead, Jake's number flashed up, along with the information that she'd already missed two of his calls. She sat bolt upright and picked up.

"Hello?" she whispered.

"Kirsty?" He sounded as if he was walking.

"Yeah."

"I need you."

It was a statement of fact.

"What for?"

"To be my witness." It felt like her heart stopped for a whole minute, along with her breath. What had he done? Where was he? What was she being dragged into? How many bodies were there? She'd evidently paused for too long because the next thing he said sounded panicky. "Are you still there, Matthews?"

She breathed out and decided to go with sardonicism.

"Do I need to fire up the chimenea? Are there clothes to burn?"

"What? Ha. Funny." He didn't sound remotely amused. Whatever was going on was too serious for humour. "No. I said witness, not cover up, smartarse. I need you to come with me. Over to big town. To Shannon's."

"What? Now? In the middle of the night? Why?"

"I think, no, actually, make that I'm pretty damn certain that she's left Sophia at home. Alone. While she's gone clubbing. So I'm going over there and I need a witness. Someone I'm not related to. Someone who hasn't got a record. Someone who's trustworthy. Actually, forget all that. I just need *you*, okay? I need you to make sure I don't lose the plot."

Halfway through his staccato explanation the background noise had changed. He didn't sound like he was moving outside any longer. He sounded as if he was stationary now, somewhere sheltered.

"Don't you think that's a bit far fetched? I mean, I'm sure if you say she's not the best mother in the world, she's not the best mother in the world, but *nobody* leaves a five-month-old baby home alone, Jake. Nobody. You're being paranoid. I mean, how do you even know? How do you *think* you know?"

Kirsty was whispering so fiercely, she felt like she was about to wake up her parents despite the hushed tones. She heard a car door being shut on the other end before he answered, his voice instantly becoming more defined and clearer in the enclosed bubble of a vehicle.

"Six months, Sophia is six months now. Shannon's done it before. Not at night, but in the daytime. I just couldn't prove it. I'll tell you about it on the way, but right now, I need to go get my baby. She'll be alone, Kirsty, and scared and hungry." There were suppressed tears in his voice. "*Please*, will you come along?"

She could hear him hold his breath and in her mind's eye she could see him clearly, sitting in a J.C. Deacon company car somewhere near his house with his eyes shut, a phone pressed to his ear, praying he had the kind of friend in her he could ring at two o'clock in the morning and go stealing babies with.

He did.

"Sure. I'll meet you at the corner of my street. I'll get some clothes on and I'll start walking."

And with that, she rang off.

∞

The doubts didn't come until she'd been standing by the roadside for a fair few minutes. Only then did her brain slow down from springing into action mode back into the land of plausibility.

It was a balmy, peaceful night, the front garden of the house on the corner smelled of jasmine and lavender, and she felt tingly all over, as if she should have been waiting for a romantic rendezvous, not going on a harebrained rescue mission. The longer she stared down the road in expectation of headlights, the more ridiculous the whole thing seemed. Still, Kirsty remained where she was and she knew she wouldn't back out, no matter what the rest of the night would bring. Questions buzzed in her mind. Like, how were they even going to get into Shannon's flat-house-houseboat if Jake was right, and Shannon was out? Or, more likely, what if she wasn't? If bumping into the woman on a Saturday shopping trip during daylight hours was a bad idea, then how great an idea was it to get her out of bed in the middle of the night accusing her of child neglect? More to the point, how bad would all of this look at Jake's next custody hearing?

Since finally introducing Sophia to the rest of Gull Cove, which had caused less of a stir than Kirsty would have expected, Jake had gradually, over the last week, become a lot more forthcoming with information about his woes. Kirsty knew a lot more about his ongoing battle for full custody of Sophia now. A fight that had always been supported fiercely by his mother and, after an initial refusal to cooperate with his son and many fights that had rocked the Deacon household to the near-divorce core, more recently also by his father, albeit still reluctantly. Jake's uncharacteristically ineloquent assessment of the mother of his baby was simply that she was unfit as a parent, which Kirsty had interpreted as completely lacking any primeval instincts towards protecting her young, based on the few choice stories he had shared with her. According to Jake, Shannon had carried on partying hard during her pregnancy, to the point where it had been almost a miracle that Sophia had been born without any serious defects aside from coming out tiny and very underweight. Next, Shannon had supposedly flat out refused to breastfeed the little girl even once, calling it filthy and disgusting. But the thing that seemed to get to Jake the most was not that Shannon continued to only ever fulfil the bare minimum of care for their baby, but the fact that she still, to this day, referred to Sophia as 'it'. Though in Kirsty's mind the saddest thing about the situation was that Sophia hadn't even been an accident. At least not for Shannon. If Jake was to be believed the woman had got herself pregnant on purpose as part of a grand plan to have her life financed. It was a cynical assessment, but when Kirsty had gently probed as to how fair he was being, and had suggested that maybe what Shannon had really needed was some postnatal counselling he'd laughed without joy.

"Been there, done that, held her hand in the waiting

room. It's not like I didn't try, you know," he'd answered. "But the problem with Shannon is, she isn't depressed, she's degenerate, and there is no therapy for that."

Still, Kirsty thought, *leaving a baby home alone?*

It remained unlikely.

But if that's what Jake had led himself to believe, she knew there was no force on earth that could keep him from checking. And she was glad he'd rung and asked her to come. On that thought she saw headlights appear in the distance, and took a deep breath.

In for a penny, in for a pound.

After a brief exchange of 'Heys', they drove in silence for most of the journey, Jake clutching the steering wheel in a way that gave the term 'white knuckle ride' an entirely new meaning. A glimpse at his clenched jaw made Kirsty's own teeth hurt in sympathy.

She felt torn between asking him all the questions that had occurred to her, and sitting quiet as a mouse, not wanting to distract him further from what little concentration he seemed to be focussing on the road. It was only when the dark A-road turned into the lamp-lit outskirts of town that she felt as if asking him something would not end up with them wound around a tree or upside down in a ditch somewhere. Still, she waited for them to hit the first red light before she opened her mouth.

"So, what's the plan?"

He didn't miss a beat.

"Go in, get Sophia, take her home, never give her back," he answered grimly.

"Okay. And how do we know Shannon isn't actually there?"

"Oh. Right. Yeah." He looked at her briefly, surprise showing in his face, before he turned back to the windscreen in time with the traffic light jumping down to green. "Do you remember Bean?" He didn't wait for her to answer as he pulled away from the lights. "My year, till he left Gull Cove for sixth form at the agricultural college. You must remember him. Smiley git. Tall, ginger, so many freckles all over it looked like he'd had a bad spray tan?"

The description was so apt, Kirsty snorted a laugh. She remembered the guy alright.

"You mean Max Wilson, right?"

"Yeah. Bean."

"What about him?"

"He's a mate. Like a real one. Best friend I've ever had. Well, until you came along anyway."

"Thanks."

"I mean it."

"Great. Carry on."

"So Bean's out clubbing tonight and guess who he bumps into?"

"Shannon."

"That's right."

He fell silent then as if that was the whole of the story. Kirsty rolled her eyes at the roof of the car.

"And? Can I have few more filler sentences here, please, Mr. Deacon, 'cause I'm not sure how that translates into how we know that Shannon is still out right this minute or why we are so certain she didn't get a babysitter, or any of this, actually."

"I just know, okay? Bean sent me a picture half an hour

ago of her slamming tequilas with her bitches. She doesn't know anyone else other than those two who she could ask to babysit. None of her family talk to her, the neighbours hate her. And I rang the landline in the flat. Repeatedly. No answer."

"Hm. Still not convinced. She could have hired someone. Someone who might be fast asleep. At two o'clock in the morning. It's not unheard of."

He snorted derisively at that.

"Forget it. She hasn't hired anyone. I know she hasn't. She just doesn't get it. She thinks this is okay. She's done it before. There've been times when I've come to pick Sophia up and Shannon wasn't there, had just left her in the flat in her crib on her own. Last one was last Thursday. I went to get Sophia a day early for the weekend 'cause Shannon had a doctor's appointment Friday morning. Got there between school and cooking and Shannon wasn't there. Sophia was though. Every time it happens Shannon comes up with some lame excuse, like she'd only popped down to the shop to buy some fags, or post a letter, or some shit like that. But last week I just didn't buy it. I was sure she'd been gone longer than a few minutes. I had no proof though. It was just, you know, in the way how Sophia felt to me when I picked her up. She felt *abandoned*." The increasingly agitated tone of his voice suddenly dropped to a hollow, defeated sound. "My baby felt like she'd been abandoned." Sometime during all of this spilling out of him, a tear had started running down the side of his nose. He swiped it away with the heel of his hand before returning the hand to the gear stick. "The thing is," he added in a small voice, "If I'm right, it's my fault. Shannon asked me to get her early again this week so she could go out. But mum couldn't look after Sophia during cooking today, so I said no. I said no."

Kirsty felt gobsmacked, outraged and sad all rolled into one. She cupped the back of his hand in her own and gave it a small squeeze.

"We'll get her," she reassured him.

He nodded curtly.

"We will. And this time, Shannon is not having her back. Ever."

∞

Sigh. There are streaks of light in the sky now and I still haven't got to the horrific bit.

It's imminent though.

We're about five minutes from serving up.

It occurs to me that writing is a lot like cooking: hours of preparation and then the finished product is devoured in a fraction of the time. Luckily, there is no washing up here.

That's not why I'm throwing in yet another interlude though. Not really big enough an observation to stop an entire story for, is it?

I just needed to back up here for a second, just to say I thought you were joking, you know.

Not about never giving Sophia back. Of course not. I knew you were deadly serious, and after all is said and done, you got what you wished for. There is no way in hell, according to your dad's lawyer, that Shannon is ever even having access now.

I thought you were joking about me.

About being your best friend other than Bean. I thought it was just a disguised way of saying 'Thank you' for coming with you. It has taken me all these words, getting my butt tattooed in a bench slat pattern and then living in your bed for two days

216

*without you to finally realise that you meant it. To realise that,
actually, I was that important in the universe of Jake Deacon.
And despite everything, that makes me happy.*

So, big breath, here goes.

∞

"You've got a key?"

Kirsty's voice couldn't have sounded more incredulous if
she'd tried.

"Of course I've got a key," Jake stated as he put the
object in question into the keyhole of the high rise's main
entrance door.

The whole scenario was entirely not what Kirsty had
expected.

She had expected grotty council housing of some
description, a flat in a dilapidated two-storey house
somewhere, maybe even the whole of a dilapidated mid-
terraced chicken coop. She had expected having to commit
the crime usually referred to as breaking and entering.

She had definitely not expected to end up standing in the
entrance way of Crimson Tower, of Crimson, Cobalt and
Emerald Towers fame, a newbuilt trio of hideous Legoland
tower blocks at the edge of big town, the erection of which
had only finished eighteen months prior, after years of
protests by surrounding residents who were having their
previously unfettered sea view stolen. Or that Jake would
come equipped with a perfectly legal method of gaining
access.

"How come?" she asked, as she followed Jake inside and
up a short staircase, deeper into the sterile hallways of the
building's inner maze.

The guts of Crimson tower were decked out from wall to ceiling in a nondescript beige stone, with a single line of blood red tiles at hip height set in between them. It looked somewhere between a nightmarish vision of a government facility where genetic experiments were being conducted, and a really big, recently refurbished, insanely posh public toilet. The smell of disinfectant that permeated the air underlined both impressions equally and made Kirsty's throat contract. They had reached the brushed steel doors of a large elevator before Jake answered, pushing the button.

"Landlord's key." The door opened immediately, and they stepped through. Jake selected the 19th floor before explaining himself further, unprompted this time and not once looking at Kirsty, but staring at the lights on the button plate as if he could will the lift to go faster. "My dad bought the flat for us when he found out Shannon was pregnant. That's dad for you. He quizzed her for about two minutes to see if she was sure she wanted to keep the baby, and for another half a minute to see if she was sure it was mine. When she said she was happy to do a paternity test, he immediately rolled over. Gave me the bollocking of the century and bought her a flat. With my uni fund. Well, no. He just took that as a deposit. An education would have been *way* cheaper than setting her up in the lap of luxury."

"Whoa."

"Yeah. Whoa. Indeed."

"You said 'us'. You said, 'He bought the flat for us'," Kirsty ventured hesitantly, not sure if the queasy feeling in her stomach was to do with what she was hearing, or just with the funny effect elevators often seemed to have on her. As if her stomach was travelling upwards more slowly than the rest of her body.

"Yeah. He had fantasies of Shannon and me and baby living together." His voice sounded as if on auto pilot.

"Did you?"

He snorted.

"No. That's where dad's fantasies, and Shannon's fantasies, and for what it's worth, my fantasies, differed *wildly*." He finally looked away from the button plate and at Kirsty, his mouth contorted into a sarcastic smile. The lift was slowing down to a halt and he gave her a resigned shrug. "I fell out of love with her the minute I realised she'd taken me for a ride. Long before Sophia was born." The door opened. "Let's go. Second on the left."

∞

The first thing that hit Kirsty's senses when they entered Shannon's flat was the stench of cold cigarette smoke paired with lily of the valley air freshener. The second was the complete absence of any sound, other than the blood rushing in her ears. She was still reeling from the heated, if whispered, argument they'd just had in the hallway.

She'd made Jake ring the doorbell a few times before she had allowed him to let them in with the key. Her insistence had almost caused a full blown hissy fit between them, with her shielding the keyhole with her body until he'd relented. Only a reminder of how this would look at his next custody hearing on the million to one chance that he was wrong and about to walk in on a perfectly respectable set up had made him see sense in the end. Kirsty knew they'd given it long enough for anyone inside to throw on some clothes and answer the door, so her heart beating high in her throat now had nothing to do with the fear of being discovered, but everything to do with the fear of him being right.

Because if he was, why was Sophia not crying?

The thought had frozen her to the spot. Standing in the dark hallway of Shannon's flat, all sorts of gruesome images flashed through her mind at record speed, while Jake stormed straight ahead without bothering with the lights. He disappeared into a room at the end of the corridor. Leaving the door ajar, he switched on the light inside, so a slant of it fell short just in front of Kirsty's feet. She took another couple of steps inside until she could make out the functions of the other rooms, two to the left and one to the right, which had been left wide open. A bathroom, a kitchen, an empty bedroom.

A few seconds later a single, subdued cry of an exhausted baby rang softly through the air and she exhaled the breath she'd been holding. The rest of her remained still though, not wanting to move further into the privacy of another person's home uninvited. Minutes passed before Jake finally appeared back in the hallway, clutching his daughter, who seemed to have gone back to sleep, to his chest.

"Let's go. We need to get her home and fed properly." He sounded choked. "She's exhausted. I bet she screamed her lungs out for hours. There was the rest of a bottle of formula left in the bed. I've just force fed her a little so she doesn't completely dehydrate. It's cold but better than nothing. But she's too tired to suck. I had to really wriggle the teat around to make her take a few sips. I'm gonna kill Shannon when I see her. Degenerate bitch."

Kirsty saw unshed tears in the corners of his eyes as he passed her in the hallway.

She hung back a bit.

"Shouldn't we write her a note or something?"

Jake stopped and turned to stare at her.

"She doesn't deserve a note."

Kirsty sighed.

"No, she doesn't. But there is a thin line between rescuing and kidnapping. You write her a note, it's a rescue. You take Sophia and don't say anything, it's kidnapping. Actually, don't make it a note, send her a text. Then you've got proof you communicated."

He took a deep breath as if to protest, but didn't. He smiled instead.

"See, and that's exactly why I asked you to come. Thank you."

He gave her Sophia to carry once they were out of the flat, and whipped out his phone. Kirsty let the baby snuggle into the crook of her neck and listened to the infant's little breaths just below her ear while he typed furiously. He wrote and rewrote the message numerous times, and when he finally got around to looking up and reading it out to her they were already back in the lift and on their way down.

"So how about this: 'Have taken Sophia away. Stopped by your place to find that you left her on her own again. Not ok. Have witness. Applying for emergency custody now," he read out what he had typed, and looked at Kirsty expectantly.

"It's good. No swearing. To the point."

He hit send.

"Done." He put the phone away and held out his arms to take Sophia back. "Mine."

"Hm." Kirsty hugged the snuffling creature a little tighter. "Can't I keep hold of her for a bit? She's so soft."

She hadn't really expected him to let her, had just

thought the remark would lighten the mood a bit, but he let his hands sink to his sides and the first warm, relaxed smile since they'd left cooking club earlier on in the night spread over his face.

"Sure," he held her eyes for a moment. "*You* can keep hold of my baby anytime."

She was still walking on the cloud carpet that his reply had conjured up when they exited the building and turned towards the visitors' car park that lay a little down the road between Crimson and Cobalt Towers. The night had stayed mild, and now that they had retrieved Sophia, and the tension that had driven Jake had drained from him, Kirsty felt a small sprinkling of spring tingles dance under her skin again. It wasn't as potent as earlier on, when she'd waited for him surrounded by the scent of jasmine and lavender under a dimly yellow street lamp, but it was almost better here, in total contradiction to the stark environment. From the outside, the towers had the distinct aura of a high security complex, with strategically placed search lights to eliminate any dark corners, and CCTV mounted on every nook and cranny. It should have given her the creeps, but walking by Jake's side and cradling Sophia, who'd gone fully back to sleep against her shoulder, all she could feel was happy.

It lasted for all of thirty seconds.

It was then they heard the car drive down the road behind them, pull up and a door open. They both looked over their shoulder simultaneously to catch a glimpse of a taxi, and of the woman exiting it, a torrent of drunken abuse spouting from her lips. Shannon was shouting after them at the top of her voice, expletive after expletive rolling off her tongue. They saw the driver get out and stall her, demanding his money.

Jake and Kirsty picked up speed.

"Shit," Jake said under his breath. "I thought that might happen. Club kicks out in half an hour. She never stays till the end so she doesn't have to wait at the taxi rank." He fumbled inside his jacket for his car keys and stuffed them into Kirsty's back pocket. "Here, take Sophia to the car. Lock yourself in. Shannon's vicious when she's pissed. Wait there. Don't come out. I'll deal with this."

He took a moment to zip his jacket up, as if putting on battle armour, rolled his shoulders, and then turned on his heels.

Kirsty marched on hurriedly towards the corner around which the car park entrance was located, Sophia getting heavier in her arms with every step. She vaguely registered that the insults still ringing endlessly through the quiet night air had now started incorporating her, and that she was being called all the names under the sun. Then it suddenly stopped. Kirsty got to the corner and turned around to see what was happening. Jake and Shannon had met halfway between where he'd turned back and the still stationary taxi. The light inside the cab was on, and Kirsty could make out the driver through the windscreen, back in his seat and speaking seemingly into the air, probably calling in to dispatch for his next pick up. Jake and Shannon were standing in full profile view facing each other. Jake's back was to the road, Shannon's to the buildings and they both had their arms crossed in front of their chests in an unmistakably hostile standoff. They were talking, surprisingly quietly. Kirsty knew she should have carried on following Jake's orders, but curiosity stapled her feet to the ground. She wanted to see how this panned out for herself. She could see Shannon's shoulder shake with the tell-tale quivers of somebody who was about to cry, and watched Jake loosen an arm to gently touch her shoulder. It was a gesture both tender and mildly condescending, and both aspects made Kirsty smile a little. That was Jake. All over. Shannon's head started bobbing up and down as if in agreement with something he'd said just as the taxi driver switched off the internal lights and pulled away with gusto.

And then it happened.

In mere seconds.

So quickly Kirsty could almost have believed that she'd known it was going to happen before it ever did.

Shannon's head jerked around to look at the approaching vehicle, her arms unfurled from the embrace she'd been giving herself, and then, with a triumphant battle cry, she shoved Jake full force out into the cab's path.

Kirsty could hear herself gasp as she instinctively moved one hand up to shield the skull of the baby in her arms, pressed Sophia tighter against her chest and looked on as the cab hit Jake side on. His body was flung into the air and somersaulted above the car's roof before disappearing from her view somewhere to the rear of the vehicle.

The next second Kirsty wasn't standing any longer.

She was running.

Carefully, because of Sophia, yet somehow still faster than she'd ever run in her life. Past the cab, past Shannon and towards the lifeless lump of human who lay across the tarmac. It seemed to take forever to reach Jake. His limp body had rolled a fair few metres before it had stopped, leaving him on his front, head resting sideways, the arm below him sprawled in an unnatural angle. By the time Kirsty and Sophia finally reached him, the taxi driver had left his car, and joined Kirsty, his hands on top of his head.

"Oh no, no, no, no, no," he sputtered, followed by something soft in another language that sounded like praying, while Kirsty sank awkwardly to her knees by Jake's side. "Is he alive?" the cabbie asked thickly.

There were scrapes all over the side of Jake's face but no serious blood anywhere that Kirsty could see immediately. She suppressed a gagging reflex and focused on Jake's nose. The sides of it fluttered.

"He's breathing," she stated, her voice unnaturally calm, as if it really belonged to someone completely different, someone observing this scene from a thousand miles away through a magic mirror. She shuffled Sophia higher up on her shoulder to free a hand and touch the side of his neck. "Jake? Jake? Can you hear me? If you can hear me, make a noise, any noise."

Nothing.

She swallowed hard, then looked up at the cabbie. He wasn't very old, of Middle Eastern origin, and with the kind of mouth that lent itself to big smiles. He looked like a really nice guy. And like one shaken to the core.

"Can you call for an ambulance?" Kirsty prompted him.

The cabbie appeared to calm down a little, propped up by her pragmatism.

"I do. Before I get out. They on the way."

"We should put him into the recovery position. Can you do that? You need to do that," Kirsty instructed helplessly, lifting Sophia a little. "I can't. I've got my hands full."

The cabbie's eyes suddenly focussed on Sophia, and surprise seemed to flicker in them, as if he'd only just realised Kirsty was holding a baby.

"Yes, yes, of course."

He nodded wildly and Kirsty got to her feet to give him space. As the cabbie stepped around and lowered himself to the ground, a movement caught the corner of Kirsty's eye, and she turned in time to see Shannon sauntering onto the scene. The woman's face held no remorse, no single emotion as she drunkenly examined the body on the floor, the cabbie, Kirsty, and her daughter, with glazed eyes. Kirsty clutched onto Sophia, fearing Shannon would try to rip the child away from her, but instead the woman just swivelled around towards the building.

"I'm going to bed," she stated coolly.

And then she staggered off.

Kirsty caught the eye of the cabbie, who'd just finished putting Jake into the recovery position. He stared at her with the same despair of the human race that she was sure she was throwing right back at him, but before they could exchange anything more, there were flashing lights and cars, and people everywhere.

Emergency services had arrived.

∞

*O*kay, *I think I've exhausted third person narrative now. I can't do it anymore. I feel too raw. And empty. Utterly drained. Whatever energy the thunderstorm infused me with is spent.*

So, let me give you a quick roundup of what happened next, and then I'll try and go back to sleep for a bit. I might get another hour in before it's up time.

Basically, the paramedics claimed you. Then a second set came and claimed the cabbie. I think they treated him for shock. They checked me over, too, but it turns out I'm psychologically more sturdy than a guy who probably joined us here from some horror war zone far, far away. Go figure. So the police claimed me. And Sophia. After some confusion, as to who belonged to whom and me trying my best to give them ungarbled information, one cop car took Sophia, and another took me home. I don't know if they arrested Shannon there and then. We were gone first. It was the hardest thing I have ever done, handing over your daughter. I made the head copper, no idea what rank he was, but he was without a doubt the boss, promise me that they would not give her back to Shannon or let her end up in the system, that they'd definitely, definitely, definitely take her to your parents. He was nice. And I believed him when he assured me they would. But I still felt like I was betraying Sophia somehow when I let them take her. And you. More to the point, I felt I was betraying you.

There was a lady cop in the car that took me home who was really nice, too. When we got to my house, she told me to stay in the car and went up to the door first, then took a fair while to explain the situation to my parents. So they wouldn't give me a hard time. Not that they would have done, but I still appreciated her concern.

So that's it. Full circle.

I got home, didn't sleep, then left the house a couple of hours later to get to the hospital and find me a friendly bench.

That's our story and here pretty much endeth the letter.

Because that's really what this is, isn't it? A letter. I feel a Box Tops hit coming on. Although I have a sinking feeling that no aeroplane will get you to me. I don't think anything will get you back to me, ever. It's seven o'clock in the morning now, and your parent's landline rang a few minutes ago.

I'm pretty sure I know what that means.

And here comes the knock on the door.

PART III : BEGINNING

So I was wrong.

I wasn't finished.

It's still the same day and I'm back at school, because that's where your mum decided to send me off to. She didn't even give me a choice. Just knocked, came in, sat on the bed, looked at me straight and said, 'You're not going to the hospital today, you're going to school with the twins'. Then she disappeared to find me your old uniform. Turns out, year eleven Kirsty and year eleven Jake are/were the same size waist and jacket. No idea how that works. Although the trousers are too long: I had to roll the legs up. Worse, my thighs are rather contained in them, and my butt is being formed into a previously unknown shape by taut fabric as we speak. Actually, it's not that bad. I just wouldn't normally let clothing show my volume off quite like this.

So I'm sitting here now, at break time, in the deepest, darkest recesses of the library where people hopefully won't find me, in your old uniform, which I'm never ever going to swap back for my own again. Not only because I actually look kind of hot in the boys' version, figure hugging though it is on me, but because it's yours. I feel like I'm sitting in your shed skin, and it's comforting and sad, both at the same time.

I was inundated with people when I turned up. All and sundry wanted an update. Seems like while they have been too shy to ask the twins any questions I'm somehow fair game. Thankfully Phoebe snarled away the worst ones, and then Simm came to shoo off the rest. He's threatened anyone who harasses me with detention, and has given me a free pass to go in and out of lessons (but not exams, he did draw the line there, those I have to sit or miss) as I see fit, and hide when I can't take it anymore.

At least until you get better.

If you get better.

I wanted to see you so badly.

But your mum was adamant. When she came back with your uniform this morning, I begged her not to send me to school, but to let me see you.

"He's awake, Kirsty, but it's early days. He's not coherent, they say," she replies, standing there in the middle of your room, holding up your old shell on a hanger. "He might never be. He might never be even remotely the same again. Apparently the first thing he did was to lash out at a nurse. Then he started ranting. It's a miracle he's talking at all, they say, that he still has any command of language, even if nothing he comes out with is making any sense. But then they said people don't normally wake up this abruptly either. There is still a chance he'll slip away again. We still don't know how much of this is temporary, and how much permanent brain damage there is. We know nothing, other than that he woke up during the thunderstorm last night, and right now he is awake, but not lucid. So go to school." She says it all so matter-of-factly that I can't even begin to get my head around it. Any of it. That you are supposed to be back, yet you're not. That I can't see you. That she is so damn calm about it. I guess she sees the desperation in my eyes, because she stops *being breezy for a second, and gives me small smile. "I tell you what, Jude and I are going to see him this morning. We'll gauge the situation. And then Jude'll pick up the twins from school and take them. That's enough visitors for one day, but tomorrow afternoon, we do a girl run. You, Sophia and me. Deal? I have a feeling you will have to be super brave, though. Can you do that?"*

No prizes for guessing what my answer was.

Even a tiny morsel of Jake Deacon is better than none.

At seven a.m. this morning, when that phone rang, I thought you were dead.

Suddenly there is hope.

All I have to do now is to somehow get through the next twenty-six hours.

∞

After almost a week of bench bumming and bed squatting, Kirsty finally moved back home. Despite the anticipation of the next day and despite missing Jake's residual presence all around her, once her head landed on her own pillow, in her own bed, she slept well for the first time since the moment Jake's body had smacked into the cab.

Her parents had welcomed her back with gentle delight, with freely dispensed hugs and squeezes, with a minimum of conversational demand, and with a delicious stew that left Kirsty a little puzzled.

"This is amazing, Mum," she'd complimented her mother over the second forkful of her dinner. "I didn't know you could cook like this."

"That's because I can't," her mum had laughed. "Caroline Connelly dropped this off for us at lunchtime. She said you needed the sustenance and that that way she felt she was *doing* something. I have an inkling the Deacons are eating the same thing right now. She's a nice woman, Caroline Connelly. So much more down to earth than you'd expect a celebrity chef to be. And she really cares."

"Yes," Kirsty had mumbled at the third forkful. "Yes, she does."

It was then that tiredness had hit her like a tidal wave. She had barely managed to keep her eyes open long enough to finish her plate before she'd stumbled upstairs and fallen into bed.

Making full use of her get out of jail free card the next morning, she decided to sleep through first period, and didn't turn up to school until the short break before third. When she finally marched in, feeling a hell of a lot more resilient than the day before, she nearly faltered as soon as she saw them. They were all hanging by the main doors, blatantly looking out for her arrival. The whole of Caroline's little club. Some were frazzled from papers they'd just finished, others seemed to have appeared outside just for her. And whereas the day before, their questions, along with everybody else's, had made Kirsty gasp for oxygen, today their company soothed her nerves. They didn't say a lot, just ringed around her as she walked up to the science lab where her biology revision was being held and then dispersed in various directions with gentle reminders that if they didn't see her before, they'd see her tonight.

It's Thursday, she thought in wonder, as she entered the lab. *Cooking night. How can it be cooking night again?*

The next hour seemed a million years long.

Kirsty barely paid attention to anything around her, at times staring at the second hand on her watch and willing it to go faster.

During lunch she hid out in the library, wondering why she was bothering. It was there that Phoebe found her, one of the warm Belgian waffles that were on offer in the cafeteria between her lips and another in her hand, much to the chagrin of Miss Austin, the librarian, who was at perpetual odds with Simm as to how well books and food mixed. Phoebe plonked herself down next to Kirsty on a bean bag in the lower years' corner. Kirsty slowly lifted her eyes from her music player.

"Hey."

"Hey."

"What are you doing?"

"Reading."

"On that thing?"

"Uh-huh."

"I didn't realise it could do anything other than play the charts from 1963."

"Funny. Sixty-three was a bad year. Just so you know. What's with the waffle?"

Phoebe examined the bakery product in her hand as if she'd only just discovered it was there, turning it critically this way and that before staring hard at its edge for a few seconds through narrowed eyes.

"Ah, there it is. Says 'Kirsty' here."

She grinned and held it out. Kirsty took it gratefully. She didn't feel hungry, but she needed the love.

"So," Phoebe said while Kirsty took the first mouthful. "You're going to see Jake after school."

"Uh-huh."

"Nervous?"

Kirsty nodded, finished chewing and swallowed.

"Terrified."

Phoebe slung her arm around Kirsty, and pulled her to her side.

"You're a braver woman than I will ever be, Kirsty Matthews, you can do this. You know what you'll need though, right?"

Kirsty let her muscles go floppy for a minute, hanging sideways in Phoebe's arms like a rag doll and stealing as much strength from her friend as Phoebe would allow. She allowed plenty. Kirsty sat upright again.

"What do I need?"

A mischievous glint appeared in her friend's eye as she barely contained a smirk.

"Clothes."

A few minutes later, they were thrown out of the library in the newfound knowledge that Miss Austin didn't just have issues with food around books, she also vehemently disapproved of beanbag fights in their vicinity.

∞

Actually, I kind of lied to Phoe when I said I was reading. Well I was, I was reading this, but only because I'd only just stopped typing. I'd literally just got to 'Kirsty barely paid attention to anything around her, at times staring at the second hand on her watch and willing it to go faster,' *when she walked in and suddenly the writing timeline and actual time collided, which was the oddest sensation ever. A bit like when Marty McFly bumps into himself in* Back to the Future.

To be honest, I don't know why I'm still chronicling this. I think I've become addicted to doing this. It should have stopped with your mangled body on the tarmac. Because that's where our story ended.

I need to remember that.

I need to remember that Jake Deacon, as he was, in all likelihood died on that road, and that what we'll eventually maybe get back is at best a bad approximation of who he was. It's what the doctors keep telling your parents, and what your mum keeps telling me, and what comaandbraininjury.org keeps telling all of us, and what seems to be the common friggin' consensus. But I guess I refuse to believe in that ending. I must be, because why else would I be sitting next to your mum right now, in the front of that silly long Mercedes, Sophia gurgling happily in her car seat just behind us?

I know I've said it before, but I'll say it again: your mum is amazing! She picked me up from school, drove me home so I could change, briefly gave me a rundown of where you're at, which can be condensed into still erratic but occasionally recognisant and responsive, but then let me be, so I could do this. I keep thinking about what she said, and I'm imagining it like a badly tuned radio station fading in and out, with varying amounts of crackle disturbing the transmission. I think I'm losing the plot. I believe I just compared you to a radio station. Jake FM.

We are nearly at the hospital now.

Give me strength.

∞

The first thing that struck Kirsty was the sheer amount of hardware he was hooked up to, despite the fact he was breathing on his own and not on life support any longer. Still, there seemed to be monitors and machines and drips and bags and tubes and cables just about everywhere. And somewhere amidst all this there was the trapped, sleeping body of a young man.

Like a Giger painting that has had a sex change.

The absurdity of the thought made her belly clench, and a choked sound emanate from somewhere deep inside her. And that seemed to be the noise that woke him. His eyes opened and his head swivelled from side to side a few times before his gaze settled on the three people hovering in the room. Kirsty had headed in first, and was standing in front of Ava, who was holding on tightly to a restless Sophia. Jake's eyes slowly came into focus and latched onto Kirsty's.

The contact struck her like a lightning bolt. She could feel it from the roots of her hair all the way down to her toe nails, and she was almost glad that it only lasted for the fraction of a second before his stare moved to look at the baby behind her. He jerked up in his bed, violently, as if a seizure had taken hold of him, his arms stretched out towards them as a primeval grunt escaped his throat, filling the room.

"Wait," Ava whispered into Kirsty's ear. "Let's give him a minute. He might lash out."

Jake's eyes found Kirsty's once more and he whimpered as he fell back onto the bed. Kirsty angled her body so she could look at Ava Deacon and held out her arms.

"Give me Sophia."

"Pardon?"

"Has he seen her since he's woken up?"

"No. We thought it was best to leave her home yesterday."

"Then give me Sophia."

The woman reluctantly handed over the baby.

"What are you doing?"

Kirsty knew she wasn't really expected to answer, so she

didn't. She could hear Ava take in a sharp breath and hold it while Kirsty made her way slowly, carefully towards the bed, laboriously navigating the machinery, tubes and cables. She could feel Jake's eyes burning holes into her while she kept hers on the floor to make sure she didn't trip or accidentally pull something out of him, like the catheter she'd just brushed past, for example. Finally, she found a small space on the side of the bed where she could have seated herself if it hadn't been for the rail in the way that kept patients from rolling out. Her heart stopped when she saw the restraints attached to it. Although presently he wasn't strapped in, clearly at some point that had been a necessary measure.

Doubt crept into her consciousness.

Or to ask it with Ava's words: *what was she doing?*

But then she dared to look at him again, and the eyes that met hers were Jake's. She hung onto them, trying hard to ignore the rest of his face, which seemed to consist solely of one large yellowing bruise decorated with crusted over scrapes.

"Hey, Deacon," she whispered quietly, and watched him try to sit up again, vaguely controlled this time but still more reminiscent of a convulsion than Kirsty would have liked to admit. "Calm. I need you stay calm. So I can put Sophia on you. Can you do that?"

She took the sound he made for a yes, and watched him try to relax. She shifted Sophia onto her hip and threw a glance over her shoulder to Ava, who was still standing where she'd left her.

"Does this side rail fold down or something?" Kirsty asked, tapping the thing.

"Yes. Yes, it does. You just need to pull it up and then it

slides down."

Kirsty managed to fumble her way through the mechanism and sat down softly by Jake's side. He raised his arms again and she complied. She gently set Sophia down onto his chest, not quite letting go of the baby, but holding on to her by the cotton of her babygrow at the small of her back. She watched his eyes fill with tears as his right arm, the one not punctured by a cannula, came up to wrap itself around his baby. He closed his eyes for a second and a sigh came out of his mouth, long and drawn out. Sophia started to wriggle, exploring her father's chest and shuffling up to his shoulders. He winced when she headbutted his chin. His eyes opened again and he smiled weakly at Kirsty, before giving her a different look. She understood. She picked Sophia back up and turned on the bed towards Ava who'd come closer by now, staring in wonder at the scene in front of her.

"Here," Kirsty lifted the baby up for Ava to take her, and then made to get up.

Her job here was done.

Only that's when his hand grabbed hers.

"Stay."

The word was almost unintelligible.

His tongue was heavy. Whether from the morphine or the brain damage she had no idea. Time would tell. But when his fingers touched hers she knew it didn't really matter either way.

Kirsty looked up at the clock above his bed, the single ornament in this otherwise utilitarian room, and smiled through held back tears.

She'd stay.

Forever and always.

And today until it was time to go cooking with Caroline.

∞

That's it. That's us. Done and dusted. I think I can stop typing now. I've recorded what needs recording.

Was that enough pathos for you right there at the end?

Actually, pathos is the wrong word. I don't feel pity or sorrow as I lie here, in my own bed, fully sated with cooking club dinner. We made burgers tonight, believe it or not. And sauces. From scratch, of course. We are *talking Caroline Connelly after all. We didn't make the buns though. She bought the buns. Shock, horror.*

But I'm digressing.

So, backtrack. No, I don't feel sad or even angry. I don't know what I feel. Grateful, for sure, a teensy bit hopeful but mostly an odd mix of both battle-fatigued and battle-ready at the same time. Because, if I am really honest, despite saying that having just a tiny piece of you back would be better than not having you at all, now that we've got the tiny piece back, I know I want it all. The whole Jake. All of you. And I understand that might never happen and I know that it'll be a long and rocky road but I meant it, the forever and always. Not just in a looking at myself from the outside, in the third person kind of way but in a me, I, the-girl-in-this-skin-looking-at-you kind of way.

I'm here.

With you.

THANK YOUS TO MY WONDERFUL TEAM OF SOUS CHEFS:

As ever, thank you to my sister Barbara, for turning my vague idea soup into a fantastic cover and for making sure the blurb is a blurb and not an essay. If you liked the cover design of any of my books you should check out her art here:
https://issuu.com/bluemoondesign

Thank you also once again to Jane Badger, without whom there would have been a massive flaw in the book, a whole load of awkward sentences and definitely not enough commas. One of the best freelance editors money can buy. You, too, can purchase her scrutiny:
https://janebadger.com

Thank you to Cheyenne 'eagle eye' Blue, final proofreader and professional finder of needles in haystacks. She is so in demand she's never got around to creating a website for her editing and proofreading services but if you are interested in hiring her you can drop her a line to
iamcheyenneblue@gmail.com

Last but not least, and new to the table: Thank you to my first ever professional beta reader, Emily May. Astute, with her finger on the book fashion pulse and worth every penny. You'll find her here:
http://thebookgeek.org

Printed in Great Britain
by Amazon